BLACK MESA

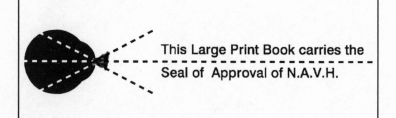

This Large Print Book carries the
Seal of Approval of N.A.V.H.

BLACK MESA

RALPH COTTON

THORNDIKE PRESS
A part of Gale, Cengage Learning

GALE
CENGAGE Learning·

Detroit • New York • San Francisco • New Haven, Conn • Waterville, Maine • London

GALE
CENGAGE Learning®

Thorndike Press® Large Print Western.
The text of this Large Print edition is unabridged.
Other aspects of the book may vary from the original edition.
Set in 16 pt. Plantin.

LIBRARY OF CONGRESS CATALOGING-IN-PUBLICATION DATA

Cotton, Ralph W.
  Black Mesa / by Ralph Cotton. — Large print edition.
    pages ; cm. — (Thorndike Press large print western)
  ISBN 978-1-4104-6483-5 (hardcover) — ISBN 1-4104-6483-0 (hardcover)
  1. Large type books. I. Title.
PS3553.O766B526 2013
813'.54—dc23   2013033180

Published in 2013 by arrangement with NAL Signet, a member of Penguin Group (USA) LLC, a Penguin Random House Company

For Mary Lynn . . . *of course*

PART 1

CHAPTER 1

"I'm taking him back," Ranger Sam Burrack said with firm resolve.

"Huh-uh. You ain't taking him nowhere, Ranger," said Alvin Krey. "You made a bad mistake tracking him here. You're a long ways off your graze," he added, his big Remington pistol already out of its holster and cocked in his hand. "Hell, I've got as much authority here as *you* do." A dark grin formed in the corner of his mouth. "*More,* come to think of it." He jiggled the Remington slightly for emphasis.

The ranger looked calmly from face to face at the three men formed in a half-circle behind Krey in the small sod and pine plank saloon. Outside, the hooves of the saloon owner's horse fell away into the distance. Sam had wondered riding in why anyone would open a saloon on such a remote spot. Perhaps the owner had suddenly asked himself that same question, Sam had thought when he stepped inside, saw the owner's eyes widen at the sight of his badge, then saw him turn and dive out a rear window.

"Authority is only what we make of it," Sam replied quietly to Alvin Krey. His Colt had also slipped its holster earlier. The big gun stood poised, cocked and ready in his gloved right hand.

"You might scare barkeeps out the back window, but you ain't taking one of our friends no-damn-where," said Krey. "That's what *I* make of it."

"Clear me a way, all of you!" Sam called out in a strong tone, ignoring Krey and talking directly to the other three men. In his left hand, Sam held Toby Burns by his shirt collar. Burns lay slumped on the dirt floor at Sam's feet, a long red welt already swelling along the side of his head where the ranger's gun barrel had struck him moments earlier.

Sensing that the men standing behind him might give in to the ranger's demand, Krey said, "Stay where you are, boys. Let one lawdog have his way, it won't be long this whole Cimarron Desert will be crawling with them." His dark grin widened and he gave Sam a cold, determined stare. "Maybe you can't count, Ranger. You've got four guns staring at you. You best turn him loose and crawl your ass out of here."

On the floor, Toby Burns moaned and shook his head slowly to clear it. *Good timing,* Sam thought, knowing how difficult it would have been to drag the knocked-out Burns across the floor and out to the hitch rail. Behind the half-circle of gunmen, sunlight rose and fell quietly as the dusty blanket hanging in the front doorway did the same.

"Are you ready to go, Sam?" his partner, Maria, asked in a level tone, stepping inside the saloon and then taking two more steps to the right of Alvin Krey, getting herself out of Sam's line of fire.

The men half turned toward the front doorway, but Krey kept his eyes riveted on the ranger, even when he heard the sound of Maria's shotgun cocking behind him. "It makes no difference who's there, Ranger," he said. "You're still outnumbered — that's a fact."

"We're through talking, Krey," Sam warned, knowing that Maria had surprised them and thrown them off for a moment; but now a move had to be made before the gunmen recovered and started listening to Krey. "Lower your gun and step aside."

"Maybe you're through, Ranger," Krey

said, still defiant, still ready for a bloody ending. His hand started to raise the big Remington. "But I've still got plenty to sa—"

His words stopped short. The ranger's bullet punched through his heart and sent shreds of it splattering on the sod wall in a wide spray of blood and bone fragments.

"Jesus!" a voice called out among the men. "You killed him!"

Maria swung the shotgun toward the other men, seeing that Sam's action had left them stunned for a second, their hands poised in reflex near their holsters. Any second she knew they would grab for their guns. "Hands up, quick!" she shouted, not wanting to give them time to think or consider anything other than what she demanded.

Hands went up chest high, then higher, seeing both the big sawed-off shotgun and the ranger's smoking Colt pointed at them in the small, confined space. "Everybody listen up," Sam said, letting the men know that the shooting had ended unless somebody else made a move to restart it. "None of you are under arrest. We're leaving here with Toby and we're taking your horses. You'll find them waiting for you a couple of miles down the trail."

"H-hold on, Ranger," said a tall, young

gunman with a deep scar across the bridge of his crooked nose. "I-I'm not a part of this bunch!" His eyes flashed around at the other faces. "For God sakes, somebody tell him! I'm just an out-of-work stage driver, stopped in for some drinks. To tell the truth I was getting worried, wondering how I was going to pull away from this bunch and get out of here."

Stepping over to him, Sam eased the young man's pistol up from his holster and pitched it over into a corner on the dirt floor. "Take it easy," Sam said to him. "You'll soon be on your way."

"You said none of us are under arrest?" an older man asked, his stubby hands raised high.

"That's right," Sam replied, "not if you do as you're told. We came here for Toby Burns. Once we're out of here, you're all free to go your own way. Just don't try to stop us." He eyed the old man closely. "You look familiar, mister. What's your name?"

"Arlo Heath," the old man said quickly. "You recognized me all right. A few years back you caught me and some others rustling goats outside of Cottonwood. Remember it?"

"Yep, I do," said Sam. "You and Gator Sal and a fellow called Frenchy. All three of you

13

attempted to rustle an old woman's milk goats."

"That's right, but our intent was never proved beyond a reasonable doubt," said Heath, unashamed.

"You had one goat slaughtered, cooked and half eaten," Sam reminded him.

Heath shrugged, conceding, "Okay, that would have been one point in the law's favor."

"Are you some sort of an attorney now?" Sam asked, knowing better.

"No, but out here a man makes do for himself," Heath said with a crafty smile. "But the point is, you had your hands full at the time, hunting Montana Red Hollis. You let us all three go, warned us to get out of the territory and stay out." Heath's smile widened, revealing a wide part in his front teeth. "So that's what I did. I ain't been back there yet, not even for visiting kin at Christmas. You've had no trouble out of me ever since."

"Good," said the ranger, looking him up and down. "Let's try to keep it that way."

The old man cocked a skeptical eye. "Do I understand you're saying that none of us are going to Judge Issac's court?" He sounded relieved but still unconvinced.

"We only want Toby Burns," the ranger

repeated, reassuring him. He watched Maria step forward and lift the older gunman's Colt from his holster and pitch it over into the corner.

"Damn, that takes a terrible load off my mind," said the old man. He gave the others a look, saying, "This is that ranger who run me out of Arizona Territory, the one who killed Montana Red Hollis deader than hell . . . who killed Bent Jackson and took his black-eyed barb!"

The other two men milled, not knowing how to respond to Heath's information. "What about me, Ranger?" the one with the scarred nose asked.

Arlo Heath jerked his head toward the younger man while Maria stepped over to the next man and disarmed him. "He's telling you the truth. He ain't nobody. Like as not one of us would have cracked his skull open before this day's over, or worse." He scowled at the young man.

"See there, Ranger?" the young man with the scarred nose asked. "Can I go now? I swear I've got nothing to do with any of this. I never should have come here."

Sam looked closer at the younger man, seeing him stare back with a blank expression. "What's your name, mister?" he asked.

"Colbert," the young man replied quickly,

"Tom Jefferson Colbert."

Sam only nodded, then turned to the others in time to see Maria disarm the last man and toss his pistol over with the rest. The last young man wore a buckskin shirt and a battered silk top hat. He stared straight ahead, sullen, trying to draw no undue attention to himself. "What's your name, mister?" Sam asked.

"What's it to you?" the man replied sharply. "You said you ain't arresting us. So keep my name out of your mouth. A man's name is his own business."

Sam stared at him for a moment until behind him the old man asked, "Well, ain't you going to let this innocent bystander leave? I already *verified on his behalf* that he ain't one of us." His voice quickly took on a semiofficial-sounding tone, but then changed back as he added, "We'll end up hurting him sure enough if you leave him here."

Sam gave the old man a look, saying, "In a minute." Turning back to the man in the silk top hat he said, "Your name *is* your own business . . . unless I match it to your face at the bottom of a pile of wanted posters."

"Like Krey said, you're too far off your graze to be making threats, Ranger," the young man sneered.

16

"Take the attitude Krey took," Sam replied, "it'll likely lead you to the same place." On the sod wall, Alvin Krey's blood ran down in long strings as the dry dirt soaked it in.

The man grew even more sullen and tight-lipped. Seeing the deadlock, Heath cut in saying, "Aw hell! His name is Bill Jones. Ain't no use in jawing back and forth about it all day."

"Keep your damn mouth shut, Heath," said the surly gunman. "Maybe you want to glad-hand this lawdog and talk like you're a big drop in the bucket, but I don't."

"All he asked was your name, fool," said Heath. "It ain't worth arguing about!"

"I said shut up, Heath!" the younger man shouted. Turning his eyes to Sam, he added in a surly tone, "Anyway, I'm clean. So go back to your own damn territory, crawl back under your rock."

Sam ignored the man's belligerent attitude. To Maria he said, "All right, let's march them outside."

Maria gave the man in the top hat a harsh glare, then motioned all the men toward the doorway, saying, "*Sí*, let's go. Everybody outside, pronto!"

Outside on the narrow dirt street, Maria kept the three men standing in front of her

17

shotgun until Sam had Toby Burns sitting slumped, handcuffed and bleary-eyed atop a big paint horse. "Where we headed next?" Burns asked with a thick tongue, still half dazed.

"All the way back to where you broke jail, Toby," the ranger said. Leaving the paint horse hitched to the rail, Sam stepped over beside Maria and said to the young man with the crooked nose, "All right, Colbert, you can go."

"Obliged, Ranger," the young man said. He stepped forward with a look of satisfaction on his face. "My gun?" He nodded toward the blanketed doorway of the saloon.

"Pick it up your next trip through here," Sam said firmly.

"I'm never coming back here," Colbert said. "Besides, one of these snakes will have stolen it before I'm a mile down the trail. Can't I just run in there, get it and —"

"You can either get on your horse and ride," Sam said, cutting him off sharply, "or you get back in line with these other two."

Without another word on the matter, Colbert turned and hurried to the hitch rail. In a moment he'd mounted, turned his horse and left a cloud of dust looming in his wake.

Stepping over beside Sam, Maria whispered just between the two of them, "You

18

did not believe a word he said, did you?"

"Nope, not a word," said Sam.

Maria nodded, then asked, "How much head start do you want to give him?"

"Just until he's out of sight," Sam whispered in reply. "I'd rather have him in front than behind us going down this high trail."

"*Sí*," Maria agreed, "that is what I thought."

CHAPTER 2

No sooner had the ranger and Maria led
their prisoner and the other horses around
the side of the sloping land near the bottom
of the tall mesa, than they caught sight of
Tom Jefferson Colbert riding three hundred
feet beneath them at a hard clip out onto
the flatlands. "He's in a hurry to meet
somebody," Sam said, scanning a few miles
farther out along a meandering trail, where
he spotted five riders rise up into sight, "and
I expect this is them."

Maria gazed out with him, judging to
herself how long it would take for Colbert
and the riders to meet on the desert floor.
"If they follow us, we have a half hour head
start at the most," she summarized, "pro-
vided we leave quickly."

"We will," Sam reassured her. With his
naked eye he still managed to see that the
riders wore blue, dust-streaked army uniforms. They rode single file, but loosely, and

had no military bearing about them. "This is interesting," he said.

"*Sí,* it is," said Maria, also staring intently at the riders on the desert floor.

Sam stepped down from his barb and led the prisoner and the horses to the side of the trail. He hitched the prisoner's horse to a rock crevice, pulled him down from the saddle and handcuffed him to a stirrup. Then he took out a dusty field lens from his saddlebags and wiped it off with his gloved hand.

"My head's killing me," Toby Burns said, his voice sounding better but still a bit groggy. "My whole right shoulder hurts like hell."

"It'll wear off soon. Stay here and don't cause us any trouble," Sam responded, ignoring Burns' aches and pains. Stepping back over to the spot that allowed a good view of the flatlands, Sam lay down on his stomach at the edge of the trail and gazed closer at the riders coming into sight. Maria had kept an eye on the desert floor. Now that Sam had returned, she stepped down from her saddle and led her horse over beside the ranger's. She came back in a crouch, slipping down beside Sam. "Do you recognize any of them?" she asked.

"Yep," said Sam, staring intently through

the field lens, "the one in front wearing a lieutenant uniform is Freeman Turnbaugh." Eyeing the heavily loaded saddlebags the first two riders carried behind their saddles, he added, "Looks like they've been busy somewhere along the way."

"*Sí*, playing soldiers," said Maria.

They watched Tom Jefferson Colbert race his horse across the flatlands toward the distant riders. Studying the faces of the riders as they grew larger, he said, "I recognize these others from some Texas wanted posters that made it into the territory. The one beside Free Turnbaugh is Max Krey, Alvin Krey's brother. He likes being called Killer Krey."

"Killer Krey." Maria's hand tightened instinctively on the small of her rifle stock. "And now that you have shot his brother, he will want revenge."

"I expect he will." Sam nodded, still studying the riders, their faces, their expressions, the condition of their horses, their armament. "The two behind Turnbaugh and Krey are the New York brothers, the ones with no names."

"The ones known as the Dead Rabbits Gang?" Maria asked, all business, studying the riders as closely as she could with her naked eye.

22

"Yep," said Sam, "they used to belong to the Dead Rabbits Gang. He lowered the lens, saying, "These two Dead Rabbits have made fools out of all the railroad detectives for the past year."

"And now we have stumbled upon them," Maria said, squinting slightly against the harsh glare of sunlight. "But are there any charges against any of them in our territory."

"None that I can think of," said Sam, staring through the lens. "But charges won't make any difference once Max Krey learns that I killed his brother." He paused, and looked over toward Colbert, still a good twenty-five minutes away from the riders, but pushing his horse hard.

"How have these men moved around so freely with so many bounty hunters and detectives ready to take off their heads?" Maria asked. "This man Turnbaugh is either very brazen or completely crazy."

"Turnbaugh's not crazy. Maybe he enjoys the thrill of it," Sam commented in speculation. "He's known to live fast and loose. Maybe he likes feeling like he can move around under everybody's noses and get by with it."

"*Sí,*" Maria said, contemplating along with him. "Where did they get those uniforms?"

she asked a moment later.

"Off dead soldiers would be my guess." Sam studied the riders. "I saw a washed-out bullet hole on the chest of one of them. It's Harvey Fanin, I believe." He turned, silent in thought for a moment, then added, "I heard about an army payroll detail getting ambushed along the border back in June."

"Let me see," said Maria.

Sam handed her the lens, rubbed his eye and watched her study the riders for a moment. "See any more bullet holes?" he asked.

"No. Wait! Yes," Maria said. "On the trouser leg of one of the Dead Rabbits. There is a bloodstain, barely visible. They did a good job patching and washing the uniforms."

"Yep," said Sam. As he spoke he reached back inside his memory and said, "So that ambush wasn't the Apache after all."

"You never thought it was for a moment, did you?" Maria said.

"Nope, not for a minute," said Sam. "Apache have no use for money — not in that sense. And they wouldn't have shot so many horses. Those army horses would have taken them deep into Mexico. The blanket Apache are much smarter than that." He pondered something, then added quietly,

"Even the *Comadrehas* wouldn't have killed the horses."

Maria lowered the lens and gave him a pointed look. "Would not those same horses have served these just as well?"

Sam took the lens as she passed it to him. But instead of looking through it, he gazed out with his naked eyes and said, "You would think so. But Free Turnbaugh and his men must have felt cocksure of themselves. They weren't worried about having to run to Mexico if something went wrong."

"Because nothing could go wrong," Maria interjected as if completing his thought for him. "They had no need for extra horses."

"That's right," said Sam, scooting back from the edge and standing, slapping dust from his chest. "We better have a little talk with Toby Burns while we're moving along, see what he can tell us about this bunch before they get too hot on our trail."

"Good idea," said Maria, also dusting herself.

But before she and the ranger could turn toward Toby Burns, Maria saw Sam stop dusting himself and look back down onto the flatlands, where a two-horse buggy raced into sight from behind a short, stubby mesa less than a hundred yards from the riders and sped toward them. "Hold on. What do we have here?" Sam asked, pondering the big buggy as it bounced and rocked back and forth along the rough, flat trail.

Maria turned the lens back to the flat-lands, studying the buggy and its driver briefly. "It is a woman, Sam," she said, sounding only a bit surprised, lowering the lens and holding it out to the ranger.

Sam took the lens, raised it to his eye for a moment, then with a stark look of surprise lowered it and said, "It's Ella Lang."

"Ella Lang?" said Maria. "*The* Ella Lang? The one who has become so popular?"

"Yep, that's her," Sam said, his voice taking on a different, softer tone. "*Lovely* Ella Lang." Sam lowered the lens for a second. "That's what the newspapers and periodicals have called her," he said tactfully, raising the lens back to his eye and adjusting it toward the buggy.

"Oh?" said Maria, coolly. "Is she indeed lovely?" Instead of a definite answer, Sam said, "She sells lots of newspapers." He lowered the lens and handed it back to Maria. "Like you said, she's very popular."

"I see," Maria said coyly, looking back through the lens, her eyes going from the riders to the fancy two-horse rig. "She is Freeman Turnbaugh's woman?"

"I wouldn't be surprised," Sam replied.

"She's known to consort with outlaws."

"Oh?" Maria caught something in Sam's voice that caused her to lower the lens an inch and give him an inquisitive look.

"Or so I've heard," Sam said. He seemed to stall for a moment, then said, "But I doubt if a woman like Ella Lang belongs to any man." He continued gazing down at the buggy as it stopped amid the riders. "I figure she's just one more member of the gang. Whatever she does, she's doing to her own advantage, like anyone else who lives that kind of life."

"Sam," said Maria, not understanding the look she saw in his eyes or the expression on his face, "you seem to know a great deal about this woman."

"I'm a lawman, Maria. I make it a point to know what I can about anybody who walks on the other side of the law," Sam replied. He added in dismissal, "Come on, we best get as far ahead of them as we can. We've done what we came here to do. So long as this bunch is in Indian Territory they belong to Judge Parker and his deputies."

"*Sí,*" said Maria, studying him closely, still uncertain of what she saw in his eyes or read in his expression. "Let's get going." She gave a curious look back down toward the flatlands floor, then turned and walked with the ranger to the horses. Whatever questions she had would have to wait for now.

On the basin floor, Ella Lang let out a short squeal of laughter, with one hand holding her hat in place, as Freeman Turnbaugh's horse spun in one last quick circle and came to a sharp halt. She kissed Turnbaugh on his dusty cheek, then spit and ran a hand across her lips. "Agh! You filthy man! Put me down!" she called out playfully.

Turnbaugh squeezed her around her waist and whispered close to her ear, "God, Ella, I have missed you something awful."

"Well, you can just stop missing me right now, Free," she whispered in reply. "I'm right here." But then she pushed him back from her with a hand and said, "Now put me down this instant. How much money did we make?"

Turnbaugh chuckled. "I never like to stop and count with *federales* shooting at us."

"That's all right," said Ella. "Max will know." She turned to Max Krey, who had stepped down from his saddle and stood holding the buggy reins.

"Then let's just ask him," said Turnbaugh. Letting Ella slip from his arm to the ground, Turnbaugh called out, "Max! Here she comes. You better tell her how much we made."

Krey gazed down, then out across the rugged terrain as if not noticing the way the two had kissed deeply upon Ella's arrival. Hearing Turnbaugh call out to him, he looked around in time to catch Ella Lang in his arms as she ran to him. Turnbaugh and the others looked on as the two kissed.

"This is the part I could do without," Harvey Fanin said sidelong and secretively to the two Dead Rabbits gunmen, who had reined their horses up beside him. He turned his eyes away from Ella and Krey.

The Dead Rabbits grinned and passed each other a glance. "Would it be a wee bit of jealousy I hear speaking?" said one to the other.

"Aye, I believe it 'tis," the other replied, neither of them looking at Fanin.

"Aw hell," Fanin growled, jerking his horse away from them, "what do you know about anything?" He gigged the horse over alongside the buggy and stopped. Peeling off his sweat-streaked wool army shirt and flinging it to the ground, he leaned low in his saddle and jerked a clean but faded plaid shirt from the pile of clothes lying behind the driver's seat.

Answering Ella, Max said, just between

the two of them, "I figure it to be thirty thousand, give or take." He held Ella around her thin waist, her hands clasped behind his dusty neck. "Damn you smell good," he said.

"Pesos or greenbacks?" Ella asked, swinging herself gently back and forth in his arms.

"Both," said Max, swaying with her. "What's the difference? They both spend the same around here." He nodded toward the bulging saddlebags. "There's also plenty of Mexican gold coins . . . if you're drawn more to beauty than you are performance." His eyes made a quick dart toward Turnbaugh, then came back to hers.

"I can enjoy both, can't I?" Ella said, smiling.

"You know you can," said Max. He squeezed her. "God, Ella, it's all I can do to keep from raising this skirt over your head and falling to the ground right here and now."

"But it will be much better tonight," she said, leaning in close to his ear, "after a hot bath, a good meal, some whiskey." She nipped firmly but gently on his earlobe.

While the two whispered quietly to each other, Turnbaugh and the Dead Rabbits rode up beside the buggy, stepped down and began pulling fresh clothes from behind the driver's seat. "All right, you two," Turn-baugh said to Ella and Krey, "keep it decent. Let's get changed and count out the money. I'm tired of sleeping outdoors."

"Go on without us," said Krey, only half joking. "We'll catch up later. You can have our share."

"Huh-uh!" said Ella, giving him a shove, coming out of his loose embrace. "All this attention feels real good, but you've been gone over a month. I'm running out of *God's own medicine.*[*] Let's go."

Turnbaugh caught her by the forearm as she tried to step back up into the buggy. "How bad is it?" he asked pointedly.

"It's under control," Ella said, resisting his hold on her arm. "I haven't tried to hide it from you."

"I know you haven't, Ella," Turnbaugh said, unbuttoning the cuff of her long blouse sleeve. "But let's just take a look."

Ella sighed, and watched him shove her sleeve up her forearm until a snaking trail of needle marks appeared raw along the faint blue vein. "See, I told you I've got it under control," she said coolly. She cupped herself low on her belly. "Want to see up here too?"

[*] A common term in the mid-1800s for morphine.

31

"Yes, later," Turnbaugh said seriously.

Ella's mood changed quickly. "Go to hell if you don't believe me," she spat at him. "The morphine is part of the deal," she said. "If you don't want it around, you don't want me around either."

"Keep pumping it this hard and you won't be around," Turnbaugh warned. "You'll be dead."

She gave Turnbaugh an obscene gesture with her hand and jerked herself away from him. But Max Krey caught her, saying, "Easy, Ella! Free is only looking out for your best interests. He's worried about you. So am I."

Ella settled, let out a breath and said, "All right, I know he is. I know you both are. But when I say I have it under control, I mean it. And I don't like being looked on and doubted by my two best friends." She glared back and forth between Krey and Turnbaugh. "Do we all understand one another?"

Freeman Turnbaugh only nodded and stepped away, saying to the other men, "All right, get a move on."

Max Krey turned a harsh glare to the Dead Rabbits and Harvey Fanin, and seeing them staring curiously, he growled, "What the hell's everybody gawking at? You

32

heard the man. Get busy!"

As the men continued changing their clothes, Harvey Fanin looked out across the desert floor and saw the rise of dust behind the tiny spec of a rider headed toward them. "Rider coming, Free!" he said.

"Damn it," Freeman Turnbaugh said, turning his gaze in the direction of the rise of dust, "I smell trouble." As he spoke, he stepped over to his horse and drew his rifle from its saddle boot.

CHAPTER 3

Tom Jefferson Colbert reined his tired horse to a halt and jerked it sideways to Freeman Turnbaugh and his men on the Cimarron Desert floor. "Damn, Cut-nose!" Max Krey said, stepping up and grabbing the worn horse by its froth-covered bridle. "You just about rode this poor sumbitch to death!"

"I know," Colbert said, panting, his face covered with a layer of red-gray dust. "I had no choice."

"This better be good, Colbert," Freeman Turnbaugh called out, riding his horse forward, staring at the worn horse and rider. "I told everybody to stay put up there."

"Unless we had trouble," Colbert reminded him, taking a half-full canteen from his saddle horn as he spoke, "which we do." He uncapped the canteen, took a mouthful of warm water, swished it around and spit it out in a long brownish stream. "I had to come tell you," he said, gasping, running a hand across his wet lips. "A lawdog rode in on us, took us by surprise and dragged Toby Burns out by the scruff of his neck!"

The men stared at him with cold expressions. "Dragged him out to where?" Turnbaugh asked coldly.

"Dragged him out and horsed him!" said Colbert. "I expect they're riding down the trail right now. That's why I got a head start and hurried down to tell you."

"You fools let one of Parker's deputies ride in and catch all of you by surprise?" said Turnbaugh.

"This ain't one of Parker's boys," said Colbert. This one is a ranger — an Arizona ranger at that."

"What the hell is an Arizona ranger doing in Indian Nations?" Max Krey asked, still holding Colbert's horse by its bridle.

Standing beside her buggy, Ella Lang had watched and listened with detached interest. But now, before Colbert could offer an answer, she stepped forward and asked with a sense of urgency, "An Arizona ranger? What's he look like? What's his name?"

"I don't recall he said his name," Colbert replied. "But he travels with a Spanish woman. Arlo said he's the one who killed Montana Red Hollis and ole Bent Jackson. He never denied it."

"Sam," Ella said in almost a whisper.

"What?" Turnbaugh said, giving her a look. "Do you know this ranger?"

Ella corrected herself quickly, "Sam Burrack. Yes, I know him, or I know of him, I should say."

"You won't be knowing of him long," said Turnbaugh, giving a glance toward the distant mesas strung out across the wide desert floor. "We've got enough lawmen on our backs. We're not letting some damned Arizona ranger ride into our territory and take a man from under our noses."

Max Krey cut in, saying, "What was my brother doing all this time? He's got himself some tall explaining to do, letting this lawman —"

"Alvin's dead, Max," Colbert said, cutting him off before he chastised his brother too harshly.

"Dead?" Max Krey stared blankly at him. "What the hell are you saying, Cut-nose?"

"He's dead, Max," Colbert repeated. "The ranger shot his heart out. It was a terrible thing to see."

Max Krey stood in stunned silence for a moment, then said in a tone of controlled rage, "My brother, Alvin, is dead, and none of you sumbitches killed the lousy lawman who shot him?"

"There was nothing we could do!" Colbert said, his voice taking on a plea. "This ranger came in drawn and cocked. He had that woman behind us with a scattergun! We couldn't make a move — I swear it!"

Linston McGinty, one of the Dead Rabbit boys, whispered to his brother, Michael, standing beside him, "Step away with me Michael *b'hoy*. There's a killing coming here."

But even as the Dead Rabbits stepped back out of the way and both Krey and Colbert closed their gun hands around their pistol butts, Turnbaugh called out, "Stand down, damn it, both of yas!"

"I come all the way down here to warn you, Free, not to get into a gunfight!" Colbert said, keeping his hand tight around his gun butt and his eyes on Krey.

"Max!" Turnbaugh shouted. "This ain't the place to do any shooting, not unless you want to warn that ranger where we are and what we're doing!"

"My brother is dead, Free, Gawddamn it! Somebody's going to pay!" Krey bellowed.

"You're right," said Turnbaugh. "This ranger *is* going to pay. We're going to ambush him when he comes down onto the trail. Now get your hand off that gun!"

Krey obeyed Turnbaugh's order, but he

did so reluctantly, his cold stare still fixed on Colbert until he stepped back and saw Colbert remove his hand as well. "Don't think it's over between you and me, Cutnose," he said to Colbert in a lowered, more controlled voice. "I ain't forgetting this."

Colbert didn't answer. Instead he cut his gaze back to Turnbaugh, saying, "I convinced him that I'm an out-of-work stage driver who had nothing to do with Burns or Alvin or anybody else." Offering a trace of a wry smile, Colbert continued. "He believed every word of it."

"Yeah, every word?" said Turnbaugh, cocking a brow slightly.

Colbert shrugged. "He must have. He cut me loose." His trace of a smile widened. "I can be pretty convincing, if I do say so myself."

"Are you sure he didn't cut you loose just so he could follow you?" asked Turnbaugh, his eyes cutting back across the flatlands and up the side of the mesa.

"Naw, he didn't suspect I was lying to him. Arlo vouched for me, said if the ranger left me there with them I might get hurt."

Turnbaugh considered everything for a moment, then said to everyone, "All right, all of yas finish dressing. Get those uniforms into the buggy. We've got some ground to cover before nightfall."

"Wait a minute," said Max Krey, sensing that Turnbaugh had changed his mind about ambushing the ranger. "What about my brother?"

"Not now, Max," said Turnbaugh. "He's laying in wait up there — you can bet on it." He turned to Ella Lang. "What do you say, Ella? You know that ranger. Did he fall for Colbert's story?"

Ella shook her head slowly. "Not a way in the world. If I know Sam Burrack, he's piecing together a big Swiss rifle right now. There's not a switchback in the mesa trail I'd want to ride right now."

"But my poor brother, Alvin!" said Max. "I want this ranger dead! I want him choking on his own blood for what he's done!"

"He'll have to keep, Max," Turnbaugh said in a stronger tone. "We know his name. We know where to find him. We're not going to play into his hand. Is that clear enough for you?"

Max Krey forced himself to settle down, seeing in Turnbaugh's eyes that there would no more discussion of the matter. "If you say so," he grumbled. He turned and stomped over to the buggy, where he threw in his army tunic, then stomped over to his horse, shoving his clean shirt into his trousers.

Standing close beside Turnbaugh, Ella Lang asked him in private, "Is he going to listen to you?"

"He better," Turnbaugh replied, a bit of a warning in his voice. "We're going to swing wide and go around to the other side of the mesa before we trail up. Even if that ranger is tracking Colbert he won't expect us to duck around him." He turned enough to look Ella up and down, and asked, "Will he?"

Ella sighed, considering it seriously. "I don't know. He might. He's a hard man to figure out."

"How well *do* you know him, Ella? And don't tell me you only know of him. I saw right through that one."

Ella stared at him. "You didn't see anything that surprised you, did you?"

"No surprise," said Turnbaugh. "Just that along with every other son of a bitch between here and Chicago, now I find out you've bedded down with a damned lawman."

"Go to hell, Free," Ella hissed. She turned to walk away, but Turnbaugh caught her by her arm and swung her back around, facing him.

"Listen to me, Gawddamn it!" said Turn-baugh. "He's slipped into the mesa and killed one of my top gunmen before anybody could put up a fight! I want to know who he is, and what I'm up against!"

Ella settled down and stared at Turn-baugh's hand on her forearm until he took the hint and loosened his grip. "Some folks in the badlands say he's half crazy. They say he's seen too much blood and it's left him as bloodthirsty as the ones he's hunting."

Studying her eyes, Turnbaugh saw that she didn't agree with those people. "But what do you think?"

"Crazy? I don't know. He never waits for a man to make the first move. He carries a list of men he's hunting, and when he catches up to them, they end up dead." She stared at him, took a breath and let it out slowly. "He's tough, Free. For my money we're better off staying away from him."

"And you and him . . . ?" Turnbaugh let his question trail.

"Yes, I bedded with him," Ella said, unashamed. She gazed off across endless mesas and rolling flatlands full of brush and barrel cactus. "The truth is, there's nights when I can still feel his arms around me . . . if I let myself."

"Oh, I see," said Turnbaugh.

She saw a spark of jealousy in his eyes. "You asked," she said, "so I told you. You did expect the truth, didn't you?" Her voice hardened as she continued. "From a woman who's bedded down with every son of a bitch between here and Chicago?"

"Damn it, Ella, that was just temper talking. You know I meant nothing by that little remark," said Turnbaugh.

Ella felt a familiar aching deep down in her stomach. She thought about the small leather bag waiting for her under the buggy seat, and raising a hand to Turnbaugh's cheek, she offered a tired smile and said, "I know, Free. Forget it ever happened."

Freeman Turnbaugh nodded and gestured his eyes toward Max, who had stepped up into his saddle along with the rest of the men. "Keep a close eye on him tonight, Ella," he said quietly. "I don't want him flaring up and doing something stupid."

"Don't worry," Ella said in a suggestive tone, turning and walking to the buggy. "I'll see to it he doesn't want to slip away in the night."

The group rode on toward the land sloping upward at the foot of the mesa. But instead of turning onto the steep trail Colbert had taken down to the flatlands, Turnbaugh led them onto another trail that swung around the belly of the mesa in an upward-reaching series of rocky switchback paths.

When the fading sunlight grew too dim to allow safe travel in the rugged land, Turnbaugh directed the riders off the trail to a secluded flat spot beneath a cliff overhang. Stepping down from their saddles, Turnbaugh said to the Dead Rabbit brothers, "Linston, you and your brother take down the buggy and roll it all the way back in there." He gestured toward the blackness beneath the overhang. "We'll leave it stashed here. Come morning, Ella will ride one of the buggy horses."

In the buggy, Ella quickly shoved the small leather bag inside her blouse and stepped down, turning the buggy over to the brothers. "M'lady," said Michael McGinty, giving her an assisting hand.

"I'm glad to see we've taken in some real gentlemen," Ella said, giving the younger of the two a smile in the grainy darkness.

"Anytime I can be of service, ma'am," Michael replied, sweeping his billed wool cap from his head.

As Ella walked away toward Max Krey, Linston McGinty said to his brother in a guarded tone, "Easy does it, *b'hoy.* All good things come to he who waits."

"Aye," said Michael, "I see how this works. I'm just letting her know I'm here." The two watched Ella and Max Krey walk away in the darkness, Max leading his horse, carrying a blanket over his shoulder.

"You know I can't stand still for this, Ella," Max said quietly as the two stepped into the deeper darkness beneath the cliff overhang. He handed Ella the blanket and she spread it on the ground while he dropped the saddle from his horse and laid the heavily loaded saddlebags beside the blanket.

"I know it's your brother, and I know how you feel," said Ella, lying down and stretching out on the blanket. "But Free is right — killing the ranger has to keep for now. We've got too much at stake."

"You know I'm going, though, don't you?" Max said, lying down beside her.

"You're putting me in a bad spot, Max," Ella whispered, her fingers reaching his shirt buttons. "I'm supposed to keep an eye on you."

"I'm making it right with you," said Max. He reached up and put a thick roll of folded dollars into her hand.

"Oh my, that feels big," Ella whispered.

As he spoke, his hand drew her riding skirt up and felt her warm skin. "All you have to do is say you had no idea what I was up to. I'll disappear in the night, kill that ranger and be back up in the mesa before midnight tomorrow." He kissed her.

But Ella cut the kiss short and said into his seeking lips, "Max, this ranger is no easy piece of work."

"I hope he's not," said Max, trying to continue the kiss as Ella pressed him back. "I want to kill him slow, him and the woman too."

"All right, Max, I've warned you," Ella said, lying back, giving in to him. "If you're not here in the morning, I didn't know a thing about it." As she unbuttoned her blouse and spread it open, she took the roll of money and the small leather bag and laid them both under the corner of the blanket.

CHAPTER 4

Earlier, Max Krey had heard Ella Lang mention the ranger's big Swiss rifle to Turnbaugh. Later in the night, Krey had listened quietly as she mentioned the big rifle again, this time warning him in a way that made him think she gave Sam Burrack more respect than any lawman had coming. Without reply, Max had listened to her in the darkness. Then he'd stood up from the blanket, slipped into his clothes and boots and slung his gun belt around his waist.

"Sounds like you had it bad for this lawdog, Ella," he'd said, buckling his belt in the dark and tying his holster string around his leg.

"I'm not denying it, Max," Ella had replied in the darkness, toying idly with the brass syringe, getting anxious for Max to leave. "But that was then and this is now. Sam Burrack is smart, Max," she warned. "Watch out for his tricks. I don't want him killing you."

"That's real sweet of you, Ella," Max had told her with a snap of sarcasm. "Any messages for him before I put that last bullet in his eye?"

He'd waited for a moment in the darkness. When she didn't answer, he said under his breath, "I thought not," then turned and walked away to the horses.

Four hours later he thought about Ella as he rode his horse quickly up the dark sloping trail toward the rising mesa, leading one of the buggy horses behind him on a rope. He had news for her, he thought to himself. This wasn't the first lawman he had ever come up against. As far as tricks . . . well, he happened to have a few of his own.

Max didn't care how deadly the ranger might be with his big Swiss rifle. In the dark, high up above the switchback trail, all the ranger could rely on would be the sound of a horse's hooves. That would be this lawdog's mistake, Max reminded himself, hurrying the horse upward to where the trail cut in around the belly of the mesa.

At a spot where a high wall of rock began running up to the left, Max slowed the two horses to halt, knowing that along the next hundred yards of rocky trail lay the most ideal position for the ranger to set up an ambush. For a moment he sat in his saddle, listening for any sounds up along the rough wall of rock.

"All right, Ranger," Max finally whispered to himself, stepping down from his horse, "it's time we let this little cat and mouse get under way."

Holding his riding horse by the reins, he took the lead rope from the buggy horse's muzzle and gave it a hard slap on its rump. The horse bolted forward up the trail, its hooves clacking loudly in the darkness. Max waited, listening intently for a gunshot from the rocky ledges above the trail.

When no gunshot came, Max smiled and let out a breath and stepped back into his saddle. He rode extra quietly to where the buggy horse stood mid-trail, resting itself. Stepping down silently from his saddle with the lead rope coiled in his gloved hand, he walked up to the buggy horse and turned it up the trail.

"One more time," he whispered to the horse, drawing back the rope and slapping the horse's rump. As the horse shot upward once again without the sound of rifle fire coming down from above, Max smiled slightly to himself. Maybe that ranger hadn't been so brave after all. Maybe he'd sensed that Colbert was lying and decided to take Toby Burns and make a run for it. That being the case, Max decided, it wouldn't be a matter of him looking out for the ranger. Once out from under this rock wall, the ranger had better worry about looking out for him.

Max turned to his horse in the darkness and started to step up into the saddle, still listening for the sound of a rifle shot as the buggy horse's hooves continued to resound along the trail. But before he could even get his foot into a stirrup, Max heard a strong, quiet voice say behind him, "Shame on you, running a good horse out on a night like this."

Before Max Krey could act or think, the ranger's rifle butt struck him hard just above his right ear and sent him sprawling on the hard rock ground.

Slipping silently out of the rocks alongside the trail, Maria stepped in beside the ranger, looked down at Max Krey and shook her head. "Now we have one more prisoner to deal with."

"Not for long with this one," said Sam. "If there's not more of them trailing us, come morning we'll be heading west, to an army camp along the Cimarron. I'll tell them about the uniforms we saw and let them have him."

"Which one do you think he is?" Maria asked, neither of them able to see very well in the darkness.

Sam looked back along the dark trail, just in case. "If he's the only one, I figure it's Max Krey. He owes me for killing his brother." Taking a pair of handcuffs from his belt, Sam stooped down, cuffed the knocked-out gunman's hands behind his back and lifted him enough to get him draped over his saddle while Maria held the horse's reins. "We'll see what Burns has to say about this. We'll collect the other horse along the trail and keep moving."

Maria gave him a look. "Do you think Burns will identify Krey for you?"

Sam gave a brief smile in the darkness. "He won't mean to, but yep, I believe he will."

Leading the knocked-out gunman across his saddle, the two walked back into a recess in the rock wall alongside the trail to where Toby Burns lay with his hands cuffed behind his back through his horse's stirrup. Sam loosened the bandanna he'd tied around Burn's mouth and said, "Give me a yes or a no, Burns. Is this Max Krey?" He raised Krey's head to give Burns a better look at the outlaw's unconscious face.

Squinting in the dark, thin light of a quarter moon, Burns stalled for a moment, then instead of a yes or no answer, he asked, "Is he dead or alive?"

"It's Krey," Sam said to Maria.

"Hold on, Ranger!" said Burns. "I never said it's Max Krey!"

"See what I mean?" Sam said confidently to Maria, hearing the fear in Burns' voice at the thought of Max Krey knowing he'd co-operated with the law.

"Think what you want to think, Ranger," said Burns. "But the fact is I never identified this man, and I don't want him thinking I did."

"Relax, Burns," Sam said. "He won't know you identified him unless I tell him you did."

"But I didn't, damn it!" said Burns. "You'll be lying if you tell him I did!" Pausing for a second as if to consider it, he added, "You won't do that, will you?" His voice sounded more and more frightened.

"It's all up to you, Burns," said Sam. "You can either tell me nothing and I'll let him think you told me everything, or you can tell me everything and I'll let him think you told me nothing."

"Damn it!" said Burns, sounding hard pressed. "How do I always manage to get

51

into a tight spot?" He shook his head and said in a lowered tone of voice, "What do you want to know?"

Sam took him by his forearm and led him a few feet away from the knocked-out gunman. Maria followed after hitching Krey's horse to a rock spur.

"First off," Burns said, "I want you to know that I haven't been riding with Turnbaugh for long. Just since I broke jail this last time. So I can't tell you much."

"Every little bit helps," said the ranger, encouraging him. "Something must've brought you all the way over here from New Mexico Territory. What was it?"

Burns shrugged. "It was mostly just something I heard from Rambling Bo Clay while him and me was cellmates in Yuma," said Burns. "He said if I ever broke out and wanted to stay out, I better find Turnbaugh over in the Indian Nations and join up with him and his gang. Said Turnbaugh and his boys have a hideout up in Black Mesa that nobody knows how to get to. I figure that's the place I want to be."

"And that's it?" Sam asked. "Rambling Bo Clay caused you to break jail, just to find yourself a good hideout? You wouldn't have needed a good hideout if you didn't break jail."

"Come on now, Ranger," said Burns. "You know nobody can take sitting around in a cell when they could be out robbing and whooping it up."

"I understand," said Sam.

"Besides, Bo also told me Turnbaugh and his boys had a good thing going on, robbing army payrolls on this side of the border and Mexican banks and trains on the other side of the border." He grinned slightly in the darkness. "Sort of the best of both countries is what Rambling Bo Clay called it."

"How would I go about finding this hideout in Black Mesa if I took a notion to?" Sam asked, realizing that if the place did exist, which he doubted, knowing its whereabouts might be information he should pass along to other lawmen.

"I've never been there yet," said Burns. "We was going to go on up there as soon as Turnbaugh and his men got back, but you came along and fouled the deal." He paused for a second, then said as if in secret among him, the ranger and Maria, "There are outlaws there that the authorities think have been dead for years. I'm talking about some mean, cold-blooded hombres!"

"Yeah? Like who?" Sam asked, getting more and more interested as Burns continued.

"Like Skin-eating Dock Dockery and Canada Paul Maple," said Burns.

"I've heard of them," Sam replied. "Who else?"

"How about Hector Montoya?" Burns said proudly, trying harder and harder to impress the ranger.

"Never heard of him," Sam said, shaking his head. But Maria saw that the ranger was only baiting Burns, keeping him naming names.

"What?" Burns seemed stunned. "You never heard of Hector the Scorpion?"

"Oh, the Scorpion," Sam replied. "Okay, now I remember him. Who else?"

Burns had to think about it. "Uh, Donnie Rice? His cousin Whit Marzell? Both of them big train robbers out of Missouri till a few years back. They disappeared when the detectives and headhunters got too hot on them."

"And all these men are living there, along with Freeman Turnbaugh and his men?" Maria asked with skepticism.

"It's no lie! Yes, they are," Burns said defiantly. "Once you get inside the place, it's nearly as large as Hole-in-the-Wall, is what I'm hearing. Like I said, I ain't been there yet, but what I've heard comes straight from the ones who knows."

"From Bo Clay?" said Sam.

"And others," said Burns hedging a bit.

"What others?" Sam asked bluntly.

"Okay, the *Midwest National Star,*" Burns said, looking embarrassed.

"Oh, now I see," said Sam. "You read about it in a news journal."

"All right, so I did," said Burns in his own defense. "Everybody reads the *National Star,* don't they?"

"They don't let it cause them to break jail though," Sam responded.

"But Bo Clay told me to," said Burns.

"Are you sure Bo Clay didn't read about it in the *National Star* himself?" Maria asked.

"I believe him — that's all I can tell you," Burns said in frustration.

"All right," said Sam, getting back on the subject, "you haven't seen the place yet, but don't tell me you don't know how to get there."

"No, I don't, Ranger," said Burns, "and that's the truth, so help me.

"Neither Bo nor the *Star* told you how to get there?" Sam asked.

"I know it's up near the top of the mesa, around on the north side somewhere. There's a big hole that goes back deep inside the mesa, big enough to hide an army if need be."

"You're telling me that all these men are living together back inside a big cave in Black Mesa?" Sam asked, giving the prisoner a doubtful look. "I'm starting to think this is all hot air talking."

"No, it's all true. But that ain't how they all live," said Burns. "They all live scattered out on the Cimarron Desert a little ways, all close around the mesa. At the first sign of trouble, they all make a run for it and go deep inside that cave. They can lay low in there from now on if need be, and never be seen or heard from again."

Sam looked at Maria in the darkness, then back at Burns. "So finding the place is not all there is to it. You have to get yourself accepted by the rest of the people living there."

"Yeah, that's how it's been for me," said Burns. "Riding with Turnbaugh gets me in. He's the big gun of the whole Cimarron Desert. So all I had to do was bide my time, make a few runs with Turnburgh, and I was in — except here you came along." His voice took on a bitter snap. "Hadn't been for you, I would never been heard of again. Would that have been so bad, Ranger?"

"You broke jail, Burns," said Sam. "That's something the law never forgets, no matter if you're heard from again or not. Besides, you would still be robbing and killing," said

56

Sam. "I know you can't see the harm in it. But the law says you have to be stopped." He paused, then added, "Nothing personal, you understand."

Burns let out a sigh. "Seems like there ought to be some middle ground. A man breaks jail, he should get a second chance or something. If he never gets caught again or heard from again, he ought to get pardoned. Is that so unfair?"

"Not for you," Sam replied. He decided not to try explaining anything more to the outlaw. Instead he said, "I won't mention you told me about Black Mesa if you won't."

"Hell, there's no way I'm going to mention telling you about it, believe me!" said Burns. "I might get a chance to go back there someday. I don't want nobody there thinking that I . . ." He let his words trail off. "Not that I would ever attempt breaking jail again — I mean, if I ever live long enough to get out of Yuma alive."

Sam nodded and turned to Maria. "Let's get going. We've got to put some distance behind us, in case Turnbaugh or any more of his men might still be trailing us."

"So you're not going to tell Max that I fingered him for you?" Burns asked.

"Not as long as you keep behaving yourself, Burns," said Sam, guiding him back

57

toward the horses. "It'll be our own little secret."

In the gray hour of dawn, Freeman Turnbaugh walked over to where Ella Lang lay wrapped in the wool blanket on the ground. Looking around, not seeing Max Krey anywhere, he grinned and started to loosen his gun belt. "Hey, lady, got room for me in there?" he said.

But Ella didn't move. He nudged her again, this time a little harder. "Hey, Ella, it's me. Wake up," he said a little louder. Still he got no response. Taking a quick look around in the gray morning light, he saw that Krey's horse and one of the buggy horses were missing. "Damn it!" he growled. He quickly stooped down and shook Ella by her shoulder, saying, "Ella, wake up! Max is gone! Come on, wake the hell up!"

A few yards away, having heard Turnbaugh trying to raise the sleeping woman, Linston McGinty stood up from his blanket and ventured over closer, saying, "Is she dead?"

His words sent a quick chill up Turnbaugh's spine; but no sooner had he asked than Ella let out a low moan and half opened her eyes. "No, she's not dead, Gawddamn it," Turnbaugh said gruffly, giving McGinty a harsh look. "Stay the hell over there."

Linston McGinty halted, but stood looking on curiously. "Did you say Max is gone?"

Turnbaugh ignored him and said to Ella, as she wiped an unsteady hand across her face, "Where the hell is he, Ella?"

"I-I don't know," Ella replied, her voice sounding blurry from the morphine.

"You were supposed to be watching him, making sure he stayed put!" he said. Taking her by her shoulders, Turnbaugh pulled her up a few inches, enough to see that beneath the blanket she lay half naked, wearing her blouse, but with the buttons undone, exposing her pale white breasts. "How long has he been gone?" he demanded.

"He's gone . . . ?" Ella asked as if speaking from within a deep sleep. The blanket fell away. Her riding skirt lay gathered high up at her waist, exposing her legs, her inner thighs.

"Oh my," Michael McGinty gasped quietly to himself. Linston McGinty kept silent but his face turned flush white at the sight of Ella's nakedness.

Turnbaugh saw the small, dried crust of blood along the vein in Ella's forearm as she struggled half-heartedly to smooth her skirt down into place. "Jesus, Ella, look at you!" said Turnbaugh, seeing her condition. A strip of rawhide she'd used to tighten around her arm spilled from the folds of the blanket. On the ground beneath the blanket the syringe lay in the dirt alongside the leather bag. "I needed to count on your help and you doped up and let him slip right past you!"

"I-I didn't take that much, Free," Ella said, her voice sounding dazed and shaky. "Just enough to help me sleep. You know I never sleep good out like this anymore." She looked all around at the staring faces of Fanin and the two Dead Rabbits. Her eyes grew misty. "I'm sorry, fellows. I've let everybody down!"

The McGintys milled in place; Fanin continued to stare with a flat expression that Ella could not interpret. Seeing her tears, Turnbaugh softened, saying, "Well, I suppose if Max wanted to slip out of here unnoticed, he would have done so, dope or no dope."

"No," said Ella, as if unwilling to forgive herself, "it's all my fault. It's this blasted dope!" She snatched up the leather bag as if ready to hurl in away. But she didn't. Instead she clenched it tightly and shook it fiercely. "Damn this stuff! I'm getting off it

60

right now."

Turnbaugh only nodded down at her, his expression saying he'd heard it all before.

"No, I mean it, Free," Ella exclaimed. She struggled to her feet with Turnbaugh's help and stood on unsteady legs for a moment. "As soon as this little bit is gone, I'm never going to use this stuff again."

"I hope you mean it, Ella," Turnbaugh said, softening further. He drew her against him and stroked a hand down her hair. "I hate seeing what this stuff does to you." He gazed off in the direction of the trail Max Krey would have taken to go after the ranger.

"All this lovey-dovey shit is starting to churn my guts," Fanin called out, taking a step forward. "If it was one of us men did something like that, you'd have already put a bullet in him."

"But Ella is not one of you men." Turnbaugh half turned, facing Fanin with Ella still in his arms, yet with his right hand lowered a bit and able to reach quickly for his Colt if need be. "Do I have to explain what the difference is to you, Fanin?" he said, offering a slight grin.

The Dead Rabbits chuckled quietly among themselves. Fanin turned a harsh eye toward them, silencing them. Then he turned his glare back to Turnbaugh. "Don't treat it like a joke, Free," he said. "It's time somebody made a decision about her."

"What do you mean, Fanin?" Turnbaugh asked. "Ella's one of us, always has been."

"One of us?" said Fanin. "Then too bad for us. This dope shooter is on a downhill slide, and she's starting to pull us all down with her." He pointed a finger at Ella. "This time she doped up and let somebody slip *out* of our midst. How long before she dopes up and lets somebody slip in?"

"Lower your finger, Fanin," said Turnbaugh, his words turning threatening. "I lead this gang." He loosened his arms from Ella and gave her a gentle nudge to the side. "Or is it time somebody made a decision about me too?"

"I'm not out to throw down with you, Free," said Fanin. "But I ain't backing off of this either. A part of every dollar I make gets split up with this woman. If she's not holding up her end of the pole, I say drop her off our payroll."

"Let me ask you this, Fanin," said Turnbaugh. "How many dollars would you be willing to split with Ella right now if you were still on that *federale* penal farm slopping hogs?"

"One thing's got nothing to do with the

other, Free," said Fanin, his face reddening a bit. "You found a way to bribe the right official for me. I'm obliged. But now —"

"No, I didn't, Fanin," said Turnbaugh, cutting him off. "That was Ella's doings. She approached the official when none of us could. She did it by throwing herself on the offering block. She did everything that turd told her to, just to save your hide. She wouldn't have had to, but she did."

"And I said I'm obliged," Fanin replied.

"Yeah, you're obliged all right," Turnbaugh said with sarcasm. He stepped closer to Fanin and the Dead Rabbits, speaking to all three of them as he stooped down, picked up a rock and tossed it over into the dirt close to Harvey Fanin's feet. "Any of yas wants to cast the first stone, there it lays."

The Dead Rabbits shrugged slightly. "Hell, mate," said Linston McGinty, "this *b'hoy* and me've got nothing but praise for the lovely Ella Lang. Do we, my brother?"

Michael McGinty said with enthusiasm, "Indeed! Nothing but praise! It's an honor to be around such a beautiful woman." He jerked his billed wool cap from his head as he spoke.

"There, you see?" said Linston. He gave Ella a smile and wink. Ella, tears glistening

63

on her cheeks, nodded her head in gratitude.

Fanin stood with a stiff, unyielding look on his face. "We're making a big mistake, is what I'm saying."

"Then there's the stone," said Turnbaugh, nodding toward Fanin's dusty boots.

Fanin stood staring as if considering it.

"Ella is having a hard time with the dope, Fanin. She's not denying it. But she's not getting cut from her share. She's never failed to meet us when we needed her somewhere, bringing us horses, clothes, whatnot. Are you wanting to take over her job? Can you ride in and out of these camps and settlements and not be looked at with suspicion?"

Instead of answering, Fanin said, "She's going to cause us big trouble, Free, and we all know it." He gave the Dead Rabbits a look of disgust, knowing he had no support from them. The two brothers only watched with detached curiosity. Fanin bit his lip and looked back and forth. Finally, he kicked the stone away from his feet. "To hell with it," he said, trying to replace his scowl with a stiff begrudging grin. "Pay me no mind, Ella. I've been sleeping too long on the hard ground."

Ella only nodded and turned away.

"We all have," said Turnbaugh, putting the

matter aside. "Let's get into the mesa, get ourselves some rest and some fresh horses." He looked off in the direction Max Krey had taken. "I'm betting Max will have that ranger and his gal chopped up and fed to the buzzards by the time we catch up to him." He looked at Ella for agreement as he spoke, but her eyes offered no reply.

CHAPTER 5

When Max Krey awakened and realized he'd been knocked cold and thrown over his saddle, he instinctively slid down off his horse's back and tried to make a run for it. But before he'd gotten fifteen feet, Maria's big paint horse bumped him soundly and sent him rolling in the dirt, his hands cuffed behind him. "Settle down, Krey," the ranger called out, stepping down from his saddle and walking over to him. "You're with us until we get to Camp Cimarron. Make the best of it." He reached down and helped the outlaw to his feet.

In the grainy light of dawn, Krey blinked dust from his eyes and looked at the ranger and Maria. "How the hell do you know my name?" he demanded. Before Sam answered, Krey turned his eyes to Toby Burns, who sit handcuffed atop his horse. "Oh, I see. This son of a bitch jackpotted me."

"Max, I never said a word!" Burns cried

out. "I swear I didn't!" He looked wild-eyed at Sam, pleading, "Ranger! Tell him I didn't say nothing to you, please!"

Sam gave Krey a shove back toward his horse. "Burns didn't have to tell me who you are. I've seen your face staring up from a Texas wanted poster for the past year. Besides, I figured you'd be coming for me, once you heard I killed your brother."

"By God you're right about that," Krey growled. He stopped short and spun facing the ranger in the dirt trail. "Take these jail-house bracelets off me and give me a gun with one shot in it. That's all I ask — you and me, right here, right now. We'll get settled up with one another."

"Stop talking out of your head, Krey," said Sam, giving him a shove that made him turn awkwardly and stumble on toward his horse. "I killed your brother because he stood between me and doing my job."

"You murdered him without giving him a chance, is what I heard!" said Krey. Instead of stopping at his horse, Krey took a sudden dive past the animal, rolled in the dirt and stopped with his cuffed hands pulled to one side, grappling with the top of his right boot.

"Here it is, Krey," Sam said calmly. He held up a small derringer he'd taken from

Krey's boot before the outlaw had awakened. Even as Sam held the gun up, Maria's rifle had already swung up from her lap and cocked in Krey's direction.

"Lousy lawdogs!" Krey sneered.

Stepping over to him, Sam dropped the derringer into his duster pocket, reached down and once again pulled the enraged gunman to his feet. "Try anything else like that, and one of us will put a bullet in you," Sam warned him. Again he shoved Krey over to his horse.

Swinging up into his saddle with Sam's help, Krey stared down at him, saying, "What you're doing is against the law, Ranger! You've got no charge against me! Even if you did, this ain't Arizona! This is illegal as hell!"

"We're taking you to the army camp over on the Cimarron," Sam said, taking up the reins to Krey's horse. "I'm going to tell them you and Turnbaugh are the ones who robbed their payroll back in June."

"That's a damn lie!" said Krey. Again his cold stare went to Toby Burns.

"I swear to God I didn't tell him that!" Burns said.

"Shut up, Burns!" Krey shouted. Then to Sam he said, "You don't have a lick of proof on any payroll robbery, Ranger."

"I won't need any," Sam replied, leading Krey's horse. "I'll tell the army to check any complaints about uniformed American cavalry troops pulling a robbery in Mexico."

"You must be as crazy as everybody says you are, Ranger," Krey responded. But his voice had lost its toughness. Sam could tell he'd pressed a nerve. Max Krey grew quiet, as if his mind had become suddenly burdened.

Maria waited, not lowering or uncocking her rifle until Sam had walked over and stepped up into his saddle beside her. Then, as the two backed their horses a step and motioned Burns and Krey onto the trail in front of them, she looked back warily along the trail they had ridden throughout the night. "I will be grateful to the army for taking this one off our hands," she said, gigging her horse forward, "the sooner, the better."

They rode on throughout the morning across sandy, rolling flatlands stretched between towering mesas and rock buttes. At noon, they stopped at a thin stream, watered themselves and their horses and grazed the animals on a pale green carpet of prairie shortgrass. As the horses finished, Maria kept a watchful eye on the back trail while Sam inspected the hooves of each animal in turn before retightening their cinches.

Max Krey had flopped back against a rock and sat slumped, his aching head lowered beneath his hat brim in the noon sunlight. "What all have you told this lawdog?" he growled sidelong to Toby Burns, who sat sprawled beside him, an uncapped canteen in his cuffed hands. Owing to Max Krey's raging temper Sam had left his hands cuffed behind his back.

"Nothing, Max!" Burns said, repeating himself. "I don't know what I can say to make you believe me. I've never spilled my guts to a lawman in my life! You can ask anybody who ever —"

"Then how does he know about the uniforms, about the robbery in Mexico?" As Max spoke, he gestured with his head for Burns to give him another sip of tepid canteen water.

"Jesus, I don't know how he knows anything, Max," said Burns, raising the canteen to Krey's lips. "I only know that I never told him anything."

Krey gave Burns a skeptical look from beneath his hat brim, checking his eyes closely as he asked, "Nothing about Mexico?"

"No, Max, nothing about Mexico," Burns repeated again.

"About the uniforms?" Krey asked quickly, giving Burns no time to stall on answering.

"No, nothing at all," Burns insisted.

"The army payroll?" Krey snapped.

"Damn it, Max! No!" said Burns, getting a bit put out, having repeatedly answered the same questions since before daylight. He gave a quick glance toward the ranger and toyed for a moment with the idea of clasping his cuffed hands around Max's throat and choking him to death before the lawman could stop him. "Are you ever going to believe me on this?" he asked.

Seeing something in Burns' eyes caused Max to settle down, let out a sigh and say, "Yeah, Burns, I believe you. We've got to think of a way to kill these folks before they turn us over to the army. If the army connects us to that payroll ambush, we'll hang for it."

"Jesus," said Burns. A troubled look came over his face as he realized that he had not even been riding with Turnbaugh and his gang during the army payroll ambush.

"That's right," said Krey, seeing his words had made a big impression on the younger outlaw. "Not only that, but the U.S. and Mexican governments have been real obliging to each other lately, delivering people like us back and forth to stand trial." He studied Burns' worried face. "Mexican rope is no better than American, I figure. Both break a man's neck the same place."

"Jesus!" Burns said again.

" 'And they shall hang by the neck until dead,' " Krey said gravely, as if echoing a judge's official decree. "We've got to break away from here before it's too late."

"Ain't Turnbaugh and the others coming to get us?" Burns asked, his voice taking on a weaker tone.

"Want to bet our lives on it?" Krey asked bluntly, gesturing for another sip of water. "I sure as hell don't."

"Jesus!" Burns said for the third time, raising the canteen to Krey's lips again. "I wasn't riding with you boys on either one of those jobs!"

"I know that," said Krey, "but these law-dogs don't. They'll hang you for it sure as hell."

"God!" said Burns, considering the dark irony of it. "I didn't escape a two-year sentence in Arizona Territory just to get myself hanged over here in no-man's-land!"

Krey gave a dark chuckle. "That's exactly what you've done if you're not ready to do whatever I tell you so's we can skin out of here when the time comes."

Before Burns could say anything more, Sam came walking closer, leading the horses, Maria trailing a few yards behind, still looking back across the rugged land. "That's enough water for now, Krey. Get on your feet," Sam said, stopping a short distance away from them. To Burns he said, "Go refill that canteen. We're heading out."

Burns shuffled to his feet and scurried away to the water's edge, feeling Krey giving him a contemptible stare. When he had refilled and capped the canteen with a shaky hand, he felt Maria walk up close behind him and keep an eye on his every move until he stood up and turned to the horses, where the ranger and Max Krey stood waiting. Just between the two of them, Maria said quietly, "Whatever Krey is telling you to do, it will only get you killed."

"He — he hasn't told me to do anything," Burns replied, shaken by the fact that this woman seemed to know what had just happened between him and Max Krey.

Maria gave him a look that told him she knew better.

"I swear he hasn't," said Burns, clenching the canteen to his chest as if it were some object upon which an oath could be declared. "All I want is to get back to New Mexico and get my time served. I don't want no more trouble."

"Good," Maria said flatly. She nodded and motioned him toward the horses.

Riding side by side a few yards ahead of the ranger and Maria, the two prisoners had nothing to say to each other for the rest of the day. Burns liked the silence and the calm monotony of the dusty trail. The calmness and easy gait settled him and gave him time to think. He realized that Killer Max Krey and he were not on the same level in the world of crime and outlawry. He knew when he'd joined up with Turnbaugh and his gang that he'd never be anything more than one of their flunkies. But that would have suited Toby Burns just fine so long as it kept him hidden and out of jail. Now that plan didn't seem to have worked. . . .

Burns swallowed and stared straight ahead along the rugged the trail rather than speculate on what dark deed Krey might demand of him. He hoped the calm and the silence would last. Krey seemed to have settled down, he noted with relief. But the following morning as they broke camp, the ranger stepped over to Krey with the handcuff key in his hands and said, "Krey, we're far enough from your pards now. I'm going to trust you to behave yourself.

Oh, Jesus! No! Burns felt like crying aloud, watching Sam reach down, uncuff Krey's hands from behind his back and re-cuff them in front of him. Looking at Burns as the ranger switched his cuffs, Krey gave him a thin trace of a smile and an ever so subtle twitch of an eye. Burns felt a tense fear begin to churn once again deep in his belly. *What the hell is wrong with this ranger?* Burns cried out inside himself. Didn't he see that Krey had nothing more in mind than to kill both him and the woman? But Burns managed to keep himself in check, watching, not saying a word.

Moments later, mounted and back on the trail across the rolling flatlands, Krey said out the corner of his mouth, "Are you with me, Burns? It won't be much longer."

Burns could do nothing other than nod slightly and continue staring straight ahead.

"What? I can't hear you?" said Krey, forcing the question on him with harsh urgency. "You better show some guts!"

"Yeah, yeah, I'm with you, Max!" said Burns. "I'm just trying to keep quiet!"

Without looking back, Krey listened to the hooves of Sam's and Maria's horses for a moment, judging how far back they were. Then he said to Burns in an even quieter, more sinister tone, "When I make my move, you take the woman."

"Take the woman?" Burns replied in a weak side-long whisper.

Krey cut his narrowed eyes to Burns. "Yeah, take her, kill her, Gawddamn it!"

"Kill her?" Burns said, sounding even weaker and less steady than before.

"Yeah, kill her!" Krey growled, getting impatient with Burns' hesitant demeanor. "What did you think you're going to do, marry her?" He cut his eyes harder to Burns, cocking a dubious brow. "Are you with me or not? Because if you're not with me, you son of a bitch, you're with these lawdogs."

"No, Max! I'm with you, not them!" Burns said quickly, to keep from upsetting him. "It's just that . . . kill her how?" he asked, sounding bewildered.

"Gawddamn it!" Krey sighed in disgust. "Jump her, choke her with your handcuffs, break her damned neck. Sink your teeth in her throat if you have to. Just hang on till she's dead."

"Teeth?" Burns said, sounding shaky.

"Damn it all to hell," said Krey. "Have you never killed a woman before?"

Burns made no reply.

"Hell no, you haven't," said Krey. "I should have seen it right off. If you can't handle her, what good are you?"

"Maybe you'd be better off alone," Burns ventured meekly.

Krey's sidelong glare caused Burns to back off.

"What I mean is, as soon as you make your move on the ranger, I'll be ready to get myself in front of her long enough for —"

"Stop right there. What's all the conversation about?" Sam asked in a raised voice. Gigging his white barb forward, switching his rifle and reins to his left hand, his right hand slipped his big Colt from his holster and cocked it. The two prisoners stopped a few feet from the crest of a low rise.

"Not a damn thing that concerns you, Ranger," Krey snarled as Sam sidled nearer to him. Burns sat nervously in his saddle, seeing Maria had cut her paint horse around to his left, lagging back a few feet opposite the ranger, keeping him and Krey gathered between them.

"Everything you say and do concerns me, Krey," Sam said. Yet as the ranger spoke, Burns couldn't help but notice that something else held his attention.

Before Krey had time to respond to the ranger, a rider stepped his horse slowly into sight at the crest of the low rise. Krey let his words stop short and stared in surprise. At the same time, ten yards on either side of the rider, two more riders appeared, forming a wide half-circle around Sam and Maria and their prisoners. Burns drew his hands taut on his reins and gave the ranger a quick glance. If the appearance of these riders surprised the ranger, Burns saw no sign of it.

"Hello the trail," said the rider in the middle, facing Sam at a distance of twenty feet. He sat relaxed atop a strong-looking buckskin, a Henry rifle in his bare right hand, his thumb lying over the hammer. His eyes went to the Colt in Sam's hand as if a drawn gun had not been expected.

"Hello as well," Sam replied curtly, seeming to have already established the riders' purpose in being there. "I'm a lawman in the midst of transporting prisoners. Clear the trail and we'll be on our way."

"Whoa now," the man responded with a slight chuckle. A smile revealed itself from behind a finely trimmed mustache. "I appreciate the seriousness of what you're doing. But we've waited nearly a half hour for you."

"Then you've already wasted half an hour of your life," Sam replied, his hand holding his cocked Colt. "Don't waste the rest of it."

"Whatever happened to hospitality to fellow travelers across this barren land?" the rider said poetically.

"I said clear this trail," Sam repeated in a stronger tone. He moved his Colt only an inch, just enough to level his aim at the rider's chest, and at the same time keep the man to his left. Maria sat as still as stone, but with both hands on her shotgun, holding it half raised toward the rider nearest her. Sam knew she had her man covered.

Burns stared wide-eyed, still taken aback by the ranger's bristly remarks and unyielding attitude. But beside him, Max Krey said in a low whisper, "Bounty hunters."

"Oh," Burns whispered in reply.

"You're making a costly mistake, Marshal," the mustached man said, raising his left hand slowly, showing Sam a small rawhide pouch he held by its drawstring. "There's some gold coins in there for your trouble." Pitching the bag to the ground alongside the trail, he added, "All I want is Killer Krey. He's worth money in Texas on the hoof or off. I'll take him from here — save you the labor and expense of taking him in yourself." He shrugged. "Hell, I always try to play squarely with you boys out of Parker's court."

Sam made no glance toward the money bag. Instead he kept his stare on the bounty hunter, saying, "I'm not one of Judge Parker's deputies. I'm an Arizona Ranger. Now take your thumb off that rifle hammer easy-like."

"Oh, a ranger," the man said, taking his thumb away from the hammer. "Then all the more reason why it would be prudent of you to take the money and give me Krey." He grinned affably. "You've really got no business over here, now, do you?"

"Lay the rifle across your lap and turn it loose," Sam said without bothering to answer the man. As he spoke, he shifted his gaze to the other man, letting his eyes issue the same command. Maria stared at the man she had covered and watched his hand slowly lower his rifle onto his lap.

As the man with the mustache raised his hand away from his lowered rifle, Max Krey called out, "Ranger, this is Crystal Jack Holder. He carries a big British pistol hanging down his chest on a lanyard."

The bounty hunter's face looked suddenly pinched and red. He glared at Krey.

Ignoring Krey, Sam said to the bounty hunter, "Now tip that rifle from your lap and let it fall."

"No way, Ranger!" said Crystal Jack. "I've gone as far with this as I'm going —"

A shot exploded from the ranger's Colt, cutting the bounty hunter off as the bullet whistled dangerously close to his ear. "Tip it," Sam demanded.

Crystal Jack tipped the rifle from his lap with a sour expression and winced as it hit the rocky ground. "You are one sly bastard, Ranger," he said, suddenly realizing he and his men had been talked out of their weapons a little at a time.

"Tell your pals to tip theirs too," Sam said matter-of-factly.

Cursing under his breath, Crystal Jack growled and said, "All right, men, you heard him."

When both men's rifles fell to the ground, Sam heeled his barb forward, sidled up against the bounty hunter, and reached over and opened his riding duster. He lifted a big British pistol by its leather strap up over Crystal Jack's head, knocking off the man's wide-brimmed hat. "I will not forget this, Ranger," Jack said in controlled rage.

"Step down off your horses, all of you," Sam demanded.

"Jack!" one of the other bounty men cried out. "We can't let them take our horses! They've already took our guns!"

"Exactly," Crystal Jack grimaced. "He has our guns! So step the hell down, Wakely. We've been had."

But Merlin Wakely wasn't taking anymore. "Aiiieee! You sonsabitches!" he screamed, diving from his saddle onto the ground, stretching his arm out for his rifle.

"Drop it!" Maria shouted, already knowing her words were useless. Her short-barreled shotgun swung upward and exploded. Merlin Wakely caught the blast in his shoulder and outstretched arm. The impact spun him off the ground and hurled him backward, leaving chewed-up fragments of his wool shirtsleeve drifting in the air.

In reflex, Crystal Jack tensed as if ready to reach for a gun before remembering Sam had disarmed him. At the same time, Sam's Colt jammed into his ribs, keeping him in check.

"Don't shoot!" the other rider bellowed, seeing Maria swing the shotgun toward him. "I'm getting down! See?" With his hands held high, the third man lifted a leg over his saddle horn and slid to the ground. He looked over at Wakely, who lay quivering and moaning, his bloody arm peppered with buckshot. "I don't want none of that," he said in earnest.

"Climb down," Sam repeated to Crystal Jack. "We'll leave your guns and horses ten miles up the trail." Nodding at the man on the ground, he said, "That one will live if you tend to him."

"What? He might live?" said Crystal Jack, sliding to the ground, sounding enraged. "You're leaving us stranded here, no guns, no horses!"

"We're leaving you alive," said the ranger, the reins to Crystal Jack's horse in hand. "That's all you get today."

CHAPTER 6

After hitching the three horses to a scrub juniper five miles along the desert trail, the ranger booted the bounty hunter's rifles and shoved their side arms down into their saddlebags. A few feet away, Krey whispered sidelong to Burns, "Get ready. We're making our move before Crystal Jack gets to these horses and guns."

Burns only nodded, hoping that by some shift of fate he wouldn't have to side with Krey and kill the woman. If worse came to worst, he thought, maybe he would come straight out and tell the ranger and Maria about Krey's intentions. But even as he contemplated doing so, the ranger walked over to him and Krey and said, "All right, both of you, down from your saddles."

"What?" Krey asked. "Why?" He looked all around as he questioned the ranger. "We're almost to the army camp."

"That's right," said Sam, his tone of voice

growing stronger. "Now step down, like I told you."

Once down from the saddle, Burns breathed a sigh of relief as he watched the ranger uncuff Max Krey and recuff his hands behind his back. Maria stood guard with her shotgun cocked and ready.

"There's no call for you doing this, Ranger," Krey growled. "We haven't done anything . . . made any attempt to escape."

"I know," said Sam, turning him and nudging him back up into his saddle. "But the closer we get to Camp Cimarron, the more tempting it's going to be, especially with you knowing there's guns and horses waiting right here."

"Gawddamn it," Krey cursed under his breath.

Burns stared almost in awe, as if the ranger had read their minds. Seeing the ranger step over in front of him, Burns stuck his cuffed hands out quickly, almost eagerly, saying, "Me too?"

"Yes, you too." Sam studied the look in the young outlaw's eyes as he unlocked his cuffs and removed them. Burns' expression was that of a man who had just had a large burden lifted from his shoulders. Yet, as he turned him around, Burns protested over his shoulder, saying, "I don't deserve this,

Ranger." His eyes went to Krey, showing his disappointment. "Haven't I done everything you or the woman told me to do?"

Nudging Burns up into his saddle, Sam said, almost in a joking manner, "That's true. You have. But I know what a powerful influence a man like Krey can have on a newcomer like yourself."

In his saddle, Burns looked down at the ranger, stunned that the lawman seemed to understand so much about what had gone on between him and Krey along the trail. "I'm no newcomer, Ranger," he said in a haughty tone, showing Krey his belligerent attitude.

Sam didn't answer. He gathered the reins to Burns' horse and handed them to Maria who stepped over beside him now that both prisoners had been recuffed and were back in their saddles.

Back on the trail, the group reached the low, winding banks of the Cimarron River by late afternoon. At dusk they came upon four rows of dust-coated army tents standing within the roped and guarded confines of the temporary desert outpost. "Here's where we'll part company, Krey," Sam said, leading the outlaw alongside him.

Krey responded with a cold, hard stare. "For now," he said in a menacing tone.

"You best to put it out of your mind," Sam warned him, giving a short jerk on his horse's reins, Maria leading Burns right behind him.

Ten yards from the camp's perimeter, the four slowed to a halt as a young sentry half turned and called out toward a command tent, "Riders coming." Then he turned and motioned for the ranger and his party to ride forward.

Once inside the perimeter, Sam and Maria waited for a moment until the sergeant of the guard, followed by two young privates, walked briskly from the command tent and stood before them. The two privates stood at attention, their rifles at port arms. The sergeant's eyes went first to Maria. Then as if having silently reprimanded himself for staring at her, he blinked hard, saying quickly, "Begging your pardon, ma'am, but it's been a long while since I've seen a woman."

Maria only gave a slight nod of her head, acknowledging him.

Immediately turning his gaze to Sam, the soldier said, "I'm Sergeant Burke. Welcome to Camp Cimarron.

"I'm Ranger Sam Burrack, Arizona Territory," Sam said cordially.

"Ah, indeed," the red-bearded sergeant

replied, noting the badge on Sam's chest. "Arizona, eh?" His eyes went to the prisoners, then back to Sam. "Then I suppose this is two more saddle tramps the army won't have to worry about."

"One anyway," Sam replied. He nodded at Maria as she led Burns forward. "This is my partner, Maria," he said. "That man is our prisoner." Pulling Krey's horse forward by its reins, Sam said, "But this is Killer Max Krey. I'm leaving him here for you."

"Oh?" the sergeant said, eyeing the sullen outlaw. "I'm familiar with Killer Krey." He stepped closer to Krey and looked up at him. "I'm familiar with Freeman Turnbaugh and his whole gang of killers and thieves." He turned to Sam, asking, "But what is the charge?"

"I have no charge against him," said Sam. "But I have some information on him and Turnbaugh that I think the army will want to hear." He motioned toward the command tent. "We'll discuss it with you and your commanding officer in private."

"Of course," said the sergeant. He turned to the two soldiers standing at attention behind him. "Guards, escort these prisoners and the horses to the livery tent. Water and feed the horses." His gaze hardened toward the prisoners. "Then do the same for these swives." Catching himself, Sergeant Burke gave Maria an apologetic look, saying, "Begging your pardon for my coarse language, ma'am."

"*Sí*, of course." Maria nodded. She and Sam stepped down from their saddles.

Sam hesitated as he handed Burke the key to the handcuffs. "Krey is a dangerous man, Sergeant Burke." He leaned in closer for privacy and asked in a lowered voice, "No offense, but are these guards going to be able to handle him?"

"Absolutely." Burke gave him a flat grin. "These are two of my best troopers. If they need any help, there are thirty-seven more troopers in camp at this minute. I'm confident that between all of us, we can handle a couple handcuffed prisoners." He took the key from Sam's hand and passed it along to one of the young guards, saying quietly, "Private Beckston, you keep your rifle cocked on these two while Private Unger releases their hands from behind their backs. Be prepared to shoot to kill at any sign of trouble. Is that clear?"

"Yes, Sergeant," the young soldier replied with a somber expression.

Turning to the other private, Burke said, "Unger, look lively when you recuff these men. As soon as they finish their last bite of grub, cuff their hands behind them again. Don't dawdle on the job, or both of you will ride the toe of my boot all the way to Fort Smith."

"Yes, Sergeant," both privates said as one. They turned to the prisoners, Unger assisting them down from their horses while Beckston held his rifle aimed and cocked at them.

"There now, Ranger Burrack," Sergeant Burke said to Sam, "are you satisfied?"

Sam cast a glance at Krey and Burns and allowed the sergeant to direct him and Maria away toward the command tent. On their way, Sam looked back once, long enough to see the two guards walking behind Krey and Burns on their way to the livery tent. Behind them a third guard led the four horses.

"You two were in luck, Ranger," said Burke as they walked on. "Tomorrow morning Camp Cimarron will start pulling up stakes and clearing out of here. This command is on its way back to Fort Smith for a much needed furlough."

"Keep a lookout for Turnbaugh and his men," Sam warned him. "If he finds out Krey is in your custody, I believe he'll fight for him."

"Obliged for your information, Ranger Burrack," said Burke as the three walked on. "I'm hoping we'll cross the desert without Turnbaugh ever knowing." He smiled and mused quietly, "Killer Max Krey. I've always wondered how he got the name Killer. He doesn't look like much to me."

Sam and Maria gave him a look. But the sergeant only chuckled and shook his head.

Inside the command tent Sam and Maria watched a young captain stand up behind an army field desk and greet them with a brisk nod. "Captain Litchfield, sir," said Sergeant Burke, snapping to attention, "this is Ranger Sam Burrack and his partner, Maria."

Upon seeing Maria, the captain resisted an urge to run a smoothing hand along his prematurely graying temple. He smiled cordially and said, "Captain Martin Litchfield at your service." He acknowledged Sam with a curt nod and made a sweeping gesture toward two wooden army folding stools standing in front of his desk. "Both of you, please do be seated."

"Obliged," said Sam, "but we won't take up your time. I only want to report what we saw on the desert the other day."

"Oh?" The captain looked to Sergeant Burke as if seeking either affirmation or assistance on the matter.

"Aye, Captain, these two have brought in Killer Max Krey."

"I see," said the captain. "Is Max Krey among the outlaws we've been sent to roust out of these Indian Nations?"

"Well, he isn't wanted by Judge Parker's federal district court, sir," said Burke, "but he rides with an awfully dangerous lot. Texas has a price on his head. He's wanted lots of other places too."

Sam cut in, saying, "Captain Litchfield, I'll tell you what we saw out on the desert beneath Black Mesa. You can judge whether or not you have an interest in Max Krey after that."

Sam spent the next few minutes telling the captain and Sergeant Burke about the uniforms Turnbaugh and his men had worn the day he and Maria had spotted them on the flatlands. He told them about the bulging saddlebags and the way Ella Lang had met the men with a change of clothes in the two-horse buggy.

"Lovely Ella Lang," the captain said, a wistful look coming to his face as he spoke her name. "One must wonder why such a beautiful and charming lady would lower herself to consorting with such hardcases as Freeman Turnbaugh and Killer Krey."

"I couldn't guess, Captain," Sam replied, offering nothing more on the subject of Ella Lang.

Maria gave Sam a curious look, noting how his voice had grown a bit tight at the mention of Ella's name. Sam must have seen how he'd drawn her attention, she thought, watching him clear his throat and continue, saying to Litchfield, "But we thought you might want to question Krey about the army payroll robbery last spring — the one the Apaches took the blame for?"

The captain winced, then said, "Yes, I will definitely want to question Krey. And I'm certain my superiors will want to do so as well, first thing when we've returned to Fort Smith.

"Good," said Sam. "Then I'm turning him over to you. That will make our trip to Arizona much easier." He paused, then said, "I ought to mention to you that a bounty hunter named Crystal Jack Holder and a couple other men will be coming along the same trail you'll be riding out of here. They want Krey pretty bad. We couldn't turn him over to them."

"Crystal Jack Holder, you say?" the captain remarked, suddenly looking impressed. "Now that's one name I'm quite familiar with! He's a violent, ruthless manhunter indeed!"

"Well," Sam said matter-of-factly, "we slowed him down, disarmed him and two other men. But we left their guns and horses where they could find them after we're gone —"

"Wait!" said Captain Litchfield, cutting Sam off. He shook his head slightly as if to clear it of any misunderstood information, then said with a slight chuckle of disbelief, "You two disarmed Jack Holder and his henchmen, Merlin Wakely and Moe Pitch?"

"Maria had to nick Wakely a little to settle him down," Sam said. "But yes, we took their guns and horses." He gave Litchfield a level gaze. "I don't turn prisoners over to a bounty hunter."

Captain Litchfield and Sergeant Burke gave each other looks of guarded disbelief. Finally, as if having decided he had no choice but to take the ranger's word for it, Captain Litchfield remarked with an expelled breath, "Of course not. I appreciate your position on that."

Maria kept her smile to herself, watching Sam look from one soldier to the other, as he said, "Now that this business with Krey is taken care of, if you'll excuse us, Captain, we'll take our prisoner and be on our way."

"So soon?" the captain said, using much

effort to keep his eyes off of Maria and on the ranger. "I had hoped you and this charming lady might join me for dinner."

"Obliged, Captain," Sam replied, realizing how greatly his dinner invitations increased when Maria rode with him. "But we have another prisoner to deliver all the way to Yuma. We best get as many miles behind us as we can before dark."

"If the captain doesn't mind me saying so," said Sergeant Burke, "I believe Ranger Burrack is concerned with how capable my troopers are at guarding the prisoners."

"I see," said Litchfield. Smiling tightly, he said to Sam, "Let me assure you, Ranger Burrack, while our troopers are young, the pursuit of outlaws in this desert has sharpened their wits to a fine edge."

"I'm certain that's true, sir," Sam replied courteously, "but all the same, I believe it's time we moved on with our prisoner."

While Sam and Maria spoke to Sergeant Burke and the captain, less than fifty yards away inside the livery tent, Max Krey and Toby Burns stood leaning back to back against a tent post eating beans from tin plates, their hands having been uncuffed from behind their backs and cuffed in front of them. Turning his head slightly while the two guards looked over toward the horses that stood eating grain from canvas muzzle bags, Krey whispered near Burns' ear, "When they go to recuff us, we make our move."

"Huh?" Burns seemed startled at the prospect. "They're ordered to shoot us!" he whispered.

"That's the breaks," said Krey. "Be ready. When you hear me draw their attention, move!"

Hearing their whispers, Private Unger turned away from the horses and said with his rifle pointing back at Krey and Burns, "No talking over there! Eat your supper!"

Without replying, Krey gave the young soldiers a scowl and spooned up another mouthful of beans.

Moments later, the two soldiers stepped in closer, took the tin plates from the prisoners and laid them aside. "All right, one at a time," Unger said, taking the key from his tunic. He waited until Beckston cocked his rifle and gave him a go-ahead nod before he reached out and stuck the key into the cuffs on Burns' outstretched hands. Freeing the cuffs, then giving Burns a nudge, Unger said, "Now turn around."

Listening and judging their moves behind him, Krey waited until just the right second, then staring wide-eyed and fearfully at the ground near Beckston's boots, he shouted, "What the hell is that?"

Beckston jerked sideways in reflex, looking down at the ground. Then he caught himself, getting a glimpse of Burns shoving Unger backward and spinning toward him. But Beckston recovered too late. As both his eyes and rifle barrel snapped back toward the prisoners, a nameless fist smashed into his face and sent him backward just as his finger pulled back on his rifle trigger.

On their way to the livery tent, Sam and Maria ducked slightly at the sound of the rifle shot coming from inside the livery tent. Sam's Colt streaked up from his holster; Maria's shotgun cocked in her gloved hands. In an instant, soldiers ran to the spot from all directions. In the next instant, Sam crouched and leveled his Colt at the tent as a horse reared, nickered wildly and bolted from the tent at a full run.

Seeing the horse charging at him, Sam timed his move to the split second. He slipped his Colt back into his holster, stepped sideways just out of the animal's path and leapt upward, diving into the rider as the horse streaked by. Watching, Maria saw both lawman and outlaw crash to the ground and roll away in a large plume of dust. At the end of the roll, seeing that Sam had the rider pinned to the ground, she rushed to the open tent fly, then moved inside slowly, the shotgun up, cocked and ready to fire.

Inside the tent, the two soldiers had already risen to their feet from the straw-covered floor, Private Unger wiping wet straw and horse matter from his cheek. Around Unger's feet lay blacksmith tools that had spilled from an overturned cart when Burns had shoved him backward. He held a cocked Army Colt in his shaking right hand. Fifteen feet away, Beckston had risen from his knees, his nose pouring blood, but his rifle still in hand.

"We've got this one!" Beckston called out, his rifle recocked and pointed at Max Krey's stomach.

Seeing the shotgun come into the tent, Unger said to Maria, "The other one is on horseback!"

"Sam has him," Maria responded, relaxing the shotgun a little, seeing the two soldiers had Krey covered. She stared at Max Krey almost in disbelief, not expecting Toby Burns to be the one attempting to make a break with rifles pointed at him.

Leaning against the tent pole, his hands still cuffed in front of him, Krey saw the look on her face and shrugged, saying with a chuckle, "I don't know what got into that fool. I told this soldier about a lizard I saw near his feet. Burns took advantage of the situation, shoved one guard away, punched the other in the face and hightailed it out of here!" Nodding toward the commotion outside the livery tent, he added, "I see he didn't get very far."

"No, he didn't," said Maria, eyeing him with suspicion. She turned as Burns came falling through the tent fly to the ground, Sam stepping inside right behind him. Burns spit dirt from his lips and struggled to his feet, his handcuffs hanging freely from one wrist.

"Which one hit you?" Maria asked Beckston, her gaze fixing coldly on Max Krey.

Private Beckston wiped his bleeding nose and said with an embarrassed look, "I-I can't really say, ma'am. It all happened awfully fast. I looked away for a second. Next thing I saw was a big fist coming at me."

"It was you, Krey," Sam said, stepping over to him as Unger pulled Burns' hands behind his back and cuffed him.

"You've got me wrong, Ranger," Krey sneered. "If that was me trying to escape, you'd be laying dead and I'd be out of this camp and cutting a trail across country."

99

Sam heard boots hurrying across the ground toward the tent. "I'm glad to get rid of you, Krey," he said. "I'm leaving you here with the army."

"The army might keep me for a while, Ranger," said Krey. "But sooner or later, I'll come looking for you." He leaned back against the tent pole and watched Sam and Maria gather Burns and their horses and leave, meeting Burke and the captain right outside the open tent fly. As the two soldiers and Sam and Maria talked for a moment, Krey stood watching, half smiling to himself. Burns' attempted escape had proved to him that this was going to be easy — *Real easy,* he thought — once the ranger and the woman got out of his way.

CHAPTER 7

After each of them separately told Captain Litchfield and Sergeant Burke their versions of what had happened, Privates Beckston and Unger reunited and stood outside the command tent awaiting Sergeant Burke's decision as to what their disciplinary would be for almost losing a prisoner under guard. As darkness set in, they gazed out across the desert in the direction the ranger, Maria and their prisoner had taken.

"All I did was tell the captain the truth as I saw it," Unger said quietly to Beckston.

"So did I," said Beckston. "I didn't say nothing that would put all the blame on you."

"Neither did I," said Unger. "Blame you, that is." He paused for a second, then added, "We'll be all right. It ain't like we actually lost the prisoners."

"We came mighty damned near losing one," said Beckston. "It still looks awfully bad on us."

"Oh, we'll never hear the end of it, I'm sure," said Unger. He paused as if considering it, then said, "But since he didn't get away, I figure the worst we'll get is a few days of slop labor and some deep teeth marks on the seat of our britches every move we make for the next month."

"I can take the slop labor. It's the ass chewing I dread." Private Beckston stared off toward the livery tent as he spoke. Inside the livery tent two other soldiers now guarded Max Krey. Beckston couldn't stand the humiliation of having been relieved of his duty. His swollen nose ached with each beat of his pulse. "I know which one hit me," he muttered almost to himself, his gazed turning harder and colder toward the livery tent. "But I didn't tell Burke or the captain."

"I don't know why," said Unger.

"I just didn't," said Beckston. "You didn't, did you?"

"No," Unger shrugged, "because I don't know which one hit you. All I said was that it happened awfully fast. The one named Burns shoved me backward over the tool cart. I lost the grip on my rifle. Next thing I saw, you was down, and he was horsed and gone!"

"Yeah." Beckston nodded. "If that's all you saw, then you did the right thing. You told them what you should have. So did I." He continued staring toward the livery tent. "Leave the rest of this up to me."

"The rest of what?" asked Unger. "What the hell is that supposed to mean?"

"Nothing," Beckston said flatly.

"Heck, you're just sore because that outlaw made us both look bad," said Unger.

Taking a deep breath and settling himself, Beckston said, "Yeah, you're right. I suppose I am. So forget it."

"It's forgotten," Unger said good-naturedly. The two stood in silence for a moment; then Unger sighed and said, "I know one thing. I'm glad Burns is out of here. Looks like Killer Max Krey won't be no trouble at all."

"Yeah, no trouble at all," Beckston murmered, still staring hard at the livery tent.

Behind them, Sergeant Burke stepped out of the command tent with a battered briar pipe clamped between his teeth and his reading spectacles perched low on the bridge of his lumpy nose. "Both of yas inside *now*," he said gruffly.

Following him into the tent, the two stood at attention in front of a smaller folding

103

desk across the tent from the captain's. Beckston and Unger both glanced toward Captain Litchfield's vacant desk and looked surprised that the captain had left through the rear fly. But they quickly turned their attention back to Burke as the gruff sergeant saw their surprise and said to them, "You can thank your patron saints that the captain turned this entire matter over to me. Since neither prisoner got away, and since we'll be pulling out of here tomorrow and need every hand we can put to labor, I'm going to postpone any disciplinary measures against yas until we arrive back at Fort Smith."

Unger looked relieved, but Beckston only winced and stood with a tight expression on his face.

"All right, Private Beckston, spit it out," Burke demanded.

"Begging your pardon, Sergeant," said Beckston, "but does that mean that Unger and I will have to go back and guard the other prisoner the rest the night? My nose hurts something awful."

"Oh, your nose hurts," Burke said with sarcasm. Seeing Beckston's obvious displeasure at returning to guard duty, he considered the private's question for a moment, then said, "Indeed you are both guarding the prisoner for the rest of the night. I see no reason to change a thing." He grinned wryly. "That shiny nose of yours will keep you on your toes, I wager."

Unger felt like saying something about the way Beckston had been talking outside the tent, but a piercing look from the other private stopped him.

Seeing the strange look on Unger's face, Burke asked, "Is there something on your mind, Private Unger?"

"No, Sergeant," Unger replied, dismissing any suspicious thoughts he'd just had about Beckston. He and Beckston both snapped back to attention.

"Then the two of yas gather your rifles and be gone," Burke said, nodding toward their rifles, which stood against the side of his small field desk. "Relieve the two guards in the livery tent and resume your prisoner guarding detail."

"Yes, Sergeant," the two privates said as one.

They each picked up their rifles and checked them. As they turned and walked toward the tent fly, Burke called out to Beckston in a chastising tone, "And don't fret, Beckston. The one who caused all the trouble is now a long ways down the trail."

"Yes, Sergeant," said Beckston, following

Unger out the tent fly.

Walking along to the livery tent, Unger said quietly, "All right, what are you up to?"

"*Me?* Nothing," said Beckston, his swollen nose giving his tone of voice a nasal twang. "I just wanted to get us both out of guarding Krey's lousy ass the rest of the night."

"That's not the way I took it," said Unger, the two walking along briskly. "It sounded to me like you wanted us to guard Krey and was afraid if you didn't remind the sergeant about it, he might let us off the rest of the night."

Beckston chuckled and gave Unger an exaggerated look. "Whoa now. You sound like you've been soldiering in the sun too long!"

Arriving at the tent fly, Unger stopped and gave Beckston a pointed look. "I'm warning you. If you're up to something, I'm not going along with it. I've been busted back to private three times in three years. I can't spend my whole career without stripes on my sleeves."

"What the hell is it you think I'm up to, Unger?" Beckston asked, giving him an incredulous look.

"I don't know," said Unger. "But if it's got something to do with beating and kick-

106

ing Krey around some because of what the other man did, I'm not being a part of it."

Beckston grinned beneath his swollen nose and said as he stepped into the livery tent, "I swear to you, beating on Krey for something the other man did is the farthest thing from my mind."

Inside the tent, his hands cuffed around a thick tent pole, Max Krey smiled to himself upon seeing Beckston's face appear through the front fly into the dimly lit interior. Beckston's and Max Krey's eyes met for a moment, each of them offering the other no more than a flat, guarded expression. "Sergeant Burke sent us to relieve you, Connelly," Beckston said to one of the two bedraggled guards standing at ease a few feet from the prisoner, their rifles held loosely at port arms.

"Oh? Well, that suits me to a fine point," said Connelly, smiling at his good fortune, already reaching up and buttoning the top button of his tunic as he spoke. "What about you, Morris?"

"I'm already gone," said the other private, shouldering his rifle. He flipped the key to Krey's cuffs to Unger and turned toward the front fly. Unger caught the key and tucked it down inside his cavalry glove.

On the ground at the base of the tent pole,

Max Krey stared in silence until the other two guards were gone. Then he said, "Well, well, my two closest friends, come back here to keep me company through this long desert night." His eyes locked on Beckston's. "How's that nose, soldier?" he asked. "It looks real painful."

Before Beckston could step forward or offer any reply, Unger cut in, saying, "Krey, we've got orders to shoot you if you cause us any trouble. You'd be wise to shut your mouth and get yourself some sleep. You've got a long ride ahead of you come morning."

"That sounds like good advice, Private," Krey said. He lowered himself back down the tent pole and made himself as comfortable as possible on a pile of fresh straw. "I always try to follow good advice." He offered a slight smile and closed his eyes.

For a few minutes the two privates stood at ease in the dim flickering glow of the lantern light, their rifles at port arms. Finally Beckston took a step back, lowered his rifle butt to the floor and leaned the rifle against his leg while he took out a bag of chewing tobacco, pulled out a wad and stuck it in his jaw. "You know," he said quietly as he wallowed the wad into place, "most officers I've soldiered under always

108

allowed men guarding prisoners to keep a deck of cards or a checker board or something on hand." He looked all around and shook his head slowly. "Not Captain Litchfield though."

"It's because we're moving out tomorrow and we've got no real facilities for prisoners," said Unger in the captain's defense.

"Yeah," said Beckston, "I suppose that's it." He spit a stream of tobacco juice and stared in silence at the sleeping outlaw as he walked over to a straight-backed chair the other guards had taken turns sitting in. "I'm going to close my eyes and chew tobacco for a while. Then we'll swap off every hour."

"Go ahead." Unger nodded, keeping his rifle at port arms and his eyes on the sleeping prisoner. "Just make sure Burke doesn't walk in and catch you sound asleep."

"It's up to you to make sure that doesn't happen." Beckston grinned. He pulled his hat low over his eyes and relaxed. But before a full hour had passed, he spit out his wad of spent tobacco, raised his hat brim and stood up in the dim light of the trimmed lantern. He walked to an overnight pot in the rear corner of the tent and, after relieving himself, walked back to Unger. He handed Unger his tobacco pouch and said,

"Here, sit down and take yourself a breather."

"Thanks," said Unger, lowering his rifle and taking the tobacco pouch. He slumped down and leaned his rifle against his leg. "See you in an hour."

Beckston nodded and stared down at the prisoner for a few minutes until he saw Unger lower his hat brim. Then he stepped forward silently and poked Krey with the toe of his boot until the outlaw opened his eyes and looked up at him. "You're not asleep, you son of a bitch. Stop acting like it." He toed him harder, this time giving him more of a kick, causing Krey to scoot around on the straw to avoid another.

"Hey, hold on, Beckston! What are you doing?" said Unger, raising his hat brim quickly and half rising from the straight-backed chair.

"Relax," said Beckston, waving him back down. "I'm just making sure this bummer ain't laying here getting any ideas for himself."

"Hell," said Unger, relaxing again, "leave well enough alone. I just want to get through this night and leave him to the next guards."

"Yeah, me too," said Beckston, staring down hard at Krey as if giving him an invitation to make a wrong move.

Returning Beckston's stare, Krey said, "Now that you woke me up, I got to relieve myself."

"Hold it till morning," Beckston replied.

"I'm not holding it," said Krey, scooting himself up the tent pole as he spoke. "When a man has to piss, he's got a right to piss anywhere." With his hands cuffed around the thick oak pole, he struggled to position himself in a stance that might enable him to unbutton his fly.

"What's he doing?" asked Unger, again lifting his hat brim. "Don't let him piss on the straw!"

Beckston poked the outlaw in his ribs with the rifle barrel. "That's enough out of you, Krey! Keep them buttoned." He turned to Unger and said, "Give me the key. I'll walk him to the pot."

"Bring the pot over here," said Unger.

"He'd still mess all over the straw. Give me the key," Beckston coaxed.

"Damn it," said Unger, shaking the key from his glove, again half rising from the chair. "I better go with you."

"Go with me?" Beckston growled. He took the key and shoved down firmly on Unger's shoulder, pressing him back into the chair. "It's twenty feet away. Don't insult me."

Krey stared at the two with a flat expression. "I never seen two such chicken-shit poltroons in my life. I ain't even the one who tried to make a break for it, you jack legs!"

"Keep your mouth shut, Krey," Beckston growled, "before I break your teeth for you!" He leaned his rifle over into Unger's hand and drew his pistol from its holster. Cocking the pistol, he stepped over with the key, unlocked the handcuffs from around the pole and locked them in front of Krey. "We're not as concerned as you might think about you making a break for it." He jiggled the pistol in his hand. "In fact, if you feel like trying something fancy, go right ahead." He pulled Krey away from the pole and shoved him toward the pot in the corner.

"No, sir, not me," said Krey over his shoulder, stumbling a bit and stopping. "I can see you're just itching to backshoot me."

"Maybe you're not as stupid as you look, Killer Krey," Beckston said, grinning, stepping forward to give Krey another shove. "But I have to admit, nothing would suit me better than for you to try to —" His words stopped abruptly as Krey suddenly turned to face him. A sharp, eight-inch hoof pick flashed in Krey's cuffed hands as he swung hard, plunged it into the side of the

112

unsuspecting soldier's throat and ripped his Adam's apple sideways.

"Jesus!" cried Unger, catching a glimpse of what had happened. He rose quickly to his feet, yet he fumbled as he shoved Beckston's rifle away and raised his own toward Krey.

Beckston had sunk to his knees before Krey as if paying homage to the man who had just spilled his life onto the straw-covered floor. He held his hands clasped tightly to his gaping throat, trying uselessly to stop the spewing blood. Krey stood straight and tall, his cuffed hands holding Beckston's Army Colt out at arm's length, cocked and pointed at Unger's face.

"Halt!" Unger shouted, his thumb cocking his rifle hammer instinctively, his finger already squeezing the trigger.

"Yeah, sure," Krey said flatly, beneath the roar and the fiery flash of the Army Colt.

CHAPTER 8

At the sound of the pistol shot, Sergeant Burke snapped up from his cot and into his boots ahead of the rest of the camp. Before he could swing his gun belt around his thick waist, he heard pounding hooves from the livery barn toward the outer perimeter of the camp. "Halt," he heard a guard call out in the distance.

"Damn it!" Burke shouted when another pistol shot answered the guard's command. Noting the horse's hooves hadn't slowed down for a second, Burke snapped his belt buckle shut and raced out into the darkness, wearing only his boots and long underwear.

Ahead of him in the dim starlit night, Burke saw soldiers running from their tents and guard positions and bunching up in the middle of the trail leading south out of the camp. "Clear the way! Step aside!" he shouted, shoving and elbowing his way until

114

he stared down at the dazed and wounded guard sitting in the dirt, holding a hand to his left shoulder. "Private Maize!" he shouted at the wounded man. "How bad are you wounded?"

"Just a flesh wound, Sergeant," the young man said in a shaken voice. "I tried to stop him. I swear I did! It happened too fast. I never expected anybody to go charging out of camp!"

Burke cursed under his breath and turned toward the livery barn, saying over his shoulder, "Corporal Risling! Form a squad, six men, boots and saddles!"

"Yes, Sergeant!" a voice called out in the moonlight.

Burke hurried to the livery tent and arrived in time to see another sergeant raise the lowered wick in the lantern and expose the grizzly scene on the straw-covered floor. "Oh, these poor lads," he murmured in remorse, letting go of his rigid authoritarian manner for a moment, seeing the dead faces of Unger and Beckston stare blankly up into the gloom above the lantern's glow.

Behind him, Captain Litchfield stepped into the tent buttoning his tunic, his eyes still misted with sleep. "Did he get past our perimeter guards?" he asked, looking all around at the blood and the bodies, seeing the gaping hole in the center of Unger's forehead. He saw the reddish spray of blood, brain and bone matter slung across the yellow straw.

"Yes, sir," said Burke. "He wounded one of them and got away." Nodding toward the row of horses in temporary stalls outside the open rear fly, he said, "It appears he took our dispatch rider's horses with him. So he is armed and equipped for a long ride."

"For God sakes!" the captain said. "What are the dispatch rider's horses doing saddled at this time of night?"

"He always leaves in the middle of the night, sir," Burke reminded him.

"Form a detail of riders, Sergeant," Litchfield ordered, ignoring Burke's answer. "I want this murderer caught, dead or alive, before this night is over."

"It's done, Cap'n," Burke replied quickly. "I'll be leading the party myself."

Pounding a fist into the palm of his bare hand, the captain said, "We never should have kept these same two men guarding him after the other man tried to escape. It goes against army policy."

"Aye, and I take full responsibility for that, Cap'n, sir," said Burke. He looked down at Beckston's torn-open throat and added, "I believe that Krey himself could not have asked for a better situation. He used that attempted escape as a chance to check these men out and get himself a weapon up his sleeve." The bloody hoof pick lay in the straw. "Killer Krey," he said. "I should have doubled the guard on such a man, sir. I bear all the blame."

In the starlit darkness beyond the perimeter of Camp Cimarron, Max Krey raced along, his cuffed hands leading the spare horse by its reins. He knew the cavalry would have soldiers on his trail no sooner than he'd left the livery tent. But with a little luck and an extra horse to his advantage, he could get across the flatlands and into the shelter of the rocks and mesas before daylight revealed him to his pursuers.

He dared not slow down or stop even long enough to change horses until he'd ridden more than a hard ten miles. When he finally did slide the horses to a halt, he jumped down from his saddle and took stock of both animals and the gear he'd taken in his escape. From his waist he pulled up Beckston's Army Colt, checked it, found four shots left in its cylinder, and put it away, smelling the lingering scent of burned powder from the two shots he'd fired.

While he'd awaited his chance to make a

break, he had singled out the big duns. Now he smiled to himself as he looked more closely at the horses and equipment he'd stolen. Both horses wore McClelland U.S. Army saddles and full U.S. Army tack and bridles, including a rifle hanging from one saddle by its steel ring. "All right!" he said aloud, taking the rifle down and checking it, finding it fully loaded.

Krey hurriedly rummaged through the horses' saddlebags, finding dried food, coffee and even three thin black cigars and sulfur matches inside a cigar tin. He stuck one of the cigars in his mouth and reached deeper into the saddlebags, pulling up a bandoleer of extra rifle ammunition. Examining the ammunition, he draped the bandoleer quickly across his saddle. He jiggled a canteen hanging from one saddle and judged it to be full. Grinning with satisfaction, the loaded rifle in hand, he said to the horses, "Boys, we're going to get along just fine."

Krey stepped up into the saddle of the fresh horse, the reins to the other one in his cuffed hand, and looked back on the trail toward Camp Cimarron. His eyes followed the dark sky beyond the camp in the direction the ranger and Maria had taken. For a moment he thought seriously about turning the big duns wide of the trail the cavalry would be on behind him, and going straight after the ranger. But fumbling with a sulfur match in his cuffed hands reminded him that he better not push his luck just now.

"I ain't forgetting you, lawdog," he said, striking the match on the hard saddle frame, keeping his eyes on the distant night sky. He lit the cigar, and let a long stream of smoke drift and spiral on the dark air. Then he turned the horses and rode away at a hasty clip across the hard rocky ground.

Without pushing the animals too hard across the rough terrain, he rode on through the night, following a wide trail atop a long land fault above the Cimarron River until the fault ran out and left him skylighted against the thin quarter moon. Dropping down to a more narrow trail, but one that ran protected from sight by a ten-foot wall of earth and rock, he followed the black snaking outline of the river another five miles, then stopped suddenly when the glow of a campfire came into sight along the river's edge.

"Well, well, boys," Krey murmured to the horses, staring at the distant firelight like a wolf staring at prey, "what have we here?" Pausing, he gazed at the first thin silver glow of morning far off on the eastern horizon, considering how close the cavalry might be behind him and how long it would take him to reach the campfire.

"Everybody's hunting everybody else." He chuckled grimly. Only a few seconds passed before he shrugged slightly to himself and nudged the big dun forward, leading the other horse beside him. "Nothing like a good ready-made breakfast and a cup of coffee to start off a new day," he said.

Crystal Jack Holder had fallen asleep on the ground, wrapped in a wool blanket against the crisp desert air. Yet when he awakened, he did so in a sweat, the length of him feeling scorched by crackling flames. His first jumbled, groggy thoughts were that he had slipped into hell in the midst of some dark terrible dream. But when his thoughts became more lucid, he scooted back quickly from the licking flames of hell and rolled to his feet, cursing, "Gawddamn it! Moe! Who built this damn fire?"

Moe Pitch rolled to his feet too, sitting halfway around the circled campfire. Dusting his trouser seat he said, "Merlin needed it, Jack! I built it for him! He's in awful pain!"

"Christ almighty!" Holder raged, looking all around as if wondering how many miles away a fire this size could be seen. With a sarcastic snap he said, "Do you think you could have built it any bigger?"

"There's more downed cedar over along that ridge," said Moe, not taking Holder's words in the manner they were intended. "I could go chop off some branches —"

"Hush, Moe," said Merlin Wakely, lying flat on his back, staring straight up. "Jack's dogging you for helping me, is all." He paused, then said bitterly, "I suppose he's never took a load of buckshot and still had to walk ten miles to get to his damn horse."

"Don't call that a load of buckshot, Merlin, you sniveler," said Crystal Jack. "Hell, a load of buckshot would have ripped your arm off and slapped you in the face with it." He walked over, rubbing his hot face, and looked down at Merlin's bloody shirt and forearm. "That's about the same kinda wound we used to give chicken thieves back home when I was a kid." He gave a tight, cruel grin. "Maybe that's what she thought you are — some kind of chicken thief."

"She'll think chicken thief," Merlin said, "once I get my hands around her throat."

"You're lucky the woman didn't decide to blow your head off," said Holder. He'd offered Wakely no sympathy since Maria's shotgun had slammed him to the ground

121

and left him incapacitated. "I wouldn't go making a lot of threats if I was you. She might hear about it and come to finish you off."

"You've acted like a real hard ass toward me ever since the shooting," said Merlin Wakely, rising slightly on his left elbow, his left hand also holding his pistol. "I want to know what the hell you mean by it."

"Let me make it plain, then," said Holder. "You're no good to me anymore. This is a business operation and you're down to carrying only half your load."

"I can still do my share," Wakely insisted, letting himself back down off his elbow and taking a better grip on the pistol. "I'll do better yet after a few days of healing — you'll see!"

"Shit," Holder sneered. "Who do you think you're fooling? Your right arm is as useless as a sleeve full of sausage." His expression grew more cruel and intense. "It ain't coming back!"

"Yes, it is!" Wakely cried out. "I feel it getting better already!"

"Oh, do you?" Holder said flatly, giving Moe Pitch a skeptical look as he continued speaking to Wakely. "Well, tell me how this feels." He reached out and pressed a boot down firmly on the limp bloody arm.

"Good God, Jack!" said Moe Pitch, wincing. "Cut it out! He's in enough pain!"

"Not from this he ain't," said Holder. He held his boot down on Wakely's forearm and said to him, "Come on, Merlin, tell us how bad that hurts."

"You go to hell, Jack," Wakely suddenly sobbed, raising his wobbling Smith & Wesson pistol in his left hand. "I'll blow your head off!"

"Not until you learn to shoot left-handed, you won't," said Holder. He pulled his boot back from Wakely's wounded right arm. "You never could do anything with your left hand. If we had to wait for you to skin a jackrabbit with it, we'd all starve to death."

"Damn it, Jack," said Moe, "why be so hard on the man? Merlin always carries his own weight. He's fine — right, Merlin?"

"Just like always, damn it," said Wakely.

"Fine, your lying ass," Holder hissed. He turned to Moe Pitch, ignoring the gun waving back and forth at him in Wakely's left hand. "He can't feel shit in his right hand, Moe," said Holder.

"It'll come back!" said Wakely, trying to steady his gun at Holder, but unable to do so.

"Yeah," Holder sneered, "so will your sister's cherry."

"Gawddamn you!" Wakely raged, unable to take any more of Holder's insults. He tried hard to squeeze off a round, but before he could, a rifle shot roared down from the grainy morning light, hit Moe Pitch from behind and sent pieces of his heart exploding from his chest.

With Moe's blood splattered on him, Crystal Jack Holder instinctively hurled himself over the fire and rolled and scrambled out of the firelight into the cover of rock. Merlin Wakely dropped his pistol and scooted frantically backward on his rear, his limp right hand dragging a trail in the dirt as another shot slammed into the hard dirt between his bootheels. From the far edge of the firelight, the horses spooked, jerked their reins free from a brittle stand of juniper and bolted away. "There go our horses again," Holder growled in disgust.

The two men huddled close together behind the low rocks, staring up along the edge of a rocky cliff that lay half shrouded in a silver morning mist. "See anything?" Wakely asked, his breath coming in fast gulps.

"No!" Holder said flatly, squinting, searching along the cliff. "Not a damn thing!"

"Is it the ranger?" Wakely asked, panting, staring helplessly, his limp right arm dan-

124

gling in the dirt at his side.

"Who the hell else could it be?" said Holder. "Somehow that sneaking son of a bitch has circled back on us!" A third shot exploded, this one ricocheting off the rock and whistling away. Holder ducked, then called out, "Ranger! Don't shoot! We wasn't following you! We're no longer interested in Max Krey's reward money! We're just trying to get on out of here and get poor Merlin here some medical attention. His arm is greening up and starting to stink!"

"Yeah. Thanks to that shotgunning woman of yours!" Wakely bellowed."

"Shut up, Merlin!" Holder warned him in a harsh whisper. "This ain't the time to bring up grudges. They've got us in their sights!" He turned and called up to the cliff, "What is it you want from us, Ranger? You've ruined Merlin's arm. You've killed Moe Pitch!"

"I want your pot of coffee!" Krey called out, grinning to himself behind a cover of rock along the cliff. "And I want whatever else you've got cooked up down there."

"That cold-blooded son of a bitch," Holder said to Wakely in a whisper. "He'd kill a man over a pot of coffee and salt pork!" He gave Merlin Wakely a look of contempt. "You and Moe had to build a

Gawddamn fire, didn't you?"

Levering another round up into his rifle chamber, Krey shouted from his lofty perch, "I'm going to count to ten, bounty hunters. If you're still down there, me and the woman's going to start shooting. We won't stop until you're both dead."

"So help me, God!" Jack Holder said to Wakely in a voice rasping with rage. "If I never do another thing in this life, I will find a way to kill that lousy lawdog!" Turning his face up toward the cliff line, he called out in a whole different voice, "All right, Ranger, don't shoot! We're clearing out of here! You can have it all!"

Max Krey lay waiting for a full ten minutes in the growing morning light, his rifle in hand and a grim smile on his face. He watched Holder and his wounded partner slip from rock to rock until the distance between them grew too far for observation. Then he stood up and led the two army duns down a narrow path, across a rocky draw and upward to the abandoned campsite.

CHAPTER 9

Freeman Turnbaugh and his gang had been only a couple miles away when the rifle shots resounded in the gray morning light. Following the sound, they spotted the two bounty hunters on foot as the pair tried to gather their spooked horses on a stretch of flatland a hundred yards away. Sitting atop her horse beside Turnbaugh, Ella Lang watched the two men running along behind the loose animals, Merlin Wakely's wounded arm flopping limply at his side.

"What makes you so certain that Max has anything to do with the rifle fire?" Ella asked. Her voice sounded tight and testy.

"I'm not certain." Turnbaugh looked her up and down, noting the ashen pallor on her face, the dullness in her eyes. "But we're in desolate land, Ella," he said, gesturing slightly toward the vastness surrounding them. "I'd have to say it's worth taking a look, wouldn't you?"

Ella didn't answer. Instead she said bluntly, "I'm running out of dope. It's time I go pick up my mail in Fenton."

"If you're running out, that sounds like a good time to quit," said Turnbaugh.

"Oh?" Ella said coolly. "You and the boys are all out of whiskey. This might be a good time for all of you to quit drinking."

"Drinking and doping is two whole different things and you know it, Ella," said Turnbaugh, turning his horse back to the thin trail.

"Yeah," said Ella, getting more agitated. "Doping is cheaper. Doping don't smell as bad. Doping is looked at as more legal and sociable than drinking alcohol, especially back east." She looked at Turnbaugh defiantly. "Want me to go on?"

"Pumping dope into your blood kills you," Turnbaugh said firmly.

"But whiskey doesn't?" said Ella, shaking her head with a dark chuckle. "Christ, what a self-righteous old maid you're turning in to, Free. What about all the poppycock you've smoked? I smoked it with you, remember? You, Max and me — all three of us in San Francisco. We smoked opium from one end of Chinatown to the next . . . stayed so laced and high we lost our rented carriage!" Her eyes took on a wistful, vibrant

128

gleam as she recalled the good times. "Opium and cocaine," she laughed. "I lost track of all the whores we —"

"That was some wild, fun time, Ella," Turnbaugh said bluntly, cutting her off. "But smoking opium and sniffing cocaine ain't the same as pumping morphine."

"It's all the same," said Ella. "It's all here to help you forget what needs forgetting." Her eyes took on a dark look of contemplation. Her tone turned bitter. "Morphine just helps you forget it faster . . . for a longer period of time."

"What the hell are you trying so hard to forget, Outlaw's Lady?" Turnbaugh asked, using a name often given to her by newspapers and periodicals. "You're Lovely Ella Lang. You've done it all. You've gotten everything you ever bargained for, haven't you?"

"Nobody gets everything they bargain for, Free," Ella said. Her voice darkened. "Some things slip past us in the bargaining process."

Behind Turnbaugh and Ella, the McGinty brothers gave each other guarded looks.

Turnbaugh started to say something more to Ella, but he stopped when ahead of them Harvey Fanin rode into sight from around a rocky turn in the trail. "It's about damn time," Turnbaugh said, gigging his horse forward, Ella and the others doing the same.

"You ain't going to believe this, Free," Fanin said, grinning, as Turnbaugh and the others reined up close to him.

"Spill it then," Turnbaugh said gruffly, having worn out his patience on Ella Lang.

Fanin gave Ella an accusing look, then said to Turnbaugh, "I spotted Max Krey just a ways up the trail, sitting at a fire, having himself a cup of morning coffee."

Turnbaugh only stared at Fanin for a moment until finally a wry smile came to his face. "I'll be damned. Did you talk to him, tell him we're on our way?"

"Naw," said Fanin, "I spotted him from a good ways off, didn't want to call out in case there's anybody around." He jerked his thumb in the direction of the two bounty hunters who were now gone. "I saw those two go by chasing after their horses."

"I expect those two are the ones who made Max's coffee for him," said Turnbaugh. "Let's get to him, before he drinks it all up." He batted his bootheels to his horse's sides and sent it loping forward.

At the campfire, Max Krey sat puffing his cigar and sipping coffee from a tin cup. On the ground beside his scuffed boots sat a skillet with scraps of darkened salt pork in it. He spotted Turnbaugh and the others coming toward him at a distance of fifty yards, but didn't bother standing up to greet them. Instead he shook the coffeepot, judging its contents, making sure there was at least enough for Freeman Turnbaugh and Ella Lang.

"What took yas so long?" Krey asked, giving a nodding invitation toward the coffeepot.

When the riders stopped a few feet from him, Turnbaugh looked down at him, wearing a dark scowl. "I ought to pistol-whip you till your eyes cross, running out on us that way."

"Got time for coffee first?" Krey responded with a dark chuckle, the cigar clamped between his teeth. While the rest of the riders pulled their horses up around him, Harvey Fanin passed them by and rode farther along, scouting Krey's back trail. "I suppose I should have told Harvey I've got army close behind me."

Stepping down from his saddle, Ella and the others doing the same, Turnbaugh said, "If there's army coming, he'll soon know it. Harvey doesn't miss a thing." He picked up an empty tin cup lying near the campfire, rubbed his gloved thumb around inside it and poured it full of dark strong coffee.

"Morning, Ella," said Krey, touching his hat brim as Ella stayed close to Turnbaugh's side.

"Don't morning me," Ella snapped at him, playing out their ruse for Turnbaugh's sake. "I'm hell*fire* mad at you, slipping away from me in the middle of the night!"

"I left you smiling, didn't I?" Krey grinned.

The Dead Rabbits gazed on, both of them smiling, Michael looking Ella up and down with hungry eyes.

"I'm not smiling now though," Ella said, relenting a bit, taking the hot cup from Turnbaugh into her gloved hands, blowing on it and taking a sip.

Changing the subject, Turnbaugh asked Krey, "Did you get settled with the ranger?"

Raising his cuffed hands, Krey said, "Does this look like I got settled with him?"

Turnbaugh shook his head slightly and sighed, as if still put out by his partner's actions. He spoke to Arlo Heath over his shoulder. "Old man, bring your keys. See what we've got here."

"Sure enough, Free!" The old man hurried down eagerly from his saddle and came forward, pulling a large ring of keys from his coat pocket. Fingering through keys of various shapes and sizes he asked Max Krey,

"Is them army cuffs or the ranger's?"

"Army," said Krey. "The ranger took his with him when he left me at Camp Cimarron."

"Camp Cimarron," said Turnbaugh, offering a slight grin. "I expect that was a lucky break for you."

Krey gave him a flat stare. "I make my own luck." He shrugged and said, "But it never hurts having a few wet-collared troopers standing guard."

"I bet," said Turnbaugh. "You'll have to tell me everything when we get back to the mesa." He grabbed the cup back from Ella, took a long sip and passed it on to Billy Jones, who sipped it and passed it on to the Dead Rabbits.

Linston McGinty clasped the hot cup of coffee with an expectant smile, saying, "It ain't tea, but it will do."

All eyes had turned to McGinty, but they quickly turned away at the sudden sound of Harvey Fanin's horse racing back to them from around the wide turn in the trail. Linston McGinty finished his sip of coffee and passed the cup on to his brother just as Fanin called out, "Soldiers coming! Coming fast!"

"Hurry it up, old man!" Krey said to Arlo Heath, whose hands worked feverishly, trying one key after another.

"Don't worry. I'll have one here that'll fit — that's for sure." No sooner had he said it than the cuff slid open on Krey's left hand. "There, you see?" Arlo said, beaming. He quickly unlocked the other cuff and slung the pair away. "There ain't a lock around that my babies can't shake loose." He jiggled the large ring of keys proudly and slipped them back into his dusty coat pocket.

Krey stood up quickly, rubbing his wrists. "All right, where are we going to fight them?" he said to Turnbaugh.

Turnbaugh looked all around begrudgingly and said, "Fight them?" He didn't like the predicament Krey had put them in, yet he knew he had no choice but to go along with his partner now that trouble had come riding down upon them. "What's wrong with right here?"

Sergeant Burke slowed his troops to a halt and looked up and all around the ridges and cliffs above the trail as he called back to the seven man squad, "Dismount and draw your rifles. Private Daniels, gather the horses."

"But, Sergeant!" Corporal Risling said, spurring his horse forward, staring down at Burke who had dismounted himself and taken his rifle from its saddle ring. "We're advancing on foot?" He gestured a hand toward the beginning of the long bend in the trail ahead of them. "There could be an ambush waiting around this next turn! We both know this trail. These next hundred yards are the most treacherous! One man with a rifle could take a high position and . . ."

Burke gave the corporal a stare that caused his words to trail to a halt. Being as patient as he could with a soldier of lesser rank who had just questioned his order, the big sergeant replied quietly in a voice just between the two of them, "Corporal, let the men see you dismount. This is no time for you and me to start disagreeing." He flicked a glance toward the turn in the trail and said, "Yes, you and I know how dangerous this trail gets. That's why we're going to leave our horses here, and we're going to slip around this section of trail as silent as lizards. If all is clear, we will have lost nothing more than a little extra time." He jutted his bearded chin. "I know that sounds over cautious on my part, but I'm not going to lose one more trooper to this Killer Krey."

Corporal Risling contemplated the matter for a moment, then stepped down from his saddle. "Sorry, Sergeant. I-I suppose I hadn't looked at it that way."

"I understand, Corporal," said Burke. He reached out and patted the young corporal on his shoulder. "You were only thinking about the men's safety. I commend you for it." He passed his reins off to a young private who came running forward, pulling five other horses behind him. Cradling his rifle in his arm, Burke raised the flap on his side holster, took out his big Army Colt and checked it, saying, "Now then, draw the men in close and keep them moving along on the inside of the trail. These rocks will give us cover from anyone overhead. Leave a man every ten yards apart until we've secured this section of trail. I'll bring Daniels and the horses along and pick the men up one at a time. Meanwhile we will have complete control of this trail." He paused and smiled at his craftiness. "Any questions?"

Corporal Risling returned Burke's smile, looking a bit embarrassed at having questioned the sergeant's orders in the first place. "No, Sergeant, no questions at all," he said. Turning, he took down his own rifle from its saddle ring and hurried over to the men.

"All right, men," said Risling, fanning the men over against the wall of rock reaching up along the inside edge of the trail. "We're going around the turn on foot. We'll disperse one at a time, every thirty feet apart. Daniels and the sergeant will pick us up with the horses."

"Jehoshaphat!" said a young private named Bliss. "All this for one derned man? Who does Burke think this man is, Genghis Khan?" As he spoke, he nodded toward Burke, who had joined Private Daniels and pulled the horses to the side of the trail and out of sight into a pile of rocks.

"As you were, Bliss!" Corporal Risling barked at him. "We're going on foot and that's the way it is! This man is Killer Max Krey, and you best show him some deference. Didn't you see what he did to Beckston and Unger?" Without waiting for an answer, he asked, "Want the same thing happening to us or worse?"

"No, Corporal," the young private said.

"Then let's get ourselves ready for this," said the corporal, looking from one man to the next. "Be thankful we've got Sergeant Burke leading this squad. He gives a damn about us getting killed. If it was Halloran or Gilder, they'd rush us around this bend like targets at a shooting gallery." He turned and, motioning for the men to follow him, began moving quietly along the inside of the trail, going down into a slight crouch as he entered the long bend around the rock wall.

Over the next half hour, the men dropped off one at a time into a good firing position alongside the trail until finally the only three still advancing around the bend were Corporal Risling and two young privates named Miller and Cates. Looking ahead, Risling saw where the bend in the trail straightened and sloped down toward a stretch of flatland. He let out a breath of relief and looked back in anticipation.

"Burke and the others ought to be coming anytime, shouldn't they?" said Private Cates.

"Yes, he should," said the corporal, still looking back along the trail, his gaze growing wary as he searched all around, even down and across the wide flatlands below them. Thinking about it, he said, "You two wait right here. I'm going to go back and make sure everything is all right."

The two soldiers nodded, wide-eyed, and watched Risling slip away from them, retracing his steps along the inside rock wall. They turned quickly at the sound of a horse's hoof click against a rock before falling silent. "Something ain't right," Miller whispered, his hand gripping his rifle tightly.

Thirty yards away, his cocked Colt in hand, Corporal Risling came to halt, seeing Sergeant Burke standing slumped back against a rock, his bloody hands clasped to his stomach. "They got me, Corporal," Burke said, his voice sounding strained and weak.

"Who?" Risling's eyes darted back and forth and in all directions, his Colt moving in unison. "How?" He looked completely bewildered, unable to make any sense out of Burke's words. Turning a quick cautious circle, he stared back at Burke, saying, "Wh-where are the men? Where's Daniels . . . the horses?"

"Why, I'm afraid they're all dead," said Burke, a strange, calm look coming to his eyes. His voice seemed to have regained some of its strength as he stared beyond the corporal, at something or someone that seemed to have just stepped into sight. Seeing Burke stare past him, Corporal Risling spun around quickly just as Burke's bloody hands fell away from his stomach. Was that a smile he'd just seen on Burke's face, he had to ask himself as he turned. But he had no time to wonder about it as he jolted to a sudden halt, staring into the eyes of Free Turnbaugh, Max Krey and Harvey Fanin, all holding guns aimed at his chest.

"Let it fall, soldier," Krey said in a calm voice, the same tone that Risling had just heard Sergeant Burke use.

But Risling held on to his Colt, kept it pointed but shaky as he said to Burke behind him, "Sergeant, what should I do?" Three shots rang out from the direction of the two troopers Risling had just left. Risling winced, knowing what those shots meant.

"I would drop it," Burke said in an even tone.

"Is that an order?" Risling asked, feeling his world grow smaller and smaller around him, feeling an ill icy tightness deep in his stomach.

"Yes, that's an order," said Burke.

"As you wish, Sergeant." Risling uncocked the Colt and let it drop from his fingertip. Raising his hands high above his head, he turned to face Burke, saying, "Sergeant, none of this makes sense to me. How can they all be dea—"

Burke was no longer ten feet away on the rock, nursing a wounded stomach. He stood almost nose to nose to the corporal, whose breath and voice had just stopped with a gasp.

"Sorry, Corporal," Burke said, his bloody hand gripping a knife handle tightly between them. He stared with indifference into Risling's bulging eyes and shoved the knife's blade harder and deeper into his belly. "It looks like you're dead too."

Krey stood silent, his pistol hanging loosely in his hand. "Damn, Sarge," he said, seeing Turnbaugh step forward and give Risling a shove sideways, "you killed these soldiers by yourself? No noise, no nothing?"

"Yeah, that's right," said Burke, watching Risling's body fall to the ground like a loose bundle of rags. "It's not so hard when you've gained everybody's trust." He wiped the knife blade between his thumb and finger and slung the blood to the ground. "I set them up and came behind like clockwork," he said matter-of-factly." His gaze went to Turnbaugh. "What's my services worth to yas this time?"

Turnbaugh said to Krey, "It's all coming out of your end, Max. You're the one caused it."

"I don't care," said Max, "but be careful how much you give him. He didn't do that much for me back at the camp."

Sergeant Burke pointed at the two army duns as he spoke up on his own behalf, saying, "Do you suppose those two dispatch horses saddled themselves, filled their own canteens and saddlebags and stood themselves in the livery tent?" Without waiting for an answer, he continued. "I picked Beckston and Unger to guard you, and even kept them guarding you after your friend tried to make his escape. I might add that I knew all along it was you behind that attempt." He tapped the side of his forehead. "You had Burns do it just as a practice run for yourself . . . to see what you'd be up against."

Max Krey stood silent, giving Burke a flat stare. Finally he tossed the matter aside, saying, "All right, you got me, Burke. You're a devil when it comes to keeping score."

Burke offered a crafty grin. I better be if I want to get paid." He rubbed his thumb and finger together in a universal sign of greed.

Turnbaugh chuckled under his breath, shook his head and said to Burke, "Andy, you always was a real piece of work. That's why we love you." Reaching into his duster pocket, he took out a small leather bag filled with Mexican gold coins and pitched it to Burke. Looking back at Krey, Turnbaugh said, "Forget about what this cost us in gold. We're losing a damn good connection from now on. Army connections like Burke aren't easy to come by."

Burke stood hefting the bag of gold in his

palm and said, "Who says you're losing me?"

"Oh?" Turnbaugh raised a curious brow. "Do you think you can sell all this to the army and not get yourself caught and hanged?"

"With your help, I can not only sell it," said Burke, sounding confident and turning a gaze to Krey. "I wager I can even get the ranger back over here for you to kill."

Krey's attention was piqued, but Turnbaugh said, "Forget the ranger. What kind of help are you talking about?" He noted the serious expression on Burke's face.

"I'll need you to rough me up and put a bullet in me," Burke replied.

"Hell, that would be my pleasure," said Krey with a wry grin, already drawing the stolen Army Colt from his waist.

"Hold up, Max," said Turnbaugh. He asked Burke, "What about the gold? They'll find it on you."

"Here then." Burke pitched the bag back to him. "Hang on to it for a while."

Turnbaugh held the bag, saying, "That could be quite a while. The heat's going to get bad out here, once the army finds out we've killed these soldiers."

"I know how bad it's going to get," said Burke, "but you're safer than the banks out here." He paused, then said, "Besides, you're innocent till proven guilty." Again he gave a crafty grin. "Who says it was you boys who killed these soldiers?"

PART 2

CHAPTER 10

Maria stood with the horses at the hitch rail, watching the ranger walk back toward her from the adobe building that housed the office of Captain Frank Donnely, Arizona Territory Rangers. It had been almost a month since the two had escorted Toby Burns to Arizona and watched him disappear inside the walls of the territory penitentiary in Yuma. Since then they had made a wide sweep of the badlands along the border and brought in Dick Vincent and Bobby Hermes, two hardcases who had robbed a stage coach outside of Cottonwood and made a run for Old Mexico.

Sam and Maria had brought the pair of robbers in, Vincent wearing cuffs, Hermes draped facedown over his saddle. That had only been two days ago, yet Maria knew when Captain Donnely sent for them that they were back on the trail again. "Where to?" she asked as Sam drew nearer.

147

Sam stopped a few feet from her and watched her surprised expression when he said, "It looks like we're on our way back to Indian Nations."

"Oh?" Maria asked, anticipating more.

Sam continued. "Under special request from the federal district court of Judge Isaac Parker."

"The Hanging Judge," said Maria, giving Sam a wary look. "And what do you suppose brought on this special request?"

Sam sighed and said, "It's not good news. It seems that after you and I left Camp Cimarron with Burns in custody, Max Krey killed two guards and made a break in the middle of the night. Sergeant Burke took a squad of men after him, but he was the only one to return. They found the rest of the squad lying dead along the trail."

Maria shook her head slowly, saying, "Those poor soldiers, they were not much more than children." She looked back at Sam. "Who killed them, Max Krey and his friends?"

"Nobody knows for sure, but that's the general suspicion," said Sam.

"But Sergeant Burke is still alive. Surely he knows," Maria said with an inquisitive look.

"Apparently the attack came so sudden

and hard that Sergeant Burke didn't get a look at any of the killers," Sam said.

"That's hard to believe," Maria commented, "an old fighting man like Burke."

"Yes, it's hard to believe," said Sam, "but let's take it at face value until we know something otherwise."

"*Sí*, until we know otherwise. Go on," Maria said, wearing a dubious expression.

Sam took a breath, as if sorting things out for himself, then continued, saying, "Because of the way we managed to slip in on Turnbaugh's gang, arrest Burns and take Krey prisoner, Judge Parker has asked the governor of Arizona Territory for our help in searching for the killers, whoever they might be."

"Just like that" — Maria snapped her fingers — "we become deputies for Judge Parker?"

"No, I'm afraid not," said Sam. "I won't be wearing a badge." He paused and gave her a look. "Both Captain Donnely and Judge Parker think it would be better to let the word get around that I've quit the law."

"No, I don't like it," said Maria.

"Neither do I," said Sam. "I never like playing games about who I am or whose side I'm on."

"You will be hunting for people who have

149

no formal charges brought against them. You will be riding without a badge. You realize what the law is asking you to do, don't you?" Maria asked pointedly.

"Yes, I do," said Sam. "Turnbaugh and his men have gotten too experienced and too slick to be handled inside the law. Parker and everybody else knows what it's going to take to stop them. They're asking me to find them and kill them," he said with grim finality.

"And regardless of how the chips fall, the law will have had no knowledge of it," Maria said, shaking her head slightly.

"I know this is a dirty piece of work," Sam said. "But if this is what it takes to bring down the ones who killed those soldiers, I figure it's worth doing." He looked closely at her and added, "If you'd like to sit this one out, I understand."

"No," she replied, "if you are going, I am going too. With or without a badge, we are still partners, sí?"

"Yes, we are," said Sam, "but I can't ask you to ride back into Indian Nations under these circumstances."

"Then do not ask me," Maria responded quickly, offering a trace of a smile. "When do we leave?"

"I thought you'd say something like that,"

Sam said, taking the reins to his horse. "We leave today. We'll draw what supplies we need and get going. We've got plenty of time to work out the particulars along the way." They both stepped up into their saddles and turned their horses to the dusty street. "I've got a feeling Turnbaugh's gang has broken up and spread out. We know they had plenty of stolen money last time we saw them."

"*Sí,* enough to lay low for a while if they are the ones who killed the soldiers," Maria offered.

"That's what I'm counting on," said Sam, nudging his white barb forward. "If that's the case, Indian Territory will just be our starting point. Men like Krey and Turnbaugh have lots of holes they can crawl into when the going gets tough."

"But do you know any of these places?" Maria asked, nudging her horse along beside him.

"No," said Sam, "I don't know anything about where Turnbaugh and Krey hide out. But I know where Ella Lang likes to be. Find her and we'll soon find all the others."

"But Ella is not the leader," said Maria.

"No, but you'd be surprised what the leaders will go through to stay close to her," Sam said quietly, with a reflective look in his eyes. A moment later he said, "Ella

151

always liked the cowtowns, the boomtowns, the rowdy places. I don't expect that's changed any."

Maria only looked at him, deciding that any questions she had regarding him and Ella Lang would keep until later when their supplies were drawn and they were on the trail. For the time being, she rode along quietly beside him to an adobe-and-log trading post at the far end of the ranger encampment, where within an hour they had taken on coffee, food staples, ammunition and grain for their horses.

They rode away. By late afternoon the two had traveled a respectable distance before making camp in the long shade of a tall saguaro cactus on the bank of a nameless meandering creak. When they'd finished a meal of beans and warm elk jerky, they set their empty plates aside and sipped coffee quietly until without being asked, Sam said, "I can tell you're curious to why know why I seem to know so much about Ella Lang."

Maria shrugged slightly. "Only if you want to tell me."

The ranger gave her a flat stare.

"I'm sorry," Maria said softly, cradling her coffee cup in both hands. "Yes, I am curious. I do want to know."

"Ella and I used to be together," Sam said

bluntly, letting his words spill like some heavy weight he'd suddenly let go.

"Together?" said Maria. "You mean . . ." Her words trailed.

"Yes, together," said Sam. "Just like you and I are now." He stopped for a moment, then said, "Not as close as you and I are . . . but we were together."

"I see," said Maria, not about to tell him that she had all but come to that conclusion on her own. "I am glad you told me this now, instead of me hearing it from someone else . . . perhaps from her."

Sam looked at her closely and said, "I know I should have told you sooner. I just kept hoping for the right time and place. Maybe I had to get it straight in my mind first . . . figure out what it was between her and me."

"And now you have figured it out?" Maria asked.

"Yes, I have," said Sam. "I had it figured out a long time ago, but I suppose I made myself quit thinking about it." He stared into the low flames as if reliving some shadowy scene from the past. "I loved her, Maria. I can't deny it."

"I see," Maria said almost in a whisper.

"You know how they say that most every man meets that one certain kind of woman

— the one that he knows he can never have? The one that he spends the rest of his life trying to forget?" Sam said quietly.

"*Sí,* I have heard that," Maria said softly.

"If I had never met you," Sam continued, "Ella Lang would have been that woman."

"Do you love her still?" Maria asked gently but firmly.

Sam sat silently for a moment, gazing into the flames. Finally he said with a slight sigh, "No, Maria, not anymore. You're the only woman for me."

"Because if you still love her," Maria continued, "you should not be the one hunting her down. Captain Donnely and Judge Parker would have to understand and send someone else."

Sam said, "That won't be necessary. If I dug down deep enough inside myself, I'm afraid of what I might still find there for Ella Lang. But my duty is to uphold the law. It's fallen to me to hunt down her and her friends, so that's what I'm going to do. I won't pass my duty off to somebody else."

"What if it were me instead of Ella?" Maria asked. "Would you still feel it was your duty?"

"Don't talk that way," Sam replied softly. "It would never be you I was hunting. You're not that kind of person."

"Wasn't there a time when you thought she would never be that kind of person either?" Maria asked, to make her point.

"Yes, I suppose so," said Sam. "But in El-la's case I think I always considered her as being one step away from going down the wrong path. I thought I was the one who could stop her from taking that step." He thought about it and shook his head in reflection. "Being a young lawman, I must've thought I could protect her, keep her away from all the bad elements. It seemed like those elements always sought her out." He stared deeper into the flames; his expression turned more solemn. "It took me a while before I realized that Ella herself was the bad element. She was only seeking out her own kind."

"So the things you tried to protect her from were the very things that she desired most?" Maria asked gently.

Sam nodded. "Yes. As it turns out, I was never protecting her from anything. I was no different than a man who keeps a wolf cub from returning to its litter mates."

"It's good that you do not blame Free-man Turnbaugh and his gang for what she's become," said Maria. "If she was bent on self-destruction, they had nothing to do with it."

"I know," said Sam. "She went looking for the outlaw life. It didn't pick her out of a crowd. Besides, there were others before Turnbaugh and Krey came along — a gunman named Dallas Mattingly, a card slick, a train robber named Benton O'Shey." He paused, then said, "There were others too. Too many others to remember."

"Benton O'Shey?" said Maria. "I have heard of him. He disappeared years ago and has not been seen or heard from. . . ." She let her words trail down as if struck by some dark realization. "Oh," she said as if in summary.

Sam noted the change in her voice and expression and said, "It's a long story about Ella and me. Someday I'll tell you the whole of it."

"But not now?" Maria asked. "Perhaps it would be good for you to get this off your chest."

"Sometimes it's good for a man to get a few things off his chest," Sam said quietly. "But sometimes all it does is make a mess of things." His eyes went to hers; his arms went out and around her, drawing her to his side. "I've got you now. As far as I'm concerned, Ella Lang belongs to the past." He looked off across the far sky. "If I'm destined to bring her and the rest of them

156

to justice, so be it." He smiled and felt Maria's warmth against him, liking the feel of her, her scent, her strength. "I wanted to get it talked about before we got too far down the trail. We might get too busy to talk once we meet up with these people."

The streets of Dodge City lay puddled and slick with mud from three days of rain when the two Dead Rabbits rode in from the north. Linston McGinty maneuvered his mud-splattered horse around two men fighting in front of Chambers' Opal Saloon. "I think this foolish of ya, Michael *b'hoy,*" he said to his brother, who was riding close beside him. A small gathering of spectators cheered and booed as the muddy street brawlers battered each other relentlessly. No one bothered casting a glance toward the two bedraggled newcomers.

"I know you, Linston," said Michael McGinty. "You're just cross because of that infernal rain." He grinned, raising a palm to the sky, the fingers of his woolen gloves missing. "But as you can see, it's all gone now. So buck up a bit." He maneuvered his horse around two spectators, who had stepped backward in the sloppy street as the fighters fell into them. "I've heard so much about Dodge City. Isn't it high time we saw the place?"

"Ha!" said Linston. "It's not sightseeing that draws you here, lad, and I know it." Straightening his horse, he reined the tired muddy animal toward a hitch rail a few yards from the fighters. "You knew as well as I that she'd be coming here. She told us as much the day we all took our shares and split up." He spoke above the sound of a twangy piano and rattling banjo.

"Aye, that she did," said Michael, reining his horse alongside his brother's and stepping down at the hitch rail with him. He straightened his soft-billed wool cap atop his head and grinned, saying, "And did it occur to you that she only told us that so I would be sure to know where to find her?" Hoots and laughter spilled from the batwing doors of the large clapboard saloon.

Linston shook his head with a concerned look. "Brother, I wish you would put her from your mind. You've been told that she'll get around to you soon enough. She makes it a point to bed anyone who rides with this gang. You're still a new man."

"New man, my arse!" Michael protested. "I'll not wait until she gets around to me. I'm going to have my fill of that woman, and I'm not standing in anyone's line to get it." He spun his reins quickly around the rail. "If Turnbaugh and Krey don't mind her rutting the lot of us, then they shouldn't mind *when* she does it."

"Lad, lad." Linston chuckled, shaking his head. "I daresay that Max Krey could care less who pokes his swamp duck once he's through wetting her thighs. But can you not see that it curdles Turnbaugh's soul, knowing that his lovely Ella spreads her legs for the whole bloody gang?"

"He agrees to her doing it," Michael said pointedly, "and he's the leader after all."

"He agrees to it because he knows he is powerless to stop her," said Linston. "At least this way he feels he still has control over her. Adding his rules around it makes it seem as if it's his idea somehow." He held up a finger for emphasis. "Mark my words though, he'll not stand for you jumping ahead of him on this. If you're smart, you'll wait for the right sign from him."

"To hell with waiting for a sign from him," said Michael. "I don't wait when it comes to matters of my nature."

"Aye, I've seen that," Linston said critically. "That's partly the reason we had to leave New York, where the pickings were easy, and come out here to this uncivilized shithole to scratch out a living for ourselves!"

"Scratch out a living!" Michael smiled calmly and shook his trouser pocket, conjuring up the muffled jingle of gold coins. "How many drunken throats would we have had to cut to make this sort of swag around the Points? Isn't this the kind of money it takes to satisfy your peculiarities?"

Linston settled down, managing a slight smile himself. "All right. Perhaps I spoke a bit rashly about our income." He leveled his wool cap and looked back and forth along the boardwalk. At the far end of the muddy street, he spotted two young women standing on a balcony, exposing their ample breasts in a red light's glow. "As to my peculiarities, I believe I will just stroll down to yon bawdy house and see what sort of whips and tethers they have on hand."

"Enjoy yourself, brother," Michael said, stepping onto the boardwalk and toward the swinging doors of the saloon.

CHAPTER 11

At the crowded bar of Chambers' Opal
Saloon, Michael McGinty ordered a bottle
of rye and a shot glass. He paid the bartender with a Mexican gold coin, took his
change in dollar bills, folded them and
shoved them down into his shirt pocket. He
pulled the cork from his bottle with his teeth
and filled his shot glass while the piano and
banjo came to a halt and paused momen-
tarily between songs.

"I'm looking for Ella Lang," he said to the
red-faced bartender, recorking the bottle on
the bar and tossing back a shot of rye.

"Lovely Ella?" the bartender replied
gruffly. "She's somewhere in there. Help
yourself to her. She's a handful when she's
shining on dope and whiskey." He nodded
into a thick haze of cigar smoke filled with
the sound of jingling coins, poker chips and
outbursts of cursing and laugher. "If you're
a friend of hers, you might want to tell her

161

to ease up on taunting the other players. These hombres come here to gamble, not to watch a woman make a fool of herself."

"Tell her your own bloody self!" Michael growled, cutting the bartender short. Giving the man a hateful scowl, he swiped the bottle off the bar and stomped away among the gaming tables. The bartender only shrugged, pulled four mugs from under the bar, stuck them beneath two beer taps and began filling them.

Halfway through the maze of gaming tables and milling onlookers, McGinty saw Ella seated at a poker table with her back to him. At her left side a whore stood leaning against her, a long, lithe arm across Ella's shoulders, Ella's left arm draped loosely around the whore's thin waist.

"Damn it all to hell!" Michael heard one player say as he walked up to the table. The player slapped his cards onto the tabletop and pushed his chair back. "That does it for me. I can't concentrate under these circumstances." He stood up, and straightened his vest as he said to Ella, with an expression of pity, "What in God's name has become of you, Ella Lang? You used to be a fine, willful spitfire of a woman, the kind of gal a sporting man was honored to know." He shook his head. "But not anymore . . . no, ma'am. You're not a lady anymore. You're just a woman low-down." He turned on his heel and stomped away through the looming smoke.

"Well, hell, mister! Don't go away mad," Ella called out with a drunken laugh. The remaining two players gave each other a look, neither of them sharing Ella's humor.

"Mind if I sit in?" Michael asked, stepping around to the empty chair, dropping his roll of bills on the table and staring down at Ella.

"Well, well," Ella said, recognizing Michael McGinty through a blur of morphine and whiskey, "if it isn't the Dead Rabbit himself!" As she spoke, she hugged the young whore tighter against her side. Seeing the concerned look on Michael's face, Ella laughed, saying, "Don't worry! These gentlemen don't know one dead animal from the next, do you, boys?"

Ignoring Ella's remark, a broad-shouldered man wearing a fringed buckskin coat and black flat-crowned hat said to Michael, "Sure, take a chair." He turned his gaze from Michael to Ella and said, "Now then, are we going to play serious poker or watch you pump dope and diddle that whore all night?" On the table near Ella's right elbow lay her syringe and her leather drug pouch.

"Now, gentlemen," Ella said in a taunting tone of voice, "why does it offend you to see me diddle a whore? I see you fellows do it all the time."

"Ma'am, it does not offend me," the man in the buckskin coat said. "I don't care if you lick her from her kneecaps to her naval. But don't do it whilst I'm trying to play poker. It's damn distracting, and I believe that's why you're doing it."

Michael had sat down in the empty chair, but upon hearing the conversation, he waited before pulling the chair in closer to the table.

"Maybe it doesn't offend you, sir," said the other player, a powerfully built cattle buyer named Beale Pierce, "but I was raised Christian, and it offends me to no end to —" He stopped midsentence when Ella pulled the young whore's face down to hers and kissed her full and deep on her mouth.

Michael McGinty and the other two players stared wide-eyed in disbelief. When the kiss ended, Ella grinned and licked her lips, saying in a purring tone, "Umm-umm. Boys, that was like sticking my tongue into a pot of warm honey!"

"Oh Jesus! Gawddamn!" said Pierce, a nauseated expression coming to his face.

He shoved his cards into the middle of the table, threw back his shot of whiskey and clamped his cigar between his large teeth. "That's all I can take. I'm out of this game." He scooted his chair back from the table and stood up quickly. Yanking his hat from the empty chair beside him, he held it in front of him instead of putting it atop his head. "I enjoy a whore as much as the next fellow . . . but this business of two women smearing around on one another is unnatural, and an abomination in the eyes of God."

Ella tightened her embrace around the whore's waist and responded with a drunken giggle, "Tell me something, Beale. Is it God's eyes wearing your face, or your eyes wearing God's face?"

"Huh?" Beale Pierce's face reddened in anger and confusion. "What the hell are you talking about, you dope-eating harlot! If you wasn't a woman, I'd backhand you off of every wall in this place!"

Michael McGinty rose halfway from his chair, gripping a boot knife in his right hand. But Ella's voice stopped him from going across the table for Pierce's throat. "Easy, Dead Rabbit boy. Don't stab him until I say so," she said.

Pierce stood stunned. His hand had gone

to the handle of the gun on his hip, but his appearance said that he would never get it drawn in time to save his own life should McGinty spring upon him. The other player watched closely, showing no sign of fear, only a look of disgust that the poker game had ended. "That's it for me too," he said, rising from his chair. "You folks go on and kill each other." His eyes flashed on the knife in McGinty's hand and the pistol on Pierce's hip. He shrugged as he turned away. "I'll go find myself a more serious game."

Ella ignored him and stared mockingly at Beale Pierce through dilated eyes. "Just think, Pierce," she said. "One word from me and this Dead Rabbit boy will cut your heart out and eat it if I tell him to . . . right, Michael?" She sliced a sidelong glance toward McGinty.

"Say the word, Ella," McGinty rasped under his breath, his eyes fixed coldly on Beale Pierce, his knife hand poised and ready.

Still grinning at Pierce, she reached around the young whore's waist and rubbed her flat lower stomach. "See? That's how powerful this stuff of ours is . . . men kill for it. This Dead Rabbit boy has been watching, waiting, biding his time. But not anymore. Tonight's his night."

"Say the word," McGinty whispered again, his eyes lit up with anticipation from Ella's words.

Ella gave a quick glance around the saloon, seeing that curious patrons had turned and begun staring toward their table. "Naw," she said coolly, "not right now. Maybe later if he's still in town." She gestured Beale Pierce toward the bat-wing doors. He backed away one cautious step, then another before turning and hurrying toward the doors with a look of humiliation on his reddened face.

The other player who had left the table had taken a spot for himself at the far end of the bar and watched with interest. No sooner had Beale Pierce disappeared through the bat-wing doors than Crystal Jack Holder sidled up to the crowded bar and, keeping his eyes on Ella Lang's table, asked sidelong, "Who's the man with her, Tilton? Please tell me he's one of the New Yorkers."

"All right, I will," Tilton Blackwell replied. He smiled behind his wide mustache and said without taking his eyes off of Ella and McGinty, "He's one of the New York brothers sure enough."

"What a stroke of luck for us!" said

Crystal Jack. "Are you sure?"

Blackwell stared at him before finally answering, "Hell yes, I'm sure. Two or three times she called him a Dead Rabbit. How much plainer do you need it to be?" He looked Holder up and down. "If we're going to be partners, you better understand, I don't make mistakes — mistakes get you killed in this business." He looked past Holder at Merlin Wakely, noting Wakely's empty half-rolled-up shirtsleeve and his stub of an arm inside it.

"I know, I know," said Holder. "We've been a long time hunting this bunch. I can't help getting a little excited at the prospect of watching their faces hit the dirt." He gave Wakely a quick grin, then said to him and Blackwell, "All we need to do now is stay on them until this bitch hooks us up with Turnbaugh and Krey. That's when we'll start drawing our pay."

"I say we shoot these two down like dogs and wait for Turnbaugh and Krey to come claim the bodies," said Wakely. He stared toward Ella's table with a fierce expression. "I'd like to gouge that bitch's eyes out with my thumbs," he murmured.

Blackwell looked at Wakely's empty shirtsleeve and said, "It would take you two tries to do it."

168

Wakely winced and cursed under his breath, seeing no humor in Blackwell's words.

Blackwell gave him a look and said to Holder, "Is your friend here always so bitter toward women?"

"It's gotten worse since he lost that arm to one," said Holder.

"Yeah, you told me all about it," said Blackwell; he rolled his eyes slightly as if bored with hearing the story. "The Spanish woman who rides with the ranger. I expect a load of buckshot would sour a man on the weaker sex at that, for a time at least." He smiled a bit, looking Wakely up and down again. "But surely you're not hating every woman because of what that one did?"

"Why not?" Wakley asked flatly. "I'll show her what hell feels like if I ever get my hands on her."

Blackwell looked at Wakely's empty sleeve again and started to make another smart remark; but thinking better of it, he kept quiet, smiled to himself and sipped his whiskey, looking back toward Ella Lang's table, where Ella sat drawing morphine into her syringe. Across from Ella, the young whore had taken a chair and she and McGinty sipped whiskey and watched Ella go about preparing herself a shot.

"You've got half the people in this joint staring at you, Ella," McGinty said, chuckling, watching Ella wipe the needle across the sleeve of her dress.

"They can all kiss my ass," Ella replied. "I'm doing nothing illegal. This stuff is cheaper than rye whiskey and has a much better punch to it." She looked Michael in his eyes and said, "Ever tried it? Who knows, it might be just the thing to soothe your pain," she said in a singsong voice.

McGinty grinned and said, "You know what it's going to take to soothe my pain, lovely Ella."

"Oh, yes, that's right!" Ella said as if suddenly being reminded. "You been wanting to feel my all fours wrapped around you ever since you started riding with us."

"Who's us?" the young woman cut in.

McGinty and Ella both gave her a silent look. "Michael," Ella said at length, "this is Feathers." She gestured toward the woman with the tip of the syringe needle. "Feathers, this is my ole trail pard, Michael." She offered nothing more than the introduction. But then she said to Feathers, "What about you, honey? Want some of this good stuff before we all go somewhere and get cozy?"

Feathers hesitated, saying, "Maybe later. I tried some of it back before I left Saint

Louis. It knocked me out so hard I peed myself!" She tossed a short giggle to McGinty.

"What about you, Dead Rabbit boy?" Ella asked McGinty, holding the needle toward him. "Want to feel the devil climb your ribs?"

"Sure, why not?" said McGinty. "I've always wanted to try it, see what all the fuss is about." He grinned, but held his hand up toward the needle, saying, "Not here though. You said something about going somewhere and all of us getting cozy?" he asked expectantly.

"You sure don't like wasting time, do you, Dead Rabbit?" Ella gave him a coy smile through glassy bloodshot eyes and held the sharp tip of the syringe needle closer to her pale forearm. "Give a lady time to freshen up."

"I want what I want, when I want it," said McGinty. "Are we going or not?"

"We're on our way," she said. "Just let me get fixed up first. I'm walking out of here with clouds at my feet."

In the gray hour before dawn, Merlin Wakely crawled across the sandy soil on his belly until he reached the spot beside a half-fallen burrow shack, where Holder and

171

Blackwell sat hunkered down behind a rail fence and a pile of downed white oak fire wood. "It's taking me a while to get used to being without an arm," Wakely said, struggling to his feet out of breath, a ten-inch metal file in his gloved hand.

Blackwell puffed on a thin cigar, watching with a bemused expression as Wakely stood up and swayed back and forth a bit before catching himself. Studying the tip of his glowing cigar for a second, Blackwell smiled to himself and said, "I have heard from others who have lost a limb that it ofttimes feels as if the missing appendage is still there. What is your say on that matter, Wakely, if I might be so bold?"

Wakely just stared at him as he handed Jack Holder the metal file and said almost in a whisper, "I filed a notch in both of their horses' shoes. We'll see it plain as day across the dirt."

"Good work, Merlin," said Holder, patting the file on his palm and gazing through the hazy darkness toward the shack they had followed the three to outside of the Dodge City town limits.

Blackwell blew off the tip of the cigar, still studying it. "I asked you a question, Wakely," he said gruffly, "but maybe you didn't hear me . . . so I'll ask it again." He turned his gaze from the cigar to Wakely. "Does it ever feel like that arm is still there?"

"I heard you the first time," Wakely replied, his voice just as gruff and testy as Blackwell's. "Did you ever stop and think that maybe I don't like talking about my infirmity?"

"Aw, come on, now, Merlin. Don't be like that," Blackwell said, goading him a bit. "How bad can it really be. It ain't like you made your living playing a fiddle." He drew a long puff of smoke and let it out in a slow, thin stream.

"I see what you're trying to do, Blackwell," said Wakely, controlling his anger. "But I'm not going to let you get to me. If you think it's so damned funny losing an arm, you're some sort of sick crazy sonsabitch, is all I can say."

He took a step forward, but Holder stepped in between the two saying, "All right, that's enough! Save it all for Turnbaugh and his bunch."

"Yes, or better yet," said Blackwell, grinning, his cigar clamped in his teeth, "save it for the ranger and his woman — especially his woman." His grin widened. "I never seen a woman ruin a man so bad in my life, as she did you!"

"Keep it up, Blackwell," Wakely warned.

"When the time comes, we'll see who gets ruined. I don't take any poking or prodding off of anybody, including you."

"Including me?" Blackwell offered a thin, tight smile. "Whatever *are* you talking about, Wakely? I'm just passing time here, waiting for the sun to rise. As far as that Spanish woman goes, threaten her all you want. The fact is, you're never going to see her or that ranger either one, ever again." He turned his slight smile to Holder. "So you can both forget ever reaping any vengeance there, unless you want to ride all the way to Arizona Territory —"

"Hey, pay attention!" said Holder. "A lantern just came on in the shack! They'll be heading out before long."

Inside the shack Ella Lang had awakened before Michael McGinty and Feathers. Staggering naked from the bed, Ella lit a coal-oil lantern with a shaky hand, then held it high in order to see if she could recognize who she'd spent the night with.

"Oh, Jesus, not you," Ella whispered with remorse, looking down at McGinty. In the crook of McGinty's forearm, she saw the slight crusts of dried blood and three needle marks in a row along the blue vein in his triceps.

Feathers lay beside McGinty, the two of

them naked, their limbs partially entwined. Feathers' arm also showed the red sting of the syringe needle. "You neither, you silly little harlot," Ella whispered. Reaching down with her shaky free hand, she brushed Feather's dingy blond hair from her face. She looked at two small bottles of morphine sitting on the stand beside the bed, one empty, the other one only a quarter of the way full. "You're right, Free. I ought to leave this stuff alone," she murmured. Then she picked up the one with morphine still in it and left the other where it stood.

Ella slipped into her riding skirt and blouse in the glow of the lantern light and, feeling the room began to sway around her again, scooted out a wooden chair from under a table in the middle of the floor. Hearing the chair scrape roughly on the plank floor, Michael McGinty lolled his head back and forth for a second until he managed to get his eyes open and ask, "Who the . . . hell's there?"

"It's me, Ella, remember?" she said aloud in a raspy, slurred voice. She held herself steady, one hand gripping the table's edge, the other picking up the lantern from the table and holding it up for McGinty to get a look at her. Putting on a false front, she said to him, "Don't tell me you're the kind of man who lets a little dope and whiskey keep him sleeping past sunup." She turned loose the table's edge and sat down shakily in the chair.

"Where's all the dope?" McGinty asked, reaching over, picking up an empty morphine bottle from atop the nightstand and shaking it. "Damn, don't tell me we're out of it," he moaned, "just when I'm beginning to like it."

"All right, I won't tell you then," said Ella, picking up her colorful lady's riding boots and shaking them out, "but we are out of it. And if you plan on using this stuff very often, you better learn to put aside a little eye-opener for yourself."

"Is that what you did?" McGinty asked. "You seem to be feeling pretty damn good."

"Oh, do I?" Ella said wryly. "Then I have sure fooled the hell out of you."

"Where are you going?" McGinty asked, his lips feeling numb and rubbery.

"First I'm going back to Dodge City to get some dope I have there. Then I'm going to the railhead at Buckton," Ella said flatly, pulling on a boot.

"Where the hell is Buckton?" Michael asked groggily, his eyes and hand going to the bottle of morphine again, as if he might have been mistaken about it being empty.

Watching him, Ella said, "Go on back to sleep. I'll close the door behind myself."

"Like hell I will!" said McGinty, struggling to his feet and staggering naked toward her. "We're sticking together, you and me." He threw his arms around her and pressed himself against her. "Now that I've got you, I'm not turning you loose." He nuzzled his beard-stubbed face into her throat.

She held him back as much as she could, saying, "Easy now, Dead Rabbit boy. What are the others going to say about this? I'm a member of the gang, remember. I take care of everybody."

"Not now," said McGinty. "I don't give a damn what Turnbaugh and Krey say. You belong to me."

"Whoa, hold on!" said Ella. As she spoke, her hand reached around and took the lantern firmly by its handle, ready to bash it into McGinty's head if need be. "There's a lot of dope and whiskey moving your lips right now. Maybe you better turn me loose and think about things before you make one hell of a big mistake."

McGinty sighed drunkenly and let go of her. "You're right. I've got no say so over who you're with or not with. But damn, Ella, I can't stand the thought of anybody else having their hands on you."

Ella smiled coyly and loosened her grip on the lantern handle. "Well, you'll get plenty of me, Dead Rabbit boy. But be careful you don't come to my gate so often that you wear out your welcome."

"Can I ride with you?" he asked meekly.

"What about your brother?" Ella replied, ready to give in and keep him with her a while longer.

Michael shrugged. "He's a grown boy. If he's not ready to go when we get to Dodge, he'll find me when he decides to." He nodded at Feathers Hilgi lying naked on the bed. "What about her? Think we ought to invite her along?"

Ella considered it, but only for a second, then said, "Sure, she can go with us for a while . . . but only for a while. That is, if you can drag her away from Ned Chambers. He brings these girls all the way out from Saint Louis, he expects them to make money for him."

"Don't worry about Chambers," McGinty chuckled. "I'll put a bullet in his ear if he raises any fuss." Looking back and forth between Ella Lang and Feathers Hilgi, he added, "I've seen times I would've killed just to get my hands on one pretty woman.

Damned if I haven't found myself two at
once!"

CHAPTER 12

At the outer edge of Dodge City, Maria reined her paint horse off the rutted trail and stepped down from her saddle, allowing a freight wagon and a single-horse buggy to ride past them.

Sam tipped his hat to the passing traffic, murmuring to himself, "Busy place at daylight."

Maria lifted her horse's hoof and inspected both its hoof and foreleg closely. Ahead of them Dodge's main street and walkways teemed with both wheel and pedestrian traffic in the early-morning sunlight. Lowering her horse's hoof gently and dusting her hands together, she said to Sam, "The tendons seem awfully tight. But I think perhaps it is only a stone bruise."

She liked knowing that Sam valued her opinion, enough so that he felt no need to step down and look for himself. Instead, he looked at the bustling town lying on the flat plain before them. "If it had to happen, we're lucky it happened here instead of thirty miles out." As he spoke, he reached down a hand, taking the reins to the paint horse, then helped Maria swing up behind him onto the white barb.

"*Sí,*" Maria said, wrapping her arms around Sam's waist, "it would have been hard on Black Pot, carrying us both that far." She leaned in and said a bit playfully into Sam's ear, "But I know you are not the kind of man who would have let me walk to town."

Sam smiled to himself, liking the feel of her against him, the feel of her arms encircling him. "No, ma'am," he said wryly, "I would never stand for that. Neither would Black Pot." He nudged the barb forward onto a side street and toward a livery sign hanging in front of a large barn and corral.

At the door of the barn, a young attendant stepped forward with a broom in one hand and reached up to take the reins to the paint horse, having already noted the animal's limp. "Got one feeling poorly, do yas?" the shaggy-haired young man asked, looking first at Maria, then directing his question to Sam.

"It's only a stone bruise," said Maria. She swung down from behind Sam and walked

181

around to the paint horse's muzzle and rubbed it with affection.

Speaking again to Sam, the attendant said, "We've got a horse doc in town. Want me to get him, have him to take a look at it, just in case?"

Sam didn't reply. He only stared at the man.

"Please do," said Maria, stepping around to the attendant, drawing his attention away from Sam and to herself. Showing him a gold piece that appeared as if by magic in the palm of her gloved hand, she said, "Show me the stall and the grain. I will wait here while you go get the doctor."

Sam sat watching, his wrists crossed on his saddle horn. When he saw that she'd finished with the livery man, he asked, "Are you sure you want to wait here?" As he asked, he began to rise as if to step down from his saddle.

But Maria stopped him, saying, "There's no need for us both to wait here. You go on, speak to the sheriff and see what you can find out. If I'm not along in a few minutes, I will be waiting here for you."

With no more to say, Sam touched the brim of his hat and turned Black Pot back toward the busy main street, where they had seen a wooden sign with a large badge painted on it that read SHERIFF'S OFFICE in gold letters.

On his way there, above the passing street traffic in the early-morning light, Sam spotted a man wearing a badge and a soft-billed police-style cap with a shiny black leather brim. The man trudged along a boardwalk with a battered, half-conscious man staggering along beside him, the beaten man's arm draped over the lawman's shoulders. Sam nudged Black Pot over toward the hitch rail in front of the office and stepped down. As the lawman approached, Sam opened the door and stood to the side.

"Much obliged," said the lawman, giving Sam an appraising glance as he struggled onward through the door and across the floor to an open cell. "Christ, mister, I'm not arresting you!" Sam heard him say to the man, seeing the man begin to resist at the sight of the barred cell lying before him. "I brought you here to get you cleaned up and out of town! Think the sheriff would want you stinking this place up? He'd fire me for arresting something like you." He looked the ragged, bruised and battered man up and down. "Usually Alice and her girls will clean a man up and take care of him before he leaves. What the hell did you do to cause them to treat you this way?"

"I-I was just being . . . myself," the man said in a choking voice.

"Good Lord! Don't talk, mister!" the lawman said, turning his head away from McGinty's swollen battered face and fanning a hand back and forth. "Try to keep that stinking breath contained until I get out of this cell. Whew!" He winced and blew out a breath.

"I-I was . . . just being myself," the man repeated through cracked and swollen lips as the lawman let him flop down onto a cot.

Stepping back and out of the cell, the lawman looked the man over more closely, and said, "Yeah? Well, maybe you'd be wise to just be somebody else from now on." Half turning to Sam, he gestured toward the man and said, "Look at this. Can you believe this? He's been holed up in a whorehouse like this for the past three days! He spent good money to be whipped, beaten, burned, you name it." He tossed a hand in disgust. "He couldn't get enough! The girls finally had to send for the sheriff to come get him."

"They nearly killed me," the man on the cot moaned with a wistful look on his tortured face. He leaned back tenderly against the wall. His shirt-sleeves hung in tattered shreds, the length of his exposed arms bruised and cut and covered with what appeared to be cigar burns. A thick leather cuff circled his wrist with a three-inch length of chain hanging from it.

The lawman gave a short bemused chuckle and shook his head. "Wait until the sheriff hears about this one."

"You're not the sheriff then," Sam said quietly, already knowing the answer.

"Naw, not me." The lawman sighed behind a dark, drooping mustache. "Sheriff's out of town right now. I'm one of his deputies. Deputy Dave Mather," he added, touching a finger to the leather brim of his cap. He nodded at the darkened spot on Sam's shirt in the shape of a ranger badge. "Looks like you've recently changed professions."

"I expect you could say so," Sam replied, still uncomfortable working this way. "I'm Sam Burrack, from Arizona Territory."

"Whoa, I've heard of you," said Mather, a thin but friendly smile coming to his face. "Let's see," he said as if sorting through his memory, "Montana Red Hollis? Bent Jackson?" As he mentioned each name he raised another finger as if to keep count. "Damn!" he said, as if suddenly a more important name came to mind. "Junior Lake, and his whole damn gang?"

"That's all over and done now," Sam said,

feeling a twinge of guilt. He had not lied, but he felt he'd been deliberately deceitful, evading an honest answer to a fellow lawman. "I took off my ranger badge almost three weeks ago. I've been on my way out of the territory ever since, headed for Indian Nations."

"I see." Mather nodded. "And what brings you to the sheriff's office, Rang— I mean, Mr. Burrack," Deputy Mather corrected himself.

"I'm looking for Ella Lang," Sam said.

"Oh?" said Mather with an ironic smile. "Are you wanting to take her picture for *Harper's*? Write a story about her exploits? Get her to say she likes a certain kind of bath soap?"

"Nothing like that," said Sam. "I know she used to spend time in Dodge. I thought she still might."

"You're right. She still does," said Mather, "only not as much as she used to. Once she became New York's Wild West Queen, I suppose she acquired a broader pick of places."

"How long since you've seen her?" Sam asked, finding himself uncomfortable making idle talk about Ella Lang.

Mather studied Sam's eyes for a second, not sure what he'd just seen there. He shrugged. "Not more than three, four days ago. She raised a stir at the Opal."

"What kind of a stir?" Sam asked.

Mather shook his head. "She got drunk and doped up, started performing lewdly with a young whore. Had her hands all up the whore's dress, all over her breasts, that sort of thing. Nothing I hadn't seen her do before, but some customers took offense. When she's pumping morphine, she'll do most anything."

"Oh, I see," said Sam, not knowing how else to react. "I didn't know things had gotten that bad with her . . . doping and all."

Seeing a look come to Sam's face, Mather said, "Hey, does Ella mean something to you? I mean, if you and her are close, I meant no offense. I'm only telling you what happened. I'm not judging her."

"I understand," Sam said. "There's no offense taken. It's been a long time since I've seen her. I appreciate anything you can tell me about her."

Mather seemed to consider it, then said, "I suppose that's about all I know about her. She still comes here, gambles some, mostly drinks and pumps dope. She still has mail sent here. The mercantile store owner saves it for her. It's mostly dope from the drug companies, I expect." His voice lowered. "I wonder what the good folks back east would think if they ever saw that side of lovely Ella, the Outlaw's Lady?"

"What about Freeman Turnbaugh and Max Krey? Does she still consort with them?" Sam asked, already knowing, but wanting to hear from Mather, just to check the deputy's honesty.

"Now you're sounding like a lawman," Mather said. He nodded at the dark impression of the badge on Sam's shirt. "I guess some things take longer to fade away." He smiled thinly. "I'm sure she still rides with them, but I'm careful not to say so. With all the newspapers, magazines and penny dreadfuls painting such a dashing picture of them, they've all three gotten too big for a dirt-street lawman like me to handle." He nodded toward Lintson McGinty. "So I sweep trash like this one off the street and keep my notions to myself."

"Do you know which way she headed?" Sam asked.

"No," said Mather. "Lucky for me, they'd already left the Opal before I got there. That probably kept me from locking horns with the fellow drinking with her." He gave a look of disgust. "She loaded her dope and put it in her arm right there at the table the bartender said. I know it's legal, but whatever happened to good manners?" he asked.

"She left here doped up, riding double with that whore, the bartender told me. Said they headed out in the direction of the shack where the whore lives. The fellow she'd been drinking with rode beside them. Sounded like a real party in the making."

"How far is that shack?" Sam asked.

"Three miles, maybe less," said Mather. "Ride east out of town, come to a fork about a mile out, take the right fork and follow it to a creek crossing. The shack's right on the other side of that crossing."

"Much obliged for your help, Deputy," Sam said, touching the brim of his sombrero.

"Say, this ain't going to be a matter requiring the local law, is it?" Mather asked. "Because if it is, I'll get saddled up and ride right out there with you."

"Thanks all the same, but it won't be necessary," Sam replied.

"All right," said Mather, offering a sigh. He gestured toward the cell where McGinty lay sprawled, having fallen unconscious. "In that case I better get busy getting this lunatic cleaned and fed and back on his feet."

Sam left the sheriff's office and rode back to the livery barn, where Maria stood watching a veterinarian examine the paint's

189

foreleg closely, the same way she had done, twisting and bending the lower joint expertly until satisfied with his findings. "You were right, ma'am," Sam heard the doctor say to Maria. "It's a stone bruise. The tendons are not injured, but they have been under some strain. I'm afraid there's going to be some stiffness and swelling. The horse is going to have to be stalled for a few days."

Beside the doctor, the livery attendant shook his shaggy head at the paint horse's misfortune. "It's a shame, ma'am," he said sincerely. "But don't you worry. I'll look after this animal like it's my own."

Stepping down from his saddle as the doctor set the paint's hoof back onto the dirt, Sam stepped over beside Maria. "You heard him?" Maria asked.

"Yep, I heard," said Sam. "You had already figured as much."

"*Sí,*" said Maria. "What did you find out? Are we going to be here for a while?"

"It depends," said Sam. "A deputy told me that Ella Lang still comes here for the gambling and drinking." Sam spoke low enough to exclude the livery attendant from hearing the conversation. "We only missed her by two or three days. She might still be holed up at a shack three miles from town." The two watched the doctor step around to the paint's other foreleg, stoop down and raise its hoof.

Maria nodded, then turned her gaze to the livery attendant. "Do you have a horse for me?"

"No, ma'am," said the attendant. "That's one thing I can't help you with. Horses have gotten hard to come by and as expensive as hell 'twixt here and Abilene. We don't have any we can rent out."

Maria gestured toward a big dun horse standing in a stall in a row of empty stalls inside the wide barn. "What about that one?" she asked flatly.

"That one belongs to a fellow who left it here three days ago while he went off seeking some drink and socializing." He ducked his head a bit and said to Sam, "If you know what I mean."

"I think I know who it belongs to," Sam said. "The deputy is getting him sobered up and ready to ride right now." He continued staring into the barn at the horse for a moment as if piecing something together in his mind. Finally he asked the attendant, "Was that fellow alone when he rode in?"

"He didn't ride in here," said the attendant. "One of the girls from Alice Becker's brought the horse here when this fellow left it standing at a hitch rail outside the Opal Saloon. She said the man told her he rode in with his brother, and that brother would be by to get him. But the brother never showed up, I reckon." He shrugged. "It happens all the time here. Folks get drunk, forget they ever owned a horse or had a brother." He chuckled at his own remark and drifted away toward the veterinarian, who stood dusting his hands together beside the paint horse.

Seeing the curious look on Sam's face, Maria asked, "What are you thinking?"

"I'm thinking maybe it'd be best if you wait here and keep an eye on things while I go check out that shack. It's only a short ride out there and back. I shouldn't be long."

"Keep an eye on what things?" Maria asked pointedly, needing an explanation.

"I've just had a notion that fellow in jail might be one of Turnbaugh's men," said Sam. "Maybe the man who left here with Ella Lang is too."

"I can watch for him, but what if he shows up for his horse and leaves town?" Maria asked. "I have no way to follow him."

"If that happens, don't try to follow him," said Sam. "But I've got a feeling he won't be leaving here for a day or so. He spent three rough days in a bawdy house, paid the

192

women to beat the fire out of him."

"You mean he . . . ?" Maria took a second to understand.

"That's right. He paid them to do it," Sam replied.

"He doesn't sound dangerous," Maria said. "He sounds insane."

"Yes," said Sam, "but if he's crazy enough to have something like that done to himself, think what he might do to somebody else."

Maria looked at him. "I will keep an eye on him, and I will not follow him if he leaves. But hurry back. I do not like splitting up like this when we are so close to Turnbaugh's people. There are too many things that can go wrong."

"I know," said Sam. "I don't like it either. I won't be gone any longer than I have to. I could be wrong about the fellow in jail, so sit tight here. If he leaves, let him go. We'll catch up to him if we need to."

CHAPTER 13

Amid a stand of trees along the creek bank where they had lain in wait for Ella and Michael McGinty since before daylight, Crystal Jack Holder stood up in his stirrups long enough to stretch out the filed lens in front of his eye and give a quick look at the lone rider who had just appeared off a stretch of wild grass. Closing the lens between his hands, he sat for a moment with a noticeably surprised look on his face.

"Who is it?" Wakely asked, seeing Holder's expression.

"It's nobody," said Holder, tossing the matter aside. "Maybe we ought to move closer to the shack. They'll be leaving any minute."

"What do mean, nobody?" said Wakely, straining his eyes toward the lone figure in the distance. "Let me have the filed lens." He reached his hand toward Holder.

Holder handed him the lens saying, "All

right, damn it. It's that ranger, Sam Bur-rack."

Wakely hurriedly jerked the lens open and looked through it. "It sure as hell is!" he said, getting excited.

Tilton Blackwell looked back and forth between the two bounty hunters and said, "Now hold on. I'm here to follow Ella Lang and her pal . . . have them lead us to Turn-baugh and his bunch. I've got no fight with that ranger."

"We're not going to fight him, Blackwell," Holder said, giving Wakely a firm stare. "Not right now. He'll have to keep till later."

"Like hell!" Wakely protested. He jerked his rifle from its boot before either of the two could stop him. "When that devil woman shows her head, I'm clipping it off!"

"Who's going to hold the front end of that rifle for you?" Blackwell asked with a cruel grin. "I'm sure as hell not.

"I can hold it up long enough to kill that bitch!" said Wakely, his face reddening, re-alizing that in the heat of the moment he'd forgotten about his missing arm.

"Try it. You might end up blowing a couple of your toes off." Blackwell's grin widened. "It's just my opinion, but I don't think you can afford to lose too many more parts."

Wakely gave him a look full of sharp daggers. But he lowered the rifle across his lap and drew his big Smith & Wesson revolver from its holster. "I'm still going to kill them both. Who's with me?" he asked, the heavy revolver looking unsteady in his hand.

"I'm just going to watch," Blackwell chuckled, crossing his wrists on his saddle horn.

"Damn it, Wakely!" shouted Holder. "This is not the time or place. He'll kill you, you fool!"

But Merlin Wakely would have none of it. Before Holder had even finished his warning, Wakely shouted, *"Hyiee,"* to his horse and spurred it out along the trail straight toward the ranger.

"That damn idiot! Let's stop him!" Holder shouted.

"Go ahead." Blackwell grinned. "I'm good right here."

"Gawddamn it!" Holder cursed, gigging his horse out onto the trail into Wakely's dust.

A hundred yards away, on a trail that meandered through knee-high wild prairie grass, the ranger saw the charging one-armed horseman coming at him, a pistol drawn and raised. Quickly, Sam reined the barb to a halt and drew his rifle as Wakely's first shot rang out. Seeing another rider appear behind the charging horseman and not knowing how many riders might be following, the ranger pulled hard to the left and upward on the barb's reins as he pressed his knee to its left side. Knowing what the ranger asked of him, the animal lowered onto his front knees as if in prayer, then rolled over onto its side and lay flat and still.

Sam had slipped from the stirrups and stepped off the animal at the last second, then dropped down himself, taking shelter behind the animal and leveling his rifle out across the barb's side.

With both his reins and pistol in hand, Wakely shouted as he rode forward firing wildly, "I got that bastard, one shot! Did you see it, Jack? One *Gawddamned* shot!"

Seeing what the ranger had really done, Holder called out, "You didn't hit him, Merlin! He took position! Get down before he kills you!"

"Oh shit!" Wakely shouted, suddenly realizing it himself. He quickly jerked his reins to the side and veered his horse off the trail and to a halt. Before the horse had completely stopped, Wakely flung himself from his saddle and lay flat in the thick prairie grass. "Two can play this Gawddamn game, Ranger!" he bellowed. He fired two wild rounds from the big revolver, then had to lay it on the ground while he plucked cartridges from his belt for a reload.

"Stupid sonsabitches," Blackwell chuckled from the protection of the trees. He stared toward the sound of Merlin Wakely's pistol shots and shook his head.

Jack Holder also veered his horse off the trail, but not before racing it out thirty yards in the opposite direction of Merlin Wakely. When he dropped from his saddle, he did so with his rifle and ammunition belt in hand, then slapped his horse on the rump and sent it running. He flattened onto the ground amid the cover of wild grass, then crawled a few yards just to make sure the ranger couldn't see his position.

"Gawddamn you, Merlin," Holder growled to himself, hearing Wakely's pistol start firing again. He shot a quick glance back toward the trees where Tilton Blackwell remained covered, and past the trees toward the shack, knowing that Wakely had just thrown away any chance of them following the pair unnoticed. He sighed to himself and levered a round into his rifle chamber. He hadn't wanted a fight with the ranger, not here, not now. But since Wakely had brought it on, he'd have to make the best of it.

Seating the rifle butt to his shoulder, Holder prepared to rise quickly, get a shot or two off and duck back down. But just as he poised himself to make such a move, he froze at the sound of Wakely shouting to the ranger, "Burrack! Where's the woman? Send her out to me! She owes me for my arm!"

"Jesus, what a fool," Blackwell chuckled, hearing Wakely.

Sam didn't answer right away. Instead he rolled and crawled ten yards from his downed horse, then called out, "The woman's not with me. She left for San Franciso." As soon as he spoke, he hurriedly crawled back to his first position and lay very still, listening intently for the two men's response. Immediately, three pistol shots whistled wildly through the air from Wakely. Two rifle shots from Holder kicked up dirt behind Sam, on the spot where he'd been lying.

"And that's for you killing Moe Pitch!" Holder shouted.

A silence followed as Sam watched rising gun smoke mark the spots where the two men lay forty yards apart. But this wasn't the time for him to return fire and show himself the same way they had. Besides, he told himself, if they were smart, they'd already have moved a few yards away by now. This was a time to be patient, lie still and let the silence work for him. Beneath a quiet whisper of wind across the wild grass, Wakely couldn't keep silent any longer. He finally called out to Holder, "Jack? Do you think you got him?"

"There's one," Sam said to himself, poising his rifle, getting ready to spring up onto a knee and take his shots.

"Shut up, Gawddamn it!" Holder shouted. "Can't you see he's wanting us to talk?"

"There's two," Sam said to himself, rising up smoothly and quickly, his rifle seating itself expertly into the pocket of his shoulder, his eyes scanning and taking aim at the same time. Their voices had given him their position. Now he had to move fast.

He heard gunshots explode as he felt his finger squeeze back on the rifle trigger. In the fraction of a second it took to get his shot off, he realized there were more gunshots than there should have been. Gunfire barked all across the wild grass in front of him — not one pistol and one rifle like before, but now three, perhaps four rifles all firing at once. Hearing the hail of gunfire, Sam tried ducking down quickly. But his move came too late.

Maria . . . He felt the impact of a bullet lift his sombrero from atop his head and send it spinning off across the grass. *Oh no . . .*

He felt himself rising up now, using no caution, feeling no fear. He realized he'd been shot, yet suddenly it seemed unimportant. "Maria," he heard himself say, this time aloud, yet hearing his own voice as if from a distance, from somewhere within a warm, engulfing mist. He felt his boots step forward in the wild grass, his rifle dropping from his hand. "Maria . . ." he managed to repeat. This time her name stirred across his lips as soft as a baby's breath, as he felt himself sink away into a deep silent darkness.

The first time the ranger awakened in the night, he had no idea of how long he had been unconscious. He had no recollection of his name, or of what had happened, or of anything else of any importance. Something inside him seemed satisfied for the time being with the simple fact of being alive. For now, being alive would have to do, he had thought dreamily to himself, before drifting back into the darkness. Twice more he awakened briefly. The second time he realized that he lay shirtless in a lumpy bed, a low pounding inside his left temple. He remembered only that he had stood up in the grass and felt his head explode. He told himself, *You've been shot. . . .* And with that he'd drifted off once again.

The third time he awakened in the night, he did so knowing his name and most of what had happened to him. This time he moved his eyes back and forth in the darkness, trying to get a sense of his situation. He wanted to get up from the bed and walk to the dust-streaked window, yet as he tried to push himself up, he realized that his arm didn't seem to work as it should. He lay helpless, and the feeling of lying helpless in a strange place chilled him. "Maria . . ." he whispered, before drifting out again.

But this time as he felt himself slip back into unconsciousness, he sensed her coming to his bed and leaning down over him. "Sam?" he heard her say. "Do you hear me? I'm here. You are going to be all right."

He could not answer, not right then. But he felt her hand caress his cheek and his forehead, and the familiar feel of her touch caused the chill to leave him. He breathed in the familiar scent of her and let himself continue to drift away, this time at peace, content with the knowledge that she would be there for him when he awakened again.

When he fully awakened hours later to the sound of a wild rooster crowing somewhere beyond the open window, his head pounded mercilessly. He kept his eyes closed against the pain. Raising his left hand, he touched it carefully to a soft bandage along his left temple, locating the source of the pounding. "Maria," he moaned aloud, to assure himself that her being there before had not been a dream.

To his surprise, a voice said, "No, I'm not Maria, and I'm starting to feel a little jealous that you keep calling me by her name." He felt the familiar hand again, touching a cool damp cloth to his forehead. "After all, I'm the one nursing you back from death's door."

Sam opened his eyes and saw Ella Lang sitting on the side of his bed, the damp cloth in her hand.

In his dazed state, it took him a second to recover from his surprise. The touch had been familiar, but it had been from an earlier time. The scent had been familiar, but it too had come from a time past. Now, his consciousness returning more clearly, he sorted out the scent, and the touch, and put it to the woman's face seated before him. "El— Ella?" he asked, but he had not intended it to be a question. Even as he said her name, he felt a twinge of guilt for having remembered the feel of her on his skin, for having mistaken her touch and scent for

Maria's.

But Ella gave him no time for such thoughts. "Here, drink this." She leaned in close and held a wooden cup full of water to his lips. He sipped from it, tasting the bitterness of it as she whispered into his ear, "We'll talk later, Sam. Right now you better listen and listen good." She glanced back quickly toward the closed bedroom door, then whispered with urgency, "You saw me in Dodge and came out here looking for me. You saw the bounty hunters setting a trap for me and you started shooting to try and warn me . . . okay? Have you got that?" She saw his eyes drift a bit and she shook his shoulder gently. "Do you?"

"Where are . . . the bounty hunters?" Sam asked.

Ella shrugged. "We chased them off. They'll be back more than likely. Headhunters are just a part of doing business." She sounded cavalier about it, the way she might sound had she been talking to a newspaper reporter.

Sam only nodded, feeling the pain in his head begin to subside a bit. A stillness settled over him and tried to press him back toward unconsciousness, but he fought it off. Before he could answer her, the door creaked open and Michael McGinty stepped inside the room, a rifle hanging in his hand. A step behind him, Feathers Hilgi slipped in quietly and stood to the side, hugging a blanket to her breasts to keep from exposing herself.

"I say it's time you quit cuddling this lawdog," said McGinty. "Let me put a bullet through him and we'll get on our way."

Instinctively Sam tensed, wanting to somehow defend himself. Yet, as he held his arms poised, he realized that his right wrist had been handcuffed to the iron bed railing behind his head. Now he understood why his right arm had felt helpless during the night.

"I told you he's not a ranger anymore, Dead Rabbit boy," said Ella, staring into Sam's eyes as she spoke to McGinty behind her. "Look at his shirt. He's taken off the badge, haven't you, Sam?"

Sam didn't answer; he only stared at McGinty.

"It makes no difference," said McGinty. He grinned. "Once a lawdog, always a lawdog."

"If it hadn't been for Sam warning us, you and I could both have our heads in a bag and headed off for a reward somewhere," said Ella.

"We're not wanted around here," said

McGinty.

"No, but I'd like to hear you explain that to Crystal Jack Holder and his men," Ella snapped right back at him. "They work for railroad men, business barons. We could have rewards posted from some stage line owner and not even know about it." She touched the damp cloth to Sam's forehead. "Anyway, Sam, I haven't forgotten my manners. I'm much obliged to you for tipping us off. You saved our lives."

"Yeah," Sam replied, coming out of his daze, knowing he had to play this thing out in spite of the pounding in his head. "If you're so obliged to me, how come my hands are cuffed?" He shook his right hand a little, realizing what a bad position he was in if this gunman decided to kill him in spite of Ella Lang telling him not to.

"That's just a precaution, Sam," Ella said, offering him an easy smile. "For all we knew, you might have woke up and left here thinking we're the ones who shot you."

Hearing Ella say it brought the possibility to mind. Had she or this young outlaw shot him? Sam wondered. But he quickly put the idea aside and asked, "Now that I know better, are you going to unlock these cuffs?"

Ella gave him a crafty smile, saying, "Real soon, Sam . . . maybe after Michael and I talk things over."

"Yeah," said McGinty, eyeing Sam closely, "what kind of story did he give you, Ella?"

"It's just like I told you, Dead Rabbit boy." Ella propped a hand on her hip and tossed back her hair. "Sam saw me in Dodge City and followed me out here . . . hoping to rekindle our old flame." She smiled at Sam. "He caught the bounty hunters lying in wait for us and fired on them to keep them from hurting me."

"So you two used to be together?" McGinty said, stepping closer to the bed with his right hand on the rifle stock. "Couldn't you see the lady was with me? What did you think I'd do, just stand by and let you ride off with her?"

Sam stared for a moment. He didn't like having to play this sort of game, but he realized that for the time being he had no choice. "I guess I hadn't thought it out that far, mister. Ella and I used to care a lot for one another. I saw her and started following her. Maybe I owe you both an apology." In an attempt to change the subject, Sam looked all around and asked, "Where are we anyway, the shack along the creek outside of Dodge?"

"Huh-uh," said McGinty. "We're a long way from Dodge City. We're in a mining survey shack almost to Buckton."

Sam stared at him, a bit stunned and not knowing what to say for a moment. Finally he asked Ella quietly, already realizing that things had spun out of his control, "How long have I been unconscious?"

"Almost three days," Ella replied, seeing him try to hide the surprise in his eyes. "Why? Is someone waiting for you? Maria maybe?"

"Yes, Maria," said Sam, knowing that a bad situation could be in the making. By now Maria would have decided something had gone wrong and would have already gotten onto his trail. He knew it. "She'll be worried about me, Ella." He jiggled his cuffed hand. "Why don't you turn me loose, let me ride off? There's no point in you keeping me with you. I appreciate all you've done for me . . . but let's all ride off in different directions."

Ella didn't seem to hear him. "So, Sam, now that you're not walking around behind the badge, what are you going to do to make a living?" she asked with a playful smile.

"Nothing you'd be interested in, Ella," Sam said humbly. "I've thought about prospecting . . . maybe starting a freight line."

"Whatever it is you're thinking about Ella,

I don't like it," McGinty cut in quickly.

"Why don't you go play with Feathers for a while, Dead Rabbit boy?" Ella said with a cutting tone to her voice. "Let us grown-ups do some talking."

McGinty's face reddened, but he kept his temper under control. "You know what," he said with a harsh grin, "why don't I do just that?" He turned and grabbed Feathers by the forearm and jerked her toward the door. "This little whore has turned out to be the sweetest surprise of my bloody life."

Sam watched the outlaw stomp out of the room, pulling Feathers Hilgi behind him, seeing her nakedness from behind without the blanket covering her. When the door slammed, Sam said quietly to Ella, "You still like playing with fire, I see."

Ella's tone took on a sharp edge. "I enjoy men, Sam." She nodded toward the door. "When there's none around, even a boy like the Dead Rabbit will do." She stepped over, sat down on the edge of his bed and laid her warm hand on his naked chest. "It's been a long time, Sam," she whispered. "I've always hoped that someday I'd see you again. Haven't you also hoped the same?"

The touch of her hand on his skin caused time to fall away. In spite of himself he felt remnants of the same old fire that her touch had always fanned in him. He let go of a tense breath and said, "I can't deny it, Ella. Yes, I have." He felt her finger trace outlines around the flat, hard muscles of his stomach and recognized the familiar feel of it as though it were only yesterday that they had been together.

"That's good to hear, Sam," Ella whispered, and she lowered her cheek onto his chest and lay there quietly.

Sam saw the raw red needle marks on the inside of her pale forearm and the sight of them made him look away. Suddenly he realized why his head had stopped pounding shortly after he'd drunk from the bitter cup of water. He looked across the room and out through a dusty cracked windowpane as if staring back through time. "Ella, Ella . . ." he whispered softly as if in sad resolve. He gently laid his free hand on her silken hair, recalling painfully even through a morphine glow all the reasons why they had gone their separate ways.

CHAPTER 14

Feeling Ella rise up from his chest caused Sam to stir from his drug-induced sleep, but by the time he'd fully awakened again, she'd stood up, straightened her clothes and left the room. When the door closed behind her, Sam forced himself to shake off the morphine lull and look all around the room for any chance he might have of escaping. His duster lay draped across a dusty wooden chair back. His black vest and his folded shirt lay piled on the seat; his boots stood on the floor beside them. He didn't see his gun belt or his big bone-handled Colt anywhere. Nor did he see his pearl gray sombrero.

He lay still for moment, wondering how much of his being unconscious the past three days had been caused by Ella lacing his drinking water, and how much had been caused by the severity of his wound. He touched his free hand to his head and reminded himself that no matter how taken he'd been by Ella and his memory of all they had once been to each other, he could not allow himself to trust her. *No, never again,* he reminded himself, feeling the old hurt, anger and sadness that he had felt all those years ago. The past moved across his mind and deep within him with the sharpness of a dagger in his chest.

On the front porch of the old mining survey shack, McGinty stood buttoning his shirt, gazing out through a tangle of juniper and white oak and across an endless rolling grassland toward a stretch of jagged hills. On a blanket a few feet away, Feathers Hilgi lay naked, flat on her stomach on an Indian blanket, her arms folded beneath her face.

"If you try taking him to meet Turnbaugh and the others," McGinty said to Ella, "Max will kill him, straight out. He owes it to him for killing his brother." He ran a hand back through his mussed hair and added, "Turnbaugh would probably kill us too, for bringing him there in the first place."

"You let me worry about Max Krey," said Ella. "Turnbaugh wants what's best for the gang. Having Sam ride with us would be the best thing that's happened in a long time."

"I don't see it," said McGinty, shaking his

head. "The man has lawdog written all over him. He'll never ride with the likes of us."

Ella smiled confidently and said, "Leave Sam to me too. I always managed to get my way with him."

McGinty reached out and cupped her breast firmly; she made no effort to stop him. "I bet you did," he said with a wry grin.

Ella skillfully eased away from his hand and stepped over to Feathers, who lay with a dreamy expression on her smooth young face. "Have you stopped wearing clothes altogether?" she asked, a bit sarcastically.

"Whoa now, Ella!" said McGinty, before Feathers could respond for herself. He chuckled and said, "Don't tell me that having one of your old suitors around is making you modest. I like seeing her naked. I thought you did too! Remember what you said? You think we're all put here for one another's pleasure."

"I still think it," said Ella, "but there has to be some time for clearheadedness. We've got bounty hunters dogging us." She stooped down and half patted, half slapped Feathers' round bottom. "Come on, honey, get some clothes on. We'll all play later, after the sun goes down." Then, standing, she said to McGinty, who leaned against a porch post and closed his eyes for a moment, "Pay attention, Dead Rabbit! They could be anywhere around here!"

She noticed the tension in her strained voice and the tremor in her hands. She still had a small amount of morphine hidden away, but her main supply of drugs still awaited her back in Dodge City. She knew that without the proper amount of medication it became easy for her to lose control, both on herself and her situation. She needed to keep a firm grip on things, and on the people around her. Now it disturbed her that McGinty had taken such an interest in the young whore.

Seeing the tension cloud her face, McGinty asked with a curious look, "Are you feeling all right, Ella?"

"Hell no, I'm not all right!" Ella blurted out. "I don't like being stuck out here without my morphine!" she said, realizing that McGinty didn't know about the small amount she had hidden.

"We could make a run to Dodge," McGinty offered.

"No, we can't," Ella said in a shaky tone, "not now. There's just the two of us and we don't know how many hunters Crystal Jack will round up and have riding with him next time! He won't stand for us chasing him away. He'll be back!"

"Easy now," McGinty said, seeing her growing less and less steady as she spoke. "We can slip in and out of Dodge, if you want to. I'd like to find brother Linston anyway, if he's still there. That would give us one more gun."

"Yes, damn it, and so would giving Sam Burrack back his Colt and his rifle," said Ella, trying to work out the best situation in her mind. "But Dodge City is out for now. It's too risky. We're riding on into Buckton and taking on supplies. Then we're headed on to Indian Nations as fast as we can. I won't feel safe until we've gathered Free Turnbaugh and the whole gang back together."

McGinty spit and ran his hand across his mouth. "Then what about your lawdog? I say we shoot him."

"Shut up, Dead Rabbit!" said Ella. "If you want to shoot somebody, shoot your whore!"

"What did I do?" Feathers Hilgi called out, slipping her dress down over her shoulders and wiggling into it, dressing herself without undergarments.

"Nothing, Feathers," McGinty chuckled. "Ella's just getting nervous 'cause she's run out of dope."

"Keep her away from me, Dead Rabbit!"

Ella warned McGinty. "I'm sick of listening to her. I'm sick of seeing her naked ass!"

"Yeah?" said McGinty. "Well, you seemed happy enough when you had her wrapped around you like a fur coat," he called out as Ella stomped back inside the shack.

"Maybe it's time I went on back to the saloon," said Feathers, stepping over beside McGinty.

"Naw, you're just fine where you are," McGinty said, slipping his arm around her waist and drawing her to him tightly. "Don't worry about lovely Ella. She's used to being the only one with anything worth squeezing."

Ella walked inside the shack, into a small back room full of dusty wooden crates and shut the door behind herself. With an unsteady hand she drew morphine into the syringe, capped the bottle and put it away. She eased down onto a crate, twisted a bandanna and looped it tight around her forearm. Then she took a breath to calm herself, and slid the needle into the risen blue vein on her arm. Shoving the plunger down gently, she closed her eyes and felt an immediate silky glow travel the length of her.

"Oh yes," she whispered softly as if breathing the words into a lover's ear. Her head went back and lolled over onto her shoulder, her lips parted in ecstasy. "Sam . . ." she whispered and pictured him and her together as they had been long ago; and she sat as if entranced as the glow of morphine and a thousand scenes from the past washed over her.

Moments later, when the initial rush of the powerful drug had worn off enough to allow her to stand, Ella walked through the shack, catching only a hazy glimpse of McGinty and Feathers through the front window. The two stood embraced in the dim evening light, leaning against a porch post. "Look, Michael," Feathers said quietly, seeing Ella over McGinty's shoulder. "There she goes."

"Back to the bedroom?" McGinty asked without looking back or taking his lips from Feathers' neck.

"Yes, I think so," said Feathers. She watched Ella stop and stare dreamily down at a wooden table for a moment, then pick up a canteen and a tin plate with a knife and a chunk of dried elk on it and carry them toward the bedroom door.

"Good for her. She must've took some of the morphine she hid away for herself. It's got her feeling moony-eyed over that lawdog." He chuckled onto Feathers' warm throat. "Good for us too. Maybe she'll leave us alone, quit horning in where she doesn't belong."

"But I thought you were smitten with Ella Lang," said Feathers, lifting his face and giving him a curious look.

"I had to see what all the shouting was about," McGinty grinned. "I've got to admit, for a fading old flower, she can still stir some gravy." He grinned at Feathers close up; his voice lowered to almost a whisper. "But having the two of yas has given me something to compare."

"Oh?" Feathers purred. "And what did you decide?"

He ran his hands up and down her back. "You see where I'm standing, don't you?"

"You really like me better than lovely Ella Lang?" Feathers asked, her voice taking on a slight tremble at such a possibility. "Don't toy with me, Michael," she added.

"I'm not toying with you, Feathers. You're the best," Michael whispered, his face going back to her soft warm throat, nuzzling her with his stiff beard stubble. "I'm keeping you. You're all mine now."

"But I have to get back to Dodge. I still owe him money. I have to work off my train fare from Louisville. Chambers is going to beat me as it is," Feathers said, turning her eyes down, watching herself stroke the back of his head.

"Nobody's beating you ever again," said McGinty, his voice muffled by her warm skin. "You don't owe him anything."

"But, Michael, he'll send men after me," Feathers said in a grave tone, testing to what extent McGinty would commit to her.

"Do you think he knows anybody bold enough to ride into Black Mesa country, tangle with me and the rest of the gang? Let Chambers try something. I'll ride in and put a bullet in his ear."

Feathers gasped in surprise and delight. "You mean I'll be riding with you and the gang?"

McGinty raised his face from her neck and spoke to her face. "Where I go, you go."

"Is Ella going to throw a fit?" Feathers asked.

Michael shrugged. "Who cares? For now she's got the lawdog to keep her company. Once we get back, Max is going to kill him, whether Ella wants to believe it or not." He grinned again. "But for now, let her slobber all over Burrack. It gives you and me more time alone."

In the bedroom, Sam watched quietly as Ella walked across the floor with a blissful trace of a smile on her face and held out the canteen to him without saying a word. "Obliged," he said, taking the canteen, laying it on his lap and uncapping it. He sipped the tepid water steadily, needing it, and looked her up and down closely, seeing the fresh mark on her forearm and knowing right away what had brought on her wistful demeanor.

"My," Ella said, "you were thirsty."

Sam wiped his free hand across his lips. "Hungry too," he said, nodding at the tin plate with the elk meat and the knife on it. Knowing Ella's condition, and knowing that at any time his situation could take a turn for the worse, he told himself that as long as food and water were made available he was determined to take advantage of it.

Ella sliced a thick cut of elk and handed it to him. "I'm sorry we have no biscuits or coffee. For now this will have to do." She spoke with a drowsy distant tone to her voice. "Come morning, we'll ride on to Buckton and take on supplies."

"Where to then?" Sam asked. He tore a bite of elk, ate it hastily and swallowed a mouthful of water behind it.

"That depends on you, Sam," Ella said, reaching out with a hand and brushing his hair from his forehead. She let her hand rest gently on his cheek. "I want you to come with me. I need you, Sam. I need somebody I can trust, somebody who'll take care of me."

Sam could tell she was speaking to him from within a make-believe world the morphine had created around her. He wondered how much of the drug she had used over the years and how badly it clouded her sense of reality. Still, he felt a sense of guilt and betrayal, knowing why he'd been on her trail, knowing how broken and hurt she would be when she realized what he'd come here to do.

"Listen to me, Ella," he said, taking her hand from his cheek just as gently as she had put it there. "You don't want me to be the one you turn to. I know I was once that person, but that's a long time ago. A lot has happened to both of us since then."

"No, Sam," she said, laying her other hand over his. "Nothing has changed since then. I feel the same toward you as I always have. I know it sounds foolish, but the minute I laid eyes on you, it was like you'd only walked out of my life yesterday. Didn't you feel it, Sam? I sensed that you did."

Here came the Ella Lang he remembered, Sam thought to himself, listening to her. He knew that in her drugged state of mind she meant every word she'd said. But he knew

221

from experience how quickly this woman's mind could change in the cold gray hours of the morning after. He'd heard Ella sing her song before, he told himself, or at least some variation of it.

"Ella, I have to admit, something happened the minute I saw you too," he said, slipping his hand from between hers. "But please don't talk yourself into believing your own story. I didn't see you in Dodge and follow you here. I didn't start a fight with the bounty hunters to warn you." He chose his next words carefully, to keep from revealing his purpose for showing up in her life when he did. "Your life and mine are a long ways apart. We can't put things back the way they once were."

"Yes, we can, Sam," Ella said, almost frantically, in spite of the drug's soothing affect on her. "I believe you did come here looking for me! I'm certain of it. I sense it so powerfully. Maybe you didn't even realize it yourself at first. Maybe you thought you had another reason." She calmed down and smiled. "But I know you, Sam. You loved me too deeply to have ever stopped. I know, because I love you the same way."

She moved to him and put her arms around him and held him close to her. With his free arm he returned her embrace. But as he did so, he shook his head and stared past her, unable to fathom just how far the drug had taken her from reality. It would have been easy to fashion the situation to be just the way she had explained it to McGinty. Perhaps there had been a part of him that had come here seeking her out. Her words were convincing, sincere; they would be easy to give in to if he let himself.

Yes, he finally confessed to himself, holding her tighter, wanting to feel the old warm aching he'd had for her, he still loved that Ella Lang. But there was a difference that could not be ignored. He had loved her blindly. But time had cleared his vision. At the heart and core of the love he'd felt for her back then there had been passion. At the core of the love he felt for her now, he found only pity.

"Ella," he said softly, still holding her to him with his free arm, "can you leave this? Can you get on your horse and ride away and never look back?"

For a moment she didn't answer. He felt her crying onto his bare chest until finally she collected herself and replied, "No, Sam, I can't. I wish to God I could, but I've gone too far to get up and ride away."

Sam considered her words, then said with resolve, "Ella, unlock these cuffs and turn me loose. We've both got lives to get on with."

She drew back from him and wiped her eyes and said, "I can't, Sam. I gave Michael the key."

"I see," said Sam, giving her a dubious look, unsure if he believed her or not.

"Don't look at me that way, Sam," Ella said.

"What way is that, Ella?" he asked.

"As if I'm a lying tramp! As if I'm nothing but a no-good doper! That was always our problem. I always hated it when you looked at me that way . . . like you thought you were so much better than me!" She sobbed aloud, unable to conceal her tears from him.

"Come here," he said quietly, holding out his free arm and motioning her back to him.

"Oh, Sam . . ." she wailed, pressing herself against him again, her arms going back around him, this time as if in desperation.

"Shhh, Ella," Sam whispered softly, sincerely. "I never thought I was better than you. I never meant to look at you that way. The only one of us who ever thought badly of you was yourself. Maybe that was always our problem."

CHAPTER 15

Standing on the porch of the Belmont Hotel, Maria had paced back and forth restlessly, the morning she'd watched the released prisoner walk from the jail to the livery barn. The scars and bruises on his face were still visible, even though they'd healed considerably. A half hour later, when she'd seen him ride back along the street headed out of town in the same direction Sam had taken, a sack of supplies hanging from his saddle horn, she'd told herself that enough was enough. Sam had been gone too long. Something had gone wrong between him and Ella Lang and her friends; she felt certain of it.

Since the released prisoner was headed in the same direction anyway, Maria immediately went to Deputy Dave Mather and managed to borrow his personal horse, a powerful buckskin stallion. Leaving her healing paint horse in the buckskin's place until she returned, in moments she had heeled the stallion out behind Linston McGinty before his dust had fully settled along the trail. But no sooner had she drawn nearer to the shack Mather had told Sam about than she looked around warily, realizing that somehow she'd been given the slip. The fresh tracks she'd been following seemed to have lifted from the face of the earth and disappeared.

"Easy, boy," she murmured to the big stallion, stepping down at a spot where she looked down and saw blood on the flattened grass at the stallion's hoofs. Her Colt came up from her holster smooth and expertly, cocking soundlessly in her hand as she stepped over toward something pearl-gray lying half hidden in the grass five yards from her. Her heart sank as soon as she stooped down and recognized it to be Sam's sombrero. Picking it up, examining it, she felt her heart sink even further as she saw the bullet hole through the tall crown.

But as she checked it out closely, she took solace in noting that no large dash of blood had stained the inside of the sombrero. *A good sign,* she told herself.

She'd started to stand up with the sombrero in hand when the sound of a footstep rustling in the grass behind her caused her to snap around quickly, the Colt out at arm's length, leveled less than three inches from a man's terror-stricken face.

"Oh my God, please don't shoot!" the man shrieked. His hands jerked straight up. He stared wide-eyed into the bore of the big Colt. In one of his trembling raised hands, he held a leather-bound journal; in his other hand, he held a wooden pencil. "I-I-I-I'm a journalist!" he stammered.

"You'll need a better reason than that, if you're caught sneaking up behind people!" Maria said, her voice tense. She glanced up and down at the frightened man. Seeing no sign of a weapon, she uncoiled a little, but kept her gun poised and ready. "Who are you and what are you doing here?"

"I'm — I'm Nathaniel Gilder," the man said quickly, a thin goatee bobbing with his words. "Feel free to call me Nat. I'm with the *New York Dauntless Quarterly.*" He lowered his pencil hand just enough to shove his spectacles back up onto the bridge of his sharp nose. Then he gestured toward his lapel pocket. "With your permission . . . ?" His voice quavered.

Maria only nodded. She watched his soft-looking hand slip carefully inside his wool suit coat, pull out a wrinkled business card and hand it to her. Taking it, she turned her eyes away from his face for only a second, read the card, then stared coldly into his eyes. " 'Madam Madeline's Pleasure Palace, San Francisco'?" she recited, holding the card back to him.

"Oh no! Wrong card!" Nathaniel Gilder looked stunned, his face taking on a red glow. He snatched the card back from her, shoved it inside his coat and came out with another one, all in one fast sleek move. "That's . . . uh . . . a place I . . . uh . . . recently visited in order to research an article on the urbane social climate of —"

"What are you doing here?" Maria asked again, cutting him off as if not interested in hearing his hastily made-up story. She glanced at the business card, this one with his name on it, and shoved it back into his hand.

Gilder took a breath to calm himself. Lowering his hands an inch, he nodded back in the direction of Dodge City. "I'm looking for lovely Ella Lang, of course. I learned from a reliable source in Houston that she frequents the gambling establishments along the cattle routes." He shrugged and added, "Apparently I just missed her in Dodge . . . but the deputy said she had left in this direction, on horseback with a gentleman and a young lady."

228

"You are lying," said Maria harshly. "You followed me from town." She leveled the gun in her hand once again.

Gilder tensed, his hands stretching upward. "Okay, all right. Actually, yes, I did! You're right!" he said rapidly. "But I meant you no harm, I assure you! I'm just doing my job! The deputy said that a former lawman and a dark-haired woman were both on Ella's trail." He gave Maria a scrutinizing look. "I take it you are that dark-haired woman . . . ?" Without waiting for her answer, he continued. "I thought it only wise to try and follow you, being a stranger here myself."

Maria relented a bit, not wanting to waste any more time talking to the reporter. Lowering her gun, she stooped back down and picked up the sombrero, which had she'd let fall from her hand. "I don't want you following me," she said flatly.

"Of course not, I understand," Gilder said, dismissing the matter. As he spoke, his eyes went to the sombrero. He flipped open the journal and cocked his pencil hand on it. "Who might the hat have belonged to?" He gazed at the hole in the sombrero's crown.

Maria gave him a begrudging stare and said, "It belongs to the former lawman

Deputy Mather told you about."

"Oh," said Gilder, noting the tone of Maria's voice, "so you think he's still alive, even with that nasty-looking bullet hole through the hat he was wearing?"

"*Sí,* he is still alive," Maria said, looking off along the trail winding past the shack, clutching the sombrero. In a calm tone, she said, "If I catch you trailing me, I will shoot you in your foot. Do you understand me clearly, Mr. Gilder?"

"Certainly, of course." Gilder shrugged, brushing her words aside as he scribbled on the journal pad. "Feel free to call me Nat." He glanced up with a quick grin, then lowered his eyes back to his notes. "How long have you known lovely Ella Lang? What can you tell me about her personal likes and dislikes?"

"Do not ignore what I'm telling you!" Maria reached out with her Colt and tapped the barrel against the top of his partially bald head, just hard enough to get his attention.

"Ouch, Jesus!" Gilder said in pain, rubbing the top of his head, pencil in hand. "Why did you do that? I'm only doing my job."

"Where is your horse, Mr. Gilder?" Maria asked.

"Right back there in the tall grass," he said, "but please feel free to call me Nat."

"Listen to me, *Mr. Gilder,*" Maria said clearly and deliberately. "Go get your horse and ride away. I won't waste my time with you. I am on a serious hunt."

"All right," said Gilder, "I'll stay out of your way. You have my word. But let me ask you one question first."

"I don't know anything about Ella Lang," Maria said.

"Oh, not about Ella," said Gilder, waving the idea away. "I want to know who this former lawman was — I mean, *is,*" he corrected himself quickly, "and what sort of lawman he used to be."

Maria considered it, then said, "His name is Samuel Burrack. He used to be an Arizona Territory Ranger."

Gilder ran the name through his mind, then finally asked, "Haven't I heard of him somewhere?"

"I do not know who you have or have not heard of, Mr. Gilder," she said. "But I have answered your question. Now do us both a favor and stay out of my way."

"Wait a minute," said Gilder in contemplation. "Now I remember. Sam Burrack is the ranger who killed Montana Red Hollis! The one who brought down Junior Lake's gang . . . killed Bent Jackson and took his horse! Of course, I remember him!"

"Good for you," Maria said, turning, walking away with Sam's sombrero in her hand.

Gilder tagged along with her, excited, saying, "Hey, now I get it! You're the Spanish woman who rides with the ranger, the one he saved from the *Comadrehas,* aren't you?"

"*Sí,* I am the one. Now you must go and let me go on about my business."

"But why on earth did he quit being a ranger? Did he get in trouble? Run afoul of the law himself?"

Maria gave him another cold stare, walking back to her borrowed horse. "If you say anything like that in print, I will track you down and feed the *Dauntless Quarterly* to you, one page at a time."

"I only report information as accurately as I can find it. If you want to make sure the story gets properly told, you need to tell everything you know about it."

"What story?" Maria said, stopping suddenly. "You are after a story on Ella Lang, remember?"

"Yes, true, but if by some fortuitous twist of fate, I have come upon a story involving you, Sam Burrack and Ella Lang, I think I owe it to my readers to bring it to them . . . don't you?"

"There is no story," said Maria. "Go away."

"Okay, okay, I'll go," said Gilder, "but I think you should —" He stopped suddenly. Five feet from Maria's borrowed buckskin stood a big man in a long black riding duster, holding a rifle cocked and pointed at Maria.

"That's it. Stop where you are," the big man said, staring hard at Maria, ignoring Gilder as if he weren't there. "I'm taking this horse. I'll pay you something for it."

In spite of the big man's clean-shaven face and civilian clothes, Maria recognized him. Feeling it would be wise not to say anything just yet, Maria said, "It does not look like paying is what you had in mind." She nodded at the buckskin's reins in the big man's hands.

"All right, little missy," he said, "have it your way. I'm stealing the sonsabitch." Along with the buckskin's reins, he held a lead rope to a spindly mule. The poor animal stood heavily laden with supplies. "Now you raise that Colt and toss it over on the ground."

"You cannot leave me here without a horse," Maria said. As she slowly raised the Colt, she glanced beyond the big man, making sure he had no one covering his move from within the tall grass.

"Oh yeah, I can." The man gave a dark chuckle. "It happens all the time." But then he gave a twist of his head and said curiously, "Say, you're the woman who brought in Max Krey!"

"*Sí,* Sergeant Burke," said Maria, now that he'd recognized her. She'd raised her Colt but still held it in her fingertips. "Have you retired from the army?"

"Yeah" — he grinned — "in a manner of speaking. Now pitch that gun and don't try anything. Being a woman won't keep me from —"

Maria's shot hit him square in his burly chest and sent him tumbling backward amid the frightened hooves of the buckskin and pack mule.

"Oh my God!" Gilder shouted. But instead of ducking away and hiding, he hunkered down and began writing furiously.

On the ground Burke clawed toward his rifle as Maria grabbed the loose reins and settled the animals.

Burke slumped on his back, his hand going to the gaping hole in his chest. "Damn my luck," he gasped pitifully, dark blood spewing from his lips. "I was . . . shed of this place," he whispered.

Maria looked suspiciously at the load of

supplies. "Where were you headed?" she asked.

"Black Mesa," he gasped, a faraway look coming over his face. "A place where nobody . . . would ever see me again."

Playing a sudden hunch, Maria said, "You were going to hide out with Max Krey and the others, weren't you?"

"How — how did you know that?" Burke asked.

"I thought it strange that Max escaped from your custody. You have handled too many prisoners to have let that happen."

Burke coughed and said, "Well, hell . . . what's it matter now? Yes, I let Max get away. Turnbaugh . . . has taken care of me . . . for a long time."

"You're dying, Burke," Maria said respectfully, but firmly. "Tell me how to get to that place in Black Mesa."

Burke shook his head slowly. "I . . . can't tell you."

Maria kneeled down beside him and took his head into her lap. "You must tell me. I believe Ella Lang and some of Turnbaugh's men have taken Sam hostage. If they are going to Black Mesa, I need to know the way."

Burke coughed again. "Can't help . . . you," he said, his gruff voice failing. "I'm gone . . . to hell. . . ."

"Burke, tell me! Tell me now before it's too late!" Maria shook him, hard, but to no avail.

"He's dead!" said Gilder, slipping in quietly and standing beside her. He stared down in disbelief. "My goodness, you have actually killed this man! He held a gun on you, but you actually killed him!"

"I had no choice," Maria said. "It was him or me." She let Burke's head down onto the ground and stood up.

"B-but he didn't make a move against you first," said Gilder.

"*Sí,* that is correct. He did not," said Maria. She opened the chamber of her smoking Colt and dropped the spent cartridge to the ground by Burke's head. "If he had shot first, I would be lying there. That's why I shot first." She took a fresh round from her gun belt, shoved it into the Colt's chamber, closed the chamber and slipped the colt into her holster. "He recognized me. He couldn't afford to leave me here alive to identify him — you either, for that matter."

"He mentioned going to a secret hideout in Black Mesa?" Gilder asked meekly.

Maria just nodded and looked at him.

Gilder rubbed his sweaty palms on his trousers one at a time, switching his pencil and paper back and forth. "And you believe the ranger might be a captive of Turnbaugh's men?" he asked, having heard the conversation and now having a good idea of Maria's purpose for being here. "That they might be taking him to that hideout?"

"I do not know," Maria said softly. "But if I lose these prints between here and Indian Nations, I need to know how to get to that hideout, just in case Sam has been taken there."

"Then you are in luck," Gilder said boldly. He wiped his pencil on his shirtsleeve, stuck it inside his journal, closed the journal with a brisk snap and put it away.

"Oh, and why do you say that?" Maria asked.

"Because I just happen to know where that hideout is," Gilder said, jutting his thin goatee.

Maria stared at him in silence for a moment, then asked, "How would you know where the hideout is? According to an article in the *Midwest Star,* only Turnbaugh and a few of his men know how to get to the hideout."

"Yes, that is so," said Gilder, hooking his thumbs in his vest and rocking back on his heels. "Them, and of course the man who wrote that story." He beamed.

"You? You are the one who wrote that story for the *Star,* Mr. Gilder?" Maria asked, realizing what a coincidence this had turned out to be.

"Yes, indeed I did," said Gilder. "I interviewed many outlaws and gunmen who had been there. In the process, a fellow named Dangerous Donnie Rice told me how to get there before he died."

"Quick then, you must tell me," Maria demanded. "I have no time to waste. If I do not find Sam along the trail, I am going to that hideout. Nothing will stop me. Where is it?"

Gilder wagged a smooth, pale, soft finger. "Huh-uh, not here, not now. You take me with you . . . I'll show you how to get there."

"Why should I believe you? How do I know you are not lying?" Maria asked.

"I can't answer those questions for you." Gilder shrugged, his whole demeanor taking on more confidence, his timidity and fear seeming to melt away. "But do you want to stand around here and answer them for yourself, or get on the trail and go find the ranger?"

"Then come with me, Mr. Gilder," Maria said, turning, stepping over to her horse and taking up the reins. "But I warn you for your own good to stay out of my way."

"Oh, I always stay out of the way." Gilder beamed. "I covered the entire Civil War when I was no more than a child. Never once was I accused of getting in anyone's way." He tugged his bowler hat down snuggly onto his head. "Which way are we headed?" he asked, turning toward his own horse standing a few yards away in the tall grass.

"There is a shack just over the creek, Mr. Gilder," Maria said. "Let's see what it can tell us."

"Fell free to call me Nat," Gilder said, grinning in his excitement. He hurried away to his horse.

Once Gilder had mounted, the two rode quickly until they reached the shack. Ten yards away from the dusty front porch, they stepped down from their saddles and approached the shack warily, Maria with her Colt in hand, Gilder carrying his pencil and journal.

"*Hola* inside," Maria called out, standing at the edge of the porch and watching the wind swing the front door back and forth slowly. Without calling out a second time, she eased up onto the porch and stepped inside cautiously, Nat Gilder right behind her.

In the room where Sam had spent the first

night in Feathers' shack, in her iron-rail bed with his hands cuffed, Gilder and Maria both looked at the wrinkled sheets and caught the scent of cheap perfume. "Oh, dear," said the reporter, "perhaps there has been more going on here than one cares to know about."

Maria ignored his remark and examined the scratches the handcuffs had left around the iron head rail. She breathed a sigh of relief. "He is alive," she whispered to herself.

"Boy, I'll say," said Gilder, looking all around at the mussed bed, the room, a blanket lying on the floor of the next room also wrinkled and wadded up.

"They have him prisoner, but he is alive . . . and planning to make his move," she murmured, more to herself than to Gilder.

"How do you know he's planning to make a move?" Gilder asked.

"Because I know Sam," Maria replied. "He is always planning his next move." She holstered her Colt, turned and walked back to the front porch. Gilder followed.

"They will be easier to follow from here," Maria said, stepping down off the porch and gesturing toward the hoofprints on the ground. "Someone has marked their horses' shoes. It is an old bounty hunter trick." As she spoke, her eyes swept back and forth, taking in the grassland along the trail ahead of them. "We might have trouble with these men, if they are who I think they are."

"Oh, and why's that?" Gilder asked.

"Because I shot one of them," Maria said flatly.

"Apparently shooting people comes easy to you," said Gilder.

"Only when I know they are about to shoot me," Maria responded. "These men were after our prisoner, Max Krey, and they were ready to take him from us by force."

"Max Krey?" Gilder looked impressed. "Pray, do tell," he said, his pencil and journal coming up, ready to write.

"Uncock it, Mr. Gilder," Maria said. "I'm not a story for your quarterly. Lovely Ella is the one you want to write about, remember?"

"Yes, of course," said Gilder, "But there is always room for a new Queen of the Wild West, isn't there?"

"Not if that person has to be me," Maria said, dismissing the subject. She leveled her hat on her forehead and stepped over to her horse. "We're going to have to keep a close watch for these bounty men. If they see me they will start shooting at whoever is with me."

"That's all right," said Gilder. "I don't mind getting shot at, so long as I don't have to shoot back." He gave a wide grin, also stepping up into his saddle. "You'll find we are peculiar birds, us reporters," he said.

"*Sí,* I find that already," said Maria, nudging her horse forward.

■ ■ ■ ■ ■

PART 3

■ ■ ■ ■

CHAPTER 16

The ranger had noticed that ever since they had left the mining shack and headed for Buckton, Ella had grown quiet and tried to lag back and keep to herself along the rocky trail. Sam decided she must have ran out of morphine, having shared her supply with him the past three days. He had noticed himself feeling jittery and queasy in his stomach. He had awakened unrefreshed and throughout the day his mood had been dark and ugly.

Sam realized the medicine had kept him half-conscious and out of pain the past few days; but if he now felt the consequences of having used the drug for only a short period of time, he could hardly imagine what Ella must be going through, having used it steadily for years. He rode along hand-cuffed, forcing himself to sat upright and remain alert, hoping that doing so would help dispel the aftereffects of the drug.

When they stopped at a point in the trail where to the left a wider trail led off across the flatlands and to the right a thinner trail meandered off and upward into a long high stretch of rocky hills, Ella sidled her horse up close to him and asked through watery eyes, "How are you feeling, Sam?"

"I'm feeling fine, Ella," he said, not about to even acknowledge that he knew he'd been taking morphine, let alone feeling any withdrawal effects from it. He looked her up and down and asked, "What about you?"

Ella averted her eyes from his and didn't answer. Instead she turned to Michael McGinty and said, "When we get to Buckton, the whore's going back to Dodge."

"Don't you worry yourself about Feathers," McGinty said. "I'm looking after her."

"How am I supposed to get back there anyway?" Feathers asked. "There's no stage from there to Dodge."

Sam sat quietly, listening and observing.

"I don't give a damn how you get back there," Ella shouted in a hoarse morphine voice, her ashen face turning red with rage. "On a Gawddamn goat cart as far as I'm concerned. But you *are* going back! This party has ended! Get it? You've got nothing to hold you here!" She lifted a heavy Smith & Wesson revolver from her lap with a shaking hand and shook it toward Feathers.

Seeing no one else make an effort to speak, Sam cut in, saying, "Easy, Ella. The young lady hasn't done anything. Don't do something you'll regret."

Ella wiped a hand beneath her running nose, trying to calm down and rasped, "Why would I regret shooting this trollop? I'd be doing the world a favor!" She backed her horse a step, turned it roughly and spurred it hard, kicking it out through the waist-high grass.

"What am I going to do?" Feathers asked McGinty in a broken tone. "I don't want Ella Lang having it in for me!"

"Keep quiet, Feathers," said McGinty. "I told you she gets this way when she's out of dope. She'll get over it." He watched Ella ride away with dread and after a moment said, "How am I going to ride out there and get her, the shape she's in?"

"I'll go," Sam volunteered.

"Oh, I bet you bloody well would." McGinty grinned slyly. "I let you go and you keep on going, eh?"

"You've got a rifle in your lap, McGinty," Sam said, "and I'm handcuffed. Just what kind of odds do you need before you'll play a hand?"

"Oh, I'll play my hand all right, Burrack!"

said McGinty, feeling shamed in front of Feathers. He jerked the rifle up from his lap. "Ride on out and get her, you son of a bitch! But make one false move and I'll stitch your shirt to your bloody back."

Sam turned his horse and heeled it out, seeing Ella corner her horse sharply and fall from her saddle into the wild grass. Her horse loped on a few feet, then came to a halt and reached its muzzle down into the softer, sweeter grass at ground level. Making a wide swing, careful not to run upon Ella in the tall grass, Sam halted Black Pot and led him the remaining few yards to where Ella lay panting heavily on the ground.

"I'm watching you, Burrack!" McGinty shouted from a hundred yards away, although now all he saw was Sam from the shoulders up, and the big barb walking along behind him.

"Here's your chance, Sam," Ella said, half sobbing, turning over onto her back, staring up at the sky with a look of pain and hopelessness on her pale face. "Take both horses and make a run for it! Leave me here. I want to die right here! I want to die and have nobody ever remember I was born!"

Sam stood over her, and reached his

cuffed hands down to help her up. "Come on, Ella. Get up. Let's go. McGinty has a rifle on me. Don't get me killed."

Ella looked at him squarely, sniffing as she did so. "Since when did you ever mind having a gun pointed at you?"

"I'm handcuffed, Ella, remember?" he said, showing her his gloved hands.

"I can fix that." Ella fished a hand down into her low-cut riding blouse, brought out the key to the cuffs and pitched them up to him. She watched him hurriedly uncuff himself and rub his wrists. "Now then," she said, grimly, "do me a favor. Take the horses, and my gun, and get the hell out of here."

"I can't do it, Ella," said Sam, offering no reason why he couldn't.

"Oh, Sam, sure you can do it," Ella replied, taking his words to suit herself. "I know you. You're thinking that sticking around is going to save me — save lovely Ella from herself?" She attempted a smile but the tension in her face caused it to come off tortured and sad.

"Don't even try to guess what I'm thinking, Ella," said Sam. "Get up. Let's go." He reached down again, this time with his hands freed. "Let's get your horse and get back on the trail. We'll both feel better after a while."

She stood up and slipped into his arms. "So you know what I did?" she said sheepishly. "Giving you the morphine?"

"Yeah, I got the idea," said Sam. "I couldn't figure how you slipped it to me, but this morning I felt so bad I knew you must have."

"In your water the first time," Ella said. "The last couple of times, I gave it to you up under your arm."

"With the needle?" Sam asked, sounding a bit surprised that he hadn't noticed it.

"I didn't do it to hurt you, Sam," Ella cut in. "I-I couldn't watch you lay there in pain, and do nothing to ease it."

They walked with their arms around each other, like lovers, through the tall grass until they stood beside Ella's horse. Sam saw McGinty keeping an eye on them from the trail. "You saw me in pain much worse than that before, Ella," Sam said. "You knew I could handle it."

"All right, I suppose I have," Ella said, "but I didn't want you to leave me, Sam. Not right then anyway."

"And keeping me doped on morphine was going to make me stay?" Sam asked, trying to understand her for reasons he could not even name.

"I know it was foolish, Sam," she said, stopping and turning to face him, close up. "I'm foolish, okay?" Again she tried to offer a smile. This one came off better. She reached up and looped her hand behind his neck. "The dope makes me act crazy, I know. Others have told me that. I suppose it's time I listen to them. I'm quitting it, Sam. I'm going to give it up . . . the dope, the drinking." She gestured a hand, taking in Feathers and McGinty. "All the other stuff too. It's over. I mean it."

"You don't have to tell me that, Ella," Sam said, "but for your sake I hope you do." He didn't want to tell her that changing her life for his sake would make no difference.

"Oh, I will, Sam. You'll see," she said, sounding suddenly full of hope even though the morphine had her hoarse and watery-eyed. "See? I was wrong a while ago. You did save me from myself, just like you set out to do! You arrived back in my life at the eleventh hour, just in time to save me from myself!"

Sam looked into her eyes, seeing past the darkness in them to some deep-down make-believe place where all these things were happening for lovely Ella Lang, just the way she had always known they would. "Ella," Sam said, "why don't you be the one to take the horse and ride away? I'll ride on to Buckton with McGinty. He can't stop me — you know that."

Ella cocked her head in curiosity. "Stop you from what, Sam?"

The ranger caught himself and said, "From anything, Ella. What I'm saying is, if you quit it all, ride away right now. Go start all over somewhere. Make a new life for yourself."

"You mean us, you and me, Sam . . . don't you?" she said, her watery eyes searching his. "The two of us could be just like we used to be, young, in love, not letting anything stand between us and —"

A hail of gunfire cut her words short. Hearing the shots and the thunder of hooves racing along the trail, Sam threw Ella to the ground. Jerking a rifle from her saddle boot, he turned toward the trail levering a round into the chamber, the rifle coming up instinctively to his shoulder.

McGinty and Feathers had heard the gunshots, but had not managed to get out of the line of fire. As Sam turned to the trail and took aim on one of three charging riders, he saw McGinty's horse go down from under him, a spray of blood flying up from its chest. Sam locked his sights onto the lead rider and squeezed off a round as the three bore down on McGinty, making him their sole target.

In the trail, Merlin Wakely and Crystal Jack Holder heard Sam's rifle explode and saw Tilton Blackwell rise up and fly sidelong from his saddle in a trail of blood. His horse lost its balance for a second, long enough to drop back and veer sideways into Wakely's chestnut gelding. Then the unsteady animal careened back over into Holder's horse, almost causing itself and the other two animals to tumble head-long in the dust.

"Damn it, take cover!" Holder shouted at Wakely, glancing out across the grass and seeing Sam standing with a rifle, ready to make his next shot. "He's loose and armed!"

The two remaining bounty hunters jerked their reins sideways, cutting their horses wildly through the grass, providing easy targets for the ranger, had he chosen to kill them. But upon seeing the two flee, Sam lowered the rifle from his shoulder and un-cocked it. On the ground Ella stood up, dusting her seat, knowing that Sam had saved McGinty's life, possibly her life as well. "Bounty hunters," Sam said before she had the chance to ask.

"Damn bounty hunters," Ella said, spitting in their direction. "It's got to where it doesn't matter if you're wanted in the place they find you in or not. These lying bastards will kill you and take you in, tell the law they found you wherever it suits them."

"One of them was Crystal Jack Holder," said Sam. "I didn't recognize the one I shot or the other one that got away." He held on to the rifle, ignoring Ella's hand as she reached out to get it back. He gathered the reins to Ella's horse and handed them to her. Together they walked over to Black Pot. Sam picked up the barb's reins and walked with Ella back toward the trail.

"You should have killed all three of those rats while you had them jackpotted," Ella said bitterly. "If you don't kill them, they'll just keep coming back, like coyotes on a carcass."

"Quit giving them reasons," Sam said, hearing the stern tone of his voice. No sooner had he said it than he took a breath and said, "I'm sorry, Ella. I shouldn't have said that."

"Forget it. I know it's true," she replied, sounding more calm now, and more in control than she had sounded all day. She wiped a steadier hand across her lips. "Anyway, much obliged, Sam," she said sincerely. "It's a good thing you took those cuffs off when you did or else the Dead

Rabbit boy would be splattered all over the trail."

"I'm keeping them off," Sam said, his tone of voice letting her know the matter was not open for discussion.

"McGinty might give you a hard time over the cuffs, Sam," Ella said, lowering her voice. "Watch him. He can get mean quicker than a rattlesnake if you crowd him."

"I don't plan on crowding him," Sam replied.

"Hold it!" McGinty called out, standing and dusting himself off. He saw the rifle in Sam's freed hands. Seeing the two arrive at the edge of the trail, McGinty hurried quickly over to meet them, his Colt in hand, his thumb over the trigger ready to cock it. The gun pointed squarely at Sam's chest. "I'll take the rifle before you come a step closer."

But Sam did not stop or even slow down a step when McGinty told him to. Instead he walked straight and steadily at him as if McGinty wasn't there. "I said, hold it, damn it!" McGinty shouted, seeing Sam get too close for comfort. "Hand over the rifle before I —" He backed up a step and tried to cock the Colt, but a vicious sidelong swipe of Sam's rifle barrel cracked against his fingertips and caused the Colt to tumble

255

from his hand as his words ended in a sharp yelp.

Before McGinty could retaliate in any way, Sam swung the rifle butt up, cocked it back with both hands and dealt McGinty a hard jab in the cheek, sending him sprawling stunned on the ground. Feathers and Ella both winced at the sound of hardwood striking bone. Sam stepped around quickly before McGinty could struggle up to his feet. He raised a rough boot and pressed it down on McGinty's throat, pinning him to the rocky ground.

"When you're ready to take this rifle, you let me know, Dead Rabbit boy," Sam said in an even tone, his teeth clenched. He held the tip of the rifle barrel to McGinty's eye and reached down and pulled his big Colt from McGinty's belt, where McGinty had been carrying it. "I'll take this back too," Sam said.

"I'll kill . . . you," McGinty groaned, the side of his face already swelling up beneath a red welt the shape of the rifle butt.

"Shut up, Dead Rabbit!" said Ella in disgust. "He's got you cold beneath his boot, and you're stupid enough to threaten him? For God sakes, Michael, this man just saved your life! You could at least keep your mouth shut!"

McGinty'e eyes wandered aimlessly back and forth, the blow from the rifle stock clouding his thinking. "I don't keep my mouth shut. I never have," he said groggily.

Sam checked his Colt, looked it over and shoved it down into his empty holster. With Ella's rifle in his left hand, he reached down his right hand and said to McGinty, "Come on, get up and shake it off. We need to get to Buckton before those two decide to get around us in the rocks ahead and ambush us."

McGinty staggered to his feet and wobbled back and forth until he caught his balance. "I can ride!" he blurted out, jerking his hand away from Sam's. Blood ran from inside his cheek and down his chin.

Sam reached in and took the dazed gunman's pistol from his holster without McGinty seeing a thing. "Good," he said, pitching the pistol to Ella, who caught it and stared at it for a second. "Let's get you in a saddle and see how it works out." He assisted McGinty to Feathers' horse and gave him an upward shove as Feathers scooted back off the saddle and made room for McGinty. No sooner had McGinty seated himself atop the horse, than Sam's handcuffs appeared as if out of thin air. He snapped one quickly around McGinty's

257

wrist. He jerked McGinty's wrist forward before the hapless outlaw could resist.

"Hey, damn it!" McGinty said, looking down befuddled, watching the ranger snap the other cuff around the saddle horn and draw it down tight. "You can't do this to me!"

"It's done," Sam said quietly. He looked at Feathers and said, "Sorry to unseat you from your saddle, ma'am, but it's only until we get to Buckton."

"I don't mind, really." Feathers smiled, looping her arms around McGinty, who sat swaying like a drunkard.

Turning to Ella, the ranger said, "Are you ready to ride, Ella, before those bounty hunters try something else?"

Ella had stood watching the ranger go about his business, taking McGinty down almost effortlessly. For all of McGinty's threats and warnings, in the end, the ranger had handled him quickly, without firing a shot or breaking a sweat, no differently than he'd handled a hundred other hotheaded drovers or barroom toughs over the years. McGinty had meant nothing to a man like Sam Burrack.

"Still the same ole Sam," she said with admiration. She turned and stepped up into

her saddle and kicked her horse out onto
the trail.

CHAPTER 17

Max Krey pulled his bandanna up over the bridge of his nose and said to the young man beside him, "Okay, Raymond, this one will show us what you and your boys are made of. Are all of yas ready?"

"Uh, yeah," said Raymond Philpot, not sounding real sure of himself. He looked down and out across a rolling stretch of prairie grassland. "As ready as we'll ever be, I reckon."

Staring at him, Krey almost shook his head in disgust. But instead he took a deep breath and said, "You know if you and Wilbur weren't Freeman Turnbaugh's nephews, I wouldn't have wasted my time with you, don't you?"

"Yeah, I do know that," said Raymond, "and I appreciate you and Free giving us a chance to prove ourselves. It's damn white of ya."

"All right then, let's get this thing going,"

Krey said.

"I just wish Uncle Free was here right now," said Raymond. "Are you sure he's going to be all right?"

"He'll be fine," said Krey behind his bandanna mask. "He's not the first man to ever step on a rattlesnake. Don't worry about it. Do a good job here today and you boys will be set for life." He drew his Colt and spun his horse in place. "All right now! Are you ready?"

"Ready!" shouted Raymond. He jerked his tall crowned hat from his head and waved it high in the air, signaling three other men, who sat in a grove of white oak two hundred yards across the valley, awaiting his move.

"Then let her rip!" shouted Krey.

"*Yeeehiiii!*" shouted Raymond, spurring his horse forward down the high sloping hillside.

Krey grinned to himself and deliberately let the young outlaw get ahead of him. Nudging his horse along at a slower pace, Krey came to a halt halfway down the hill and stepped down from his saddle. He stared closely at the oncoming train and jerked the bandanna down from his face.

From the oak grove, Wilbur Philpot saw his brother's gesture and he pulled his bandanna up and said to Pokey Barnes and Randall Judd beside him, "There he goes, boys! It's commenced!" He drew his big Dance Brother's revolver and spurred his horse hard, sending the animal into a run. Beside him the other two did the same.

On the valley floor, a big engine rumbled forward beneath a dark cloud of smoke, pulling hard up a long stretch of sloping terrain. The engine pointed east with determination, pulling eight cattle cars, three passenger cars, two freight cars and a red caboose. Had the robbers swooped down on the train ten minutes before or waited and made their move ten minutes later, they would never have caught up to the sleek modern engine. But on this high roll of land, for a stretch of four miles, the engine had to slow from its twenty-five miles per hour speed to a mere ten. This made all the difference in the world to the bandits.

In the open door of the express car, railroad detective Dale Peepers knew the train would slow on this long uphill pull. He knew this to be a dangerous length of rail, and he'd prepared himself for it. His orders had been to keep the door closed and bolted, but he had a better idea. Standing to one side of the open door for cover, he held a big fifty caliber rifle at port arms, a bandoleer of ammunition slung over his narrow shoulder.

At the first sound of gunfire, Peepers showed no surprise, nor did he get up in any great hurry. He calmly took a pair of darkened sun-shade spectacles from his vest pocket, wiped them on his shirtsleeve and put them on. As the gunshots drew closer, he cocked the big rifle and swung around into the open door, his feet at shoulder width for balance. As he leveled the rifle on Raymond Philpot charging down the hillside, he caught a glimpse of the horse standing halfway up the hill and realized he'd just made a mistake. Even from a distance, he recognized Max Krey standing crouched with a rifle aimed at him.

With his big rifle raised and ready, Peepers said, "Uh-oh!" a split second before Max Krey's bullet nailed him dead center, where his ribs met in the center of his chest. The shot sent him stumbling backward over a waist-high crate of valuable farming implements. He landed flat on his back on a narrow spot of grimy plank floor, hidden from sight and half-conscious, unable to move. His hand grasped his lucky Silver Rails medallion, which hung beneath his coat on a chain around his neck. "Oh God," he managed to murmur, coherent enough to realize the medallion had just saved his life.

As soon as Max Krey had made the shot, he murmured with a cruel grin, "So long, Peepers, you son of a bitch." Then he mounted his horse and raced down the hillside, his smoking rifle in hand.

Inside the engine compartment, Orville Tinker, the fireman, shoveled more coal into the already glowing belly of the firebox. "We're getting all she can give us, till we reach some flat ground!" he shouted at the engineer above the roar of the engine and the steel wheels.

Moon Decker, the engineer, looked out the open window and back along the side of the cars, seeing the riders gain on them almost effortlessly. "Stop stoking her, Orville," he said. "They've got us cold. No use in risking our boiler or our passengers' lives trying to outrun them. These rascals could ride circles around us right now, and they know it."

"Gawddamn it!" said the fireman. "Every time we've been robbed, it's been along this same stretch! What the hell is Peepers doing back there?"

"Speak thoughtfully, Orville," the engineer said. "I fear Dale Peepers may have met foul play."

As the train slowed to a halt amid a metal-to-metal screech and a hissing of steam, two young boys raised a window and shouted out at the passing riders, "Show your faces, you cowards!" But a bullet thumped into the side of the car and sent them scurrying down.

"Everybody stay down, and stay quiet," an old conductor called out along the aisle. "Keep calm and we'll all leave here unharmed. They only want the money and valuables from the express car."

"Not this time, old man," said Randall Judd, appearing in the open door at the end of the car, his bandanna up across his face. "This time I'm taking everything, rings, watches, brooches, you name it." He stepped forward and pitched a canvas bag to the engineer. "You can do the honors for me," he said. "Get collecting it up."

"You are a scoundrel, sir," said a large woman who stood up holding an ornate parasol. She wore a large ruby brooch centered on her ample bosom.

"Drop the parasol, ma'am, and give up the jewelry," Judd said in a firm tone. Raising his voice for the benefit of all, he said, "There is no one here, man, woman or child, that I won't shoot if I get any trouble from yas. Hand over your belongings and keep your mouths shut."

At the engine, Wilbur Philpot and Pokey scrambled inside and stood nervously holding their rifles cocked and pointed at the engineer and fireman. "Now what, Wilbur?" Pokey Barnes asked through his bandanna mask.

"Damn it, Pokey!" Wilbur shouted. "We're not supposed to use our names!" Everything froze for a second as a loud blast resounded from the express car. The two railroad men winced.

"I forgot," Pokey said, his voice getting more tense. "I can't remember every damn thing." He looked back and forth at the engineer and fireman and said, "Now what do we have to do, kill them?"

"Whoa, boys, you don't have to do that," said Moon Decker. "Hell, we didn't hear anything, did we, Orville?"

"Shit no!" said the fireman. "We've had these engines banging away in our noggins so long we're lucky to hear a dinnerbell!"

"We're supposed to kill them," said Wilbur. He glanced back out the open compartment door as if making sure no one could hear him. "But we're not going to. We're going to play like nothing happened. They didn't hear nothing and we didn't hear nothing. Is that all right by everybody?"

"Oh, hell yes," said the engineer, his raised

hands trembling a bit. "We won't say nothing if you won't. Right, Orville?"

"What?" Orville asked, squinting. "I can't
hear yas. I haven't heard a damn word all
day!" His raised hands also trembled.

"Is everything all right up there?" Raymond Philpot called out from back alongside the express car.

"Right as can be, Ra—" Wilbur caught
himself before saying Raymond's name
aloud. "I mean, sure thing, *Bob*. Everything's fine!"

The two railroad men gave each other
looks of relief and lowered their hands an
inch.

Standing in the express car, pitching three
large canvas bags down to Raymond on the
ground, Max Krey shook his head and said,
"Are those two monkeys going to foul this
up?" He'd looked around for Dale Peepers'
body, but hadn't seen any sign of the man.
With a shrug he'd decided the detective
must've gone backward when the bullet hit
him, then staggered forward out the door
before the car stopped.

"My brother ain't no monkey," Raymond
said in a tight voice, interrupting Max's
thoughts about Dale Peepers. It didn't matter. Krey knew he had hit Peepers dead
center.

"Whatever you say," Max chuckled. Stepping back over to the blown-open safe door, he reached in through the smoke, ran his gloved hand all around, feeling nothing, and said, "Looks like this does it. Let's see what the other monkey got off the passengers." Behind the crate of farming implements, Dale Peepers lay as silent as stone, listening, the pain in his badly bruised chest beating like a drum.

Raymond glowered at Krey, but kept silent. Krey jumped down from the express car and the two hefted the bags of money and trotted quickly to their horses and hung them from their saddle horns. "Give a whistle," said Krey. "See if everybody can find their way back here."

"I think everything went pretty damn good, Max," said Raymond.

"Hell, me too," said Krey, slapping him on the shoulder. "I'm just giving you the raspberries. No offense."

Raymond grinned. "Heck, none taken." He turned, let out a sharp whistle and gathered the other three men back to their horses. "How'd it go?" he asked his brother and Pokey as the two came running from the engine, out of breath.

"Slicker than socks on a rooster!" Wilbur replied.

"They was both too scared to fart above a whisper," Pokey laughed.

Atop his horse, Max Krey only watched the three gather their reins and mount up. His bandanna hid his expression. He turned his eyes to Randall Judd as the young outlaw jumped down from the last of the passenger cars with the canvas bag bulging in his hand. "All right, you bad desperadoes!" he called out heartily, giving a brisk jerk on his horse's reins. "Let's ride!"

In the engine compartment, the fireman and engineer, their knees still shaking, watched the robbers ride quickly up the steep hillside. No sooner were the five men out of sight than the fireman looked back along the side of the train and nudged the engineer, saying, "Look who's coming here."

Dale Peepers walked stiffly to the engine compartment, clutching his chest, his face still red, his breathing still labored.

"Are you shot, Detective?" Moon Decker called out to him.

"No, but it hurts near as bad," Peepers gasped. He held up the bent, twisted medallion in his other hand. "Take a look at this. God had a hand on me, fellows. That's all I'm saying."

"Yeah?" said the engineer, impressed but

still upset with him. "You better hope He has His hand on you when you tell Brim Willoughby why that damn express car door was open!"

Dale Peepers continued holding his sore chest and said, "They would have robbed us whether the door was open or closed, and you know it. Besides, I got a good look at who shot me," he added.

"Who?" the fireman and engineer asked as one.

"It was none other than Max Krey," Peepers said. "He must've known I was riding this run and figured it was time he took vengeance for me sending him to jail back when he was pint size."

"You know what this means?" Moon Decker asked, suddenly excited. Before either Peepers or the fireman could answer, Moon said, "It means that was Freeman Turnbaugh in the lead, sure as hell!"

"Good," said Peepers. "It's high time somebody can identify those blackguards." He gazed back along the side of the passenger cars, where heads now ventured out and stared toward the engine. "At least when I tell these folks they got robbed by Freeman Turnbaugh and Max Krey, they won't feel so bad." He grinned. "It'll give them something to talk about the rest of

270

their lives."

Max Krey led the riders two miles at a fast pace until they rode into an old abandoned stage relay station whose corrals stood empty with their rail gates lying open and sagging to the ground. "All right, boys, let's make this fast and sweet," Krey said, slipping down from his saddle and lifting the bags of money from his saddle horn. "We split this up and get on our separate ways until things cool off. Then we'll get back together and do it again." He grinned and spread his arms wide.

"*Whooiiii!* Let's get her done!" said Raymond, jumping from his saddle and taking down the bags of money he'd been carrying. Wilbur and Pokey also jumped down, both wearing wide grins. The three stepped away from their horses and formed a circle around the money bags.

"All right," said Krey, "everybody sit down and get comfortable." He stooped down as the three seated themselves on the hard ground facing him. "Here we go." He turned the first bag upside down and checked the excited looks on the three men's faces when they saw banded stacks of money spill into the dust. Seeing Randall Judd had stepped down but not joined them, Krey turned and saw him standing beside his horse, his reins in hand, the bulging canvas bag in his arm. "Hey, Judd, what do you say? Can we have some of your candy?" Krey chuckled at his own joke, but then gave Judd a curious look. "What's wrong with you? Get over here."

"I'm good here," said Judd. Taking only a step, he lowered the bag into his left hand and pitched it over at Krey's feet. "Start splitting."

Krey stared at him for a moment, then shrugged and said, "Suit yourself." He took a step backward and said, "Who's the best at counting?"

Randall Judd, watching Krey closely, saw his eyes sweep across the three seated men as they stared down at the money. He saw Krey's gun hand begin to move toward his gun butt. "Watch out!" Judd shouted at his three companions, already reaching for his own pistol.

As quick as a snake, Max Krey drew and fired, his first shot hitting Judd in the side, wounding him and sending him slamming against his horse. Without a second's hesitation, Krey swung his next shot at Pokey Barnes, nailing him in his forehead. The other two saw what had started, but they were too slow to stop it and, seated on the ground, too off guard to get away. Krey's next shot hit Raymond in his heart just as Raymond's gun started up from his holster. The next shot hit Wilbur in the chest.

Wasting no time, Krey swung back to finish off Randall Judd. Just as he turned, a shot from Judd punched him in his shoulder and sent him falling backward. The next shot from Krey's Colt went wild and thumped into a corral rail as he caught himself and steadied his pistol toward Judd.

Clutching his wound, blood running freely through his fingers, Judd had thrown himself upward into his saddle and nailed his spurs to his horse's sides. Slumping forward in his saddle, he glanced back and caught a glimpse of Max Krey raising his Colt and taking aim with both hands. Judd clenched his teeth against his pain, and against the bullet he knew would hit him in his back any second.

But instead of hearing a gunshot, Judd heard Krey shout, "Damn it to hell!" as his hammer fell on an empty chamber.

Krey stood hurriedly reloading his gun, but by the time he'd shoved the new bullets in and closed the chamber, Randall Judd had disappeared in his own wake of dust. "Son of a bitch," Krey growled, cursing his luck. He turned and walked back to the money on the ground, holding his hand, gun and all, to his bloody shoulder. He looked down at the bags of money and the bag of loose cash, watches and jewels from the passengers, and smiled to himself. After all was said and done, it hadn't been such a bad day, he told himself.

He took the bandanna from around his neck and stuffed it inside his shirt against his shoulder wound. Then he stuffed the money back into the one empty bag and hefted bag after bag over to Raymond Philpot's horse and lifted them up and hooked them back onto the saddle horn, two on either side of the animal for good balance.

Leading Raymond's horse by its reins, Krey walked over and picked up the bag Randall Judd had collected. He poked a finger around in the jeweled trinkets and smiled. "I love it when I get it all," he murmured quietly.

On the ground, in a puddle of dark blood, Wilbur Philpot struggled and managed to hold his head up inches from the dirt. "I hope my Uncle Freeman . . . ki-kills you," he stammered.

The sound of his voice caused Krey to draw his gun and turn quickly toward the dying man. But seeing his condition and that Wilbur posed no threat, he took a breath of relief and smiled, saying, "Hell, your uncle won't kill me. He trusts me."

Wilbur rasped, "I-I just hope to God . . . that he finds out what —"

Krey cut him off with a bullet to his head. "Aw, shut up and die, monkey." He hefted the bulging bag in his arm, led Raymond's horse over beside his own, stepped up into his saddle and rode away, leading the loaded horse beside him.

CHAPTER 18

Arlo Heath, Cut-nose Tom Colbert and Bill
Jones sat at a battered table in the only
saloon left in Buckton, a crumbling adobe-
and-log building looking out onto the single
rutted dirt street. Clumps of wild grass had
begun to encroach on the street from both
sides. The weathered door to an abandoned
church banged sporadically on the passing
wind. Bill Jones gave the other two a sly
look.

Pushing his last forty dollars into the
middle of the battered table, he grinned and
said, "Hell, I might as well go out in big
way." He greedily eyed the stacks of winnings in front of both Colbert and Heath.
In his hand he held three aces, and a pair of
fours. The best hand he'd had all day.

"Finally drew something, didn't you?"
Colbert grinned.

"Naw, I didn't get nothing," said Jones,
studying the cards in his hand. Then to

change the subject he said, "I wish somebody would go jerk that damn church door down and give it a heave. It's getting on my nerves something awful."

"Then you ought to be the one to go do it," said Colbert, chewing on a wooden matchstick, studying his own playing cards with only mild interest.

The street running the length of Buckton became a trail that led in from the Cimarron Desert to the south and the wide prairie grassland to the north. Looking out through a large window that had only a few shards of broken glass still clinging to its frame, Arlo Heath saw the lone rider approaching and laughed under his breath.

"Here comes Linston McGinty," he said. He pitched his worthless poker hand onto the tabletop and stood up. "This ought to be worth listening to. He said he was going to go to Dodge City and lay up at Alice's."

"No kidding!" said Colbert, also pitching his cards down as if suddenly losing interest in them. "These Dead Rabbits have turned out to be some real huckleberries. I can't wait to hear this. I've spent a night or two at Alice's myself."

"I know," said Heath. "I'm the one who showed you her place."

"So that's all of the game?" said Bill Jones.

"I finally get a hand worth playing, and you two bastards both fold on me? What the hell is all this? You pokes can't quit while you're winning!"

"That's the stupidest damn thing I ever heard of," said Heath, stuffing his winnings into his pocket. He hiked up his gun belt and headed for the door. "While I'm winning is the only time to quit.

"I never quit you boys like that when I'm winning," said Jones, pitching his cards down in disgust.

"That explains why you're such a losing sonsabitch," Arlo Heath laughed on his way outside, stepping out through the empty window frame instead of bothering to use the door. Tom Colbert gathered his lesser stack of winnings quickly, shoved them into his pocket and followed right behind him. "A man without sense enough to quit ought to never start in the first place," Colbert called back over his shoulder to Jones.

"I'm left with forty lousy damn dollars to my name," Jones cursed, slapping his cards down.

"When a man's down to forty dollars, I've no more use in playing him," Heath chuckled. "Save your money until you get some more. Then come see me."

Hurrying to catch up to Heath, Colbert

said, "I'll be glad when Free shows up with work for us. We'll be snapping at one another like bulldogs in another week."

Heath grinned. "Yep, and it'll only get worse as more of us start showing up."

On their way along the street, Colbert said to Heath, "I like hearing these Dead Rabbits talk about New York, about their Five Points territory and all that, even if half of it is lies."

"It's not lies about the Five Points area," said Heath. "And from what I've heard about it, the Dead Rabbits used to be some of the toughest gangs in town."

"Used to be don't feed a cat, far as I'm concerned," said Colbert. "I reckon I'm just hard to impress."

"The Dead Rabbit Gang once started a fight that ended with a hundred and fifty dead in the streets."

"That's a lot of dead," said Colbert, sounding a little skeptical. He gave Heath a look and said, "I can't help wondering, if these two had it so good in New York, what the hell are they doing out here?"

"Good question," said Heath, showing no interest in pursuing the subject any further. "You'll have to ask them sometime."

Ten yards up the dusty deserted street, the two stopped and stood in front of Linston McGinty as he halted his horse and turned it quarterwise to them. "Howdy, Dead Rabbit," said Heath, both him and Colbert seeing the bruises and cuts on McGinty's face and exposed forearms beneath his rolled-up shirtsleeves.

"How was Alice's?" Colbert asked, staring into McGinty's puffy, still bloodshot eyes.

McGinty swung stiffly down from his saddle with a groan. "It's not one of Big Tim Sullivan's New York brothels," he replied with a grin on his cracked lips, "but it will do."

Heath and Colbert laughed, giving each other bemused looks. "Did you tell her I said to give you the works?" Heath asked.

"Oh yes, indeed I did tell her," said McGinty. "Once I mentioned your name, those mean little creatures went crazy on me. I felt lucky to get out of there alive!" He beamed. "I assure you I'm going back as soon as I raise some more cash."

"You don't mean to tell us you spent your whole roll there?" Colbert asked with an astonished look.

"Oh no, not all of it," said McGinty. "But a pretty damn good chunk of it, for sure." He took off his bowler hat and fanned himself as the three of them walked to the adobe saloon, McGinty leading his horse.

"What I didn't give them, they stole!" He grinned, then said in reflection, "What a wonderful time I had. I am forever obliged to you for telling about the place."

"Don't mention it," Colbert said, giving Heath a curious grin.

"So back to work," said McGinty, sighing and looking all around the nearly abandoned squalor of Buckton. "Has either of you seen my brother, Michael?"

"Nope, he's not here yet," said Heath. "But everybody's started to straggle in over the past couple of days."

"Hmmm, strange," said McGinty. "I left him at Chambers' Opal Saloon in Dodge. Before I left town, the bartender there said he and Ella left together with some young whore."

"Well, there you are then," said Colbert. "If there's a young whore involved, they'll both show up once they've gotten their fill."

"You mean Ella . . . ?" McGinty let his words trail rather than finish his question.

"Oh, hell yes," said Heath. "I can't think of anything on two legs or more that Ella won't crawl on to, give her enough dope to keep her from thinking about it first." He slapped himself on his forearm, giving McGinty the idea.

McGinty grinned through his cracked lips.

"My brother is crazy about her. And he thinks there's something wrong with me for going to a place like Alice's and having them beat the hell out of me."

"Well," said Heath, hesitantly, "I have to admit I find that a little peculiar myself."

"It does take some getting used to," McGinty said, carefully touching his fingertips to his bruised forehead. He looked all around and said, "My, what a dismal shithole this appears to be. Whose idea is it that we get back together here?"

"Freeman Turnbaugh himself chose this place," said Heath.

"Oh, then never mind," said McGinty.

"Before the rails cut across from Saint Louis and bypassed this place, Buckton was one hell of a hell-raising cowtown."

"I'll have to take your word for it," McGinty chuckled, looking all around the deserted street and empty dust-streaked storefronts. "This makes me long for the bustling streets of home."

"Next time maybe we'll meet in Chicago," said Heath, a little put out with McGinty's sarcasm.

"Hey," said Colbert, cutting in, "here comes four more riders." He gestured a hand out toward another trail coming in from a different direction than the one

McGinty rode in on.

The three turned and watched in silence as the four horses drew closer at the head of their own wake of dust. After a moment, Linston McGinty said, "Speak of the devil, that looks like Brother Michael coming now." He squinted. "Yes, that's him all right, I recognize his cap. He has a woman riding double with him."

"All right," said Colbert. "Now all we need is for Turnbaugh and Krey to show up. We can haul up out of here . . . go somewhere more to our liking."

McGinty stood staring at his brother with a bemused smile until the three horses rode down the center of the dirt street, close enough for him to see Michael's swollen purple jaw. "Jesus," he said under his breath, walking forward the remaining few yards to meet him. He did so with Heath and Colbert beside him. The pair looked past Michael McGinty and recognized Sam as he stopped Black Pot and sat with his hands crossed on his saddle horn.

"Easy, boys," Sam said in a lowered tone, seeing the two lag back and to one side as if ready to go for their guns. "I didn't come here wearing a badge."

"So," said Colbert, "you're saying there's no trouble between us, after the way I lied to you and all?" He kept his gun hand poised near the Colt standing in his tied-down holster.

Linston McGinty looked back and forth quickly, not recognizing Sam Burrack or having heard much about him. But listening to Colbert and seeing the position he and Heath had taken toward this stranger, he poised his hand also, and continued talking to his brother. "Who did that to your face, Michael? This man? Was it him?" he asked sharply, giving Sam a cold stare.

"Yeah," Michael replied in a muffled voice, keeping his teeth clenched to avoid more pain. "I believe he broke my jaw."

Seated behind Michael McGinty on the horse's rump with her arms around his waist, Feathers Hilgi said, "He's right. It looks broke to me. He can't open his mouth enough to eat anything. If he tries, he can't chew it. He's like a newborn baby almost."

"Feathers, shut up," Michael grumbled over his shoulder. To Linston and the other two he said, "He snuck up in front of me and cracked me with a rifle butt."

"How the hell does somebody sneak up in front of you, less you're asleep?" Heath asked, not too keen on throwing down with the ranger if he could keep from it.

"That's not the point, though, is it?" Lin-

284

ston McGinty said, spreading his feet shoulder-width apart, facing the ranger.

"The point is," Sam said, as he reached down and raised his big Colt from his holster calmly, slowly, as if he intended only to check the gun, "instead of thumping him a little with the gun butt, I could have killed him." His thumb eased the Colt's hammer back, and without really posing a threat to any of the three gunmen, the barrel of the Colt tipped down just enough to point loosely at Linston McGinty's chest.

There it is. . . . Just the way she remembered seeing him do it countless times before, Ella told herself: Sam, taking charge, getting the drop on everybody before they knew what had happened. While the three had postured and positioned themselves and thought about what they should or shouldn't do, Sam had arrived prepared. Now they saw it, but now it was too late. Sam would kill them; she knew it.

"Everybody settle down!" Ella said harshly, eyeing Heath, Colbert and Linston McGinty. "I saw the whole thing. Do you think I would be vouching for this ranger if he'd made an underhanded move on one of our own? Hell no, I wouldn't." She gave each of the three a cold stare, then said, "What Michael didn't mention is the fact

285

that Sam here saved him from a band of bounty hunters."

Heath and Colbert needed very little coaxing to keep them from making a move on the ranger, his big Colt already drawn, cocked and ready to go to work. Seeing how reluctant they'd become, Linston McGinty relented a bit himself, looking his brother up and down as if to say maybe Michael didn't look to be too badly hurt after all. "Is that so?" Linston asked Michael. "This man saved your life?"

"Bounty hunters?" Heath asked, him and Colbert both growing wary and looking all around the endless grasslands.

"That's right," said Ella. "Crystal Jack Holder and some friends. They shot Michael's horse from under him. Sam sent them running."

"Michael?" Linston asked.

Instead of a long answer through his pain-racked jaw, Michael nodded stiffly and muttered, "It's true."

"So, then, what *are* you doing riding with the ranger, Ella," Heath asked in a wry tone, "if I may be so bold?"

"We're friends from way back," Ella said bluntly, giving Sam a proud smile. "I'm hoping he'll decide to ride with us. He's been thinking about it, right, Sam?"

The ranger didn't answer.

"He'll decide?" Heath cut in. "As best I recall, it's still Free Turnbaugh and Max *Killer* Krey who decide." Heath raised his brow toward Sam. "You know Killer Krey, I expect. The man whose brother you shot dead the last time we all met. The day you rode in on us roughshod, by surprise and dragged poor ole Toby Burns off to the Yuma Penitentiary."

"That was a bad mistake you made, Ranger," said Colbert.

"I remember," said Sam, letting his Colt sag but keeping its presence felt. "Alvin Krey drew on me. You all saw it. I had no choice but to kill him."

Arlo Heath chuckled under his breath. "You be sure and explain all that to Max Krey. I believe you'll find him to be real understanding about it." He glanced at Colbert. "Don't you think so, Cut-nose?"

"Oh yes, I'm sure of it," said Colbert. "You just stick around. I'm sure he'll want *you* to ride with us."

"I'm not sticking around, Ella," Sam said, turning to glance at her, then back to the gunmen.

"What?" said Colbert in feigned surprise. "But I thought you wanted to ride with us!"

"I never *said* I wanted to ride with you,"

287

Sam replied, jerking his head toward Ella. "She did. I rode with my friend Ella this far just to keep the bounty hunters off her back." He backed his horse a step as if ready to turn and ride away. "Far as I know I might decide to pin a badge back on." He stalled for a second as if to let something sink into their thoughts. "Now that I know how easy you boys are to find, I could go to work for Judge Parker. I think he'd hire me."

"If that's supposed to be a joke, Burrack," Heath said in a stern tone of voice, "ain't nobody here laughing."

"But, Sam," Ella said, her voice getting a little shaky at the thought of him leaving, "I thought you told me you wanted to ride with our gang!" She looked as if her feelings were hurt. "Don't you?"

"No, Ella," Sam said. "Riding with the gang is something you came up with." He shook his head, staring at Heath, then at Colbert, then at Linston McGinty. "All I said is that I might want to be a part of the gang. That's a whole other thing."

The men stood silent for a moment. Finally Heath said, "Oh, I see what it is you're getting at. You're looking for a deal like some other lawmen and soldiers have going with us." He gave a harsh little laugh. "It seems like everybody wants to get themselves a little piece of our pie."

"Now you're getting the idea," Sam replied. "Tell Free Turnbaugh I'm not wearing a badge now, but I might be willing to put one on when the right time comes."

Sam started to turn his horse and ride out, but a voice from between two weathered shacks caused him to stop. "Why don't you wait around and tell him yourself?" said Harvey Fanin. He stepped out onto the street with a cocked sawed-off shotgun in his hands, letting Sam know he'd been there listening and watching all along. As a gesture of goodwill, Fanin uncocked the shotgun and lowered the barrels. "If you're all right by Ella, you're all right by us." He stepped forward, swinging the shotgun up over his shoulder. "But when Max Krey gets here, you're on your own."

"I wouldn't have it any other way," said the ranger. He lowered the Colt into his holster, but raised his rifle from his lap and kept it in his hand as he stepped down from his saddle.

CHAPTER 19

When Freeman Turnbaugh and Lee Sugar Townsend first heard the sound come from within the brush alongside the trail, they both reined their horses to an abrupt halt, Turnbaugh drawing his big Smith & Wesson pistol, Lee "Sugar" Townsend jerking one of his big Walker Colts from their saddle rig. They sat silently, listening intently until they heard the faint sound again.

"Who's in there?" Turnbaugh demanded, once he recognized that they'd heard a human voice uttering faint pleas for help.

No response came from the brush. Turnbaugh and Townsend looked at each other. "Cover me, Sugar," Turnbaugh murmured.

"You're covered," the tall, thin outlaw whispered in reply.

Turnbaugh heeled his horse over toward the brush with caution, his Smith & Wesson cocked and ready. But when he stopped at the edge of brush, he stiffened in his saddle when he heard the voice say with much effort, "Is that you, Free? Oh God, don't shoot me. . . . I'm done for."

"Who's there?" Turnbaugh demanded again, gesturing with his gun for Townsend to come join him.

Townsend gigged his horse over to him, in time to hear a voice say within the brush, "It's me, Judd. Remember me? I . . . ride with your nephews. I'm shot bad."

"Yeah, I remember you," Turnbaugh said, swinging down from his saddle and stepping into the brush, his gun still out and pointed, just in case.

"Please don't shoot me! You keep it all. I won't tell nobody nothing!" Randall Judd begged, seeing Turnbaugh part the brush and stand over him, looking all about the small clearing. "I hurt so damn bad!" Judd said.

Turnbaugh saw a sweat-streaked horse standing in the clearing, its side covered with Randall Judd's blood.

"Take it easy, Judd," he said. "Keep all of what? Why the hell would I shoot you?" He stepped over to Judd and pressed a boot down on the gun lying loosely in his weak bloody hand. Stooping, he picked the gun up with two fingers and pitched it away.

"Be-because of what . . . I saw," Judd said

in a gravelly voice. "But I won't tell."

"He's talking out of his head," said Townsend. Reaching out with his Walker Colt, he cocked it and said, "Adios. You're off to a far better place."

"Wait, Gawddamn it, Sugar!" Turnbaugh demanded. He waved Townsend's Walker Colt away, saying, "I want to know what he's trying to say!"

"Suit yourself," said Townsend, lowering the Walker and taking a step back. "I'm just trying to do the young man a favor."

"You want to do him a favor, go get the canteen off your horse," said Turnbaugh, stepping in and stooping down beside Judd. As Townsend moved away through the brush, Turnbaugh said to Judd, "Are my nephews all right? What the hell happened here?"

"You — you don't know?" Judd asked.

"Tell me, damn it!" said Turnbaugh, propping the dying man's head up onto his lap.

"Max Krey . . . set us up. He killed Wilbur, Raymond and Pokey."

"Krey killed my nephews? You must be crazy!" Turnbaugh said, not wanting to believe it. "I asked him to stop by and tell them to hold up on joining us for a while! What do you mean he *killed* them? You're lying!" He shook the dying man, as if to do so would change what he'd just heard about his long-time partner.

Judd coughed and struggled with his words. "Krey . . . said you got snakebit. Said you sent him to check us out . . . help us rob a train. Then he killed the others . . . and me too." Judd's eyes went down to his wounded side. "I put a bullet in his gun arm, high up. But he killed us all." He nodded weakly toward his saddlebags and said, "I took some jewelry . . . while nobody was watching." He coughed and gave Turnbaugh a crooked bloody grin. "I couldn't help myself. Once a thief, always . . ." His words stopped in an exhalation of breath.

Turnbaugh felt the young outlaw's head fall limp on his knee. "Damn Max Krey," he whispered to himself.

"What about Max?" Townsend asked, stepping in with the canteen, handing it down to him.

"Never mind the canteen, Sugar," said Turnbaugh, standing up, dusting his hands. "He's dead."

"Oh," said Townsend, letting the canteen slump in his hand. "Then he saved me a bullet."

A silence passed as Turnbaugh stepped over beside the blood-caked horse and began rummaging through Judd's saddle-bags.

"What was he saying about Max Krey?" Townsend asked.

"Nothing, Sugar. Forget it," said Turnbaugh, in a tight voice, his hands feeling all around until they came upon a handful of loose jewelry, a watch and a wad of loose cash, just enough to make him believe the dead robber's story.

"Forget it?" said Townsend. He shrugged. "What is it, some big secret?"

"Yeah, it's a big secret all right," said Turnbaugh, grasping a handful of the stolen goods and holding it around toward him. "Until I say otherwise, you keep your mouth shut about all of this."

"You can count on that," said Townsend, eyeing the cash and jewelry in Turnbaugh's gloved fist. "Now are you going to tell me about it?"

"Yeah," said Turnbaugh, staring out through the thick brush toward the trail. "I'll tell you everything Judd told me before he died."

Sam stood at the open window frame and watched Ella Lang walk across the dusty street and meet Harvey Fanin on the plank boardwalk out front of a seedy run-down hotel whose faded sign read THE MONARCH. Fanin handed her a small package wrapped in brown paper and a key before he turned and walked away. Sam stepped to the side of the window frame to keep Ella from seeing him when she gave a look both ways along the street. Stepping an inch back into the window frame, Sam watched her walk inside the hotel and close the dusty door behind herself.

"So, Burrack," said Bill Jones, seated at the table less than six feet away, "do you want to play some poker? Or has spending your life behind a badge made you a little too good for us common folk?"

Sam only looked at him without replying.

"I'll warn you before you start," Heath said to Sam from his spot along the dusty bar, "this bummer is only good for forty dollars. If he was worth playing, I'd be playing him myself." He chuckled, threw back a shot of whiskey and banged his empty glass on the bar. A frail-looking old man with a thin wispy beard got up from atop an empty beer barrel and ambled over to pour him another drink.

"Why don't you mind your own business, Arlo," said Jones, "you brown-nosing sons-abitch?" He stood halfway up from his chair.

"Aw, sit your ass back down, you forty-dollar bummer," Heath laughed. Yet, as he laughed, his hand rested idly on his gun butt. Tom Colbert noted the gesture and took a step back along the bar, indicating that he had no part in anything. At a table in a far corner, the two Dead Rabbits sat watching intently, Feathers sitting asleep on Michael's lap, her arms around his neck.

Jones stood tensed for moment as if thinking things over. But then he let out a breath and cursed, "Hell with it, old man. You ain't worth killing."

His words caused Heath to roar with laughter and throw back the glass of whiskey as soon as the old bartender poured it. Tom Colbert let out a breath, hooked a bottle of rye off the dusty bar and walked over to the ranger, shaking his head. "I'm staying over here, removing myself out of the line of fire," he said. He held the bottle out toward Sam, saying, "How about a drink, Ranger? Just to show me you've no hard feelings over me lying to you that time."

"I'm not a ranger anymore, Colbert, remember?" Sam replied, turning down the offered bottle. He forced himself to show a wry smile. "If I had any hard feelings, you wouldn't be *removed* from the line of fire. You'd still be in it."

Colbert chuckled. "Fair enough, Burrack.

But let me ask you this," he said curiously. "When I told you I was a stranger passing through, did you believe me? Or did you let me go knowing I was one of the gang?"

"I figured a man consorting with a tough crowd had to have some sort of connection to them. You didn't just drop by to form a choir."

"That's a good one." Colbert grinned, throwing back a shot of rye. He wiped a hand across his lips and said, "I'll have to remember that."

Sam gave a glance through the empty window frame toward the hotel and said, "You do that, Colbert. Now, if you'll excuse me . . ."

He started to turn and walk away toward the front door, but Colbert caught him by the forearm, having seen the way he'd been watching Ella only moments earlier. "Burrack, forget her. She'll eat you alive."

Sam gave a harsh stare at Colbert's hand on his forearm, causing the outlaw to turn him loose quickly. "I've known her a lot longer than you have, Colbert," Sam responded. "When I say she and I are friends . . . *friends* is all I mean by it."

Colbert stepped back with a nod and watched Sam walk away. When Sam had left the saloon, Arlo Heath sidled over drunkenly from the bar with his empty shot glass in his hand, and held it out toward Colbert's bottle of rye. "Did I just see you and the ranger having words?" he said.

Colbert filled his glass. "He just reminded me that he's not a ranger anymore."

"So he says." Heath grinned. He raised the glass toward Colbert as if in a toast and said, "Ranger or not, we'll see how well he can manage to keep himself alive once Max Krey shows up."

"Ha!" said Colbert. "If Free Turnbaugh thinks this man can do us some good, I've got a hundred dollars that says he ain't about to let Max Krey kill him."

"You're making the wrong bet with me," Heath chuckled. He threw back a drink of the strong rye. "But I'll for damn sure bet you a hundred dollars Max Krey *can't* kill him."

Outside the run-down saloon, Sam walked straight to the Monarch Hotel and through the creaking front door. On the counter stood a wooden box with a small sign on its lid that read: PAY HERE ONE DOLLAR. Next to it stood another box bearing a sign of its own, which read: TAKE KEY. Sam looked down at the floor, saw the fresh set of a lady's footprints in the dust leading up the stairs and followed them upward to a door halfway down a long empty hallway.

He knocked lightly on the door and felt it open slightly. "Ella?" he called into the room. He knocked again. "Ella?" When a few seconds had passed with no reply, he pushed the door open gently and stepped inside. He saw Ella sitting with her head bowed in an overstuffed chair to his right, her arms spread over the thick arms of the chair, and a bandanna lying on the floor beneath her dangling right hand. He saw the fresh red needle mark on her left forearm. "Oh, Ella," he murmured, stepping over to her.

"Hmmm?" Ella said dreamily, barely raising her eyes to him, a trace of a blissful smile on her face.

"I thought you quit this stuff, Ella," Sam said, stooping down in front of her and lightly tipping her chin up in order to face her.

"Oh, I have, Sam," she said, her brow clouding for a moment as if she remembered what she'd said about giving up the powerful drug. But her thought only lasted a second. "It's just that . . . Harvey brought me some I ordered from Chicago. . . ."

"I understand," Sam said quietly. He let her chin down gently, stood up and took a step back.

Ella seemed to come around a little, enough to raise her face and stare at him through glassy eyes, her pupils as tiny as pinpoints. "No, Sam, you don't," she whispered. "You *can't* understand. Nobody can."

"All right then," said Sam, "maybe I don't. Maybe I'm only saying it because I don't know what else to say."

She closed her eyes and smiled dreamily. "Where I am right now, Sam, is in a place where nothing hurts . . . where everything feels and looks too beautiful to even describe. . . ." Her words lingered, and she appeared to be asleep. But then she continued, raising a limp hand to him as if to draw him down to her. "Oh, Sam, if only you could feel this with me . . . be here with me. I know you would love it here. . . ."

"Don't, Ella. You know better than this." Sam took another short step backward. Her fingertips fluttered lightly toward him, but in a moment she lowered her hand and opened her eyes slightly.

"Yes," she said softly, "I know better. I see the look on your face. I know what you're thinking. You think what all of you think — that you're all so damn superior. . . ." She closed her eyes and seemed to drift off with that thought foremost on her mind.

Sam studied her sleeping face for a moment. "That's what you must've thought all along, lovely Ella," he whispered. "Nobody has ever been able to convince you otherwise."

He turned and started for the door; but, in spite of how soundly she seemed to have fallen asleep, Ella rose up unsteadily from the chair and said, "Sam . . . wait. I am going to quit. Right now. I promise this is the last time. I'm quitting, for *you*!"

"I told you before, Ella," said Sam without stopping, "don't quit for me. Quit for your own sake."

"Stay here with me, Sam. Don't leave," she called out to him, making it as far as the open door before she swayed and had to catch herself against the doorframe. "Please don't . . ." she whispered, hearing his boots move farther away from her down the dusty stairs.

On the front porch of the hotel, Sam stopped and gazed at the saloon, where two men in long riding dusters stood beside their sweat-streaked horses listening to the rest of the gang. Sam knew what they were telling the new arrivals. Michael McGinty held a hand to his swollen jaw as if showing them the damage.

At the sight of the ranger, Heath drew the two men's attention in his direction, pointing toward him with his bottle of rye. Sam watched one of the men snatch the bottle from Heath's hand, take a long swig and pass it to the man beside him. Seeing the entire group form up and come walking toward him, Sam stepped down off the hotel porch and stood facing them, his Colt coming up easily from his holster and hanging in his hand.

"See there, Free?" said Heath, taking his bottle back from Sugar Townsend. "That's the way this sumbitch acts. It's hard to get within a mile of him without that Colt getting into his hand some way."

"Shut up, Heath, you swine," said Bill Jones. "It ain't black magic. He just draws the gun in a way that you don't take exception to why he's doing it till it's done."

"Have a drink, Jones," said Turnbaugh, walking straight and deliberately without turning toward him. "You sound like you need it."

"He better have his gun out if he's of a mind to give me any sass," said Sugar Townsend, flipping his duster lapel back behind one of the big saddle Walkers he'd shoved down behind his belt.

"There you go," said Colbert, giving a trace of a grin. "Let Sugar face off with him."

"No," said Turnbaugh, "none of yas better make a move unless I make one first." He walked on until he stopped ten feet from the ranger, seeing something in the ranger's bearing that told him that he'd come close enough. "Ranger Sam Burrack!" he called out. "I understand you brought Ella and Michael McGinty here."

"Not 'Ranger' anymore," Sam replied. "But yes, I brought Ella here, to keep some bounty men off her." He nodded at Michael McGinty. "I've already explained what happened to this man more times than I ever cared to."

Turnbaugh dismissed McGinty's misfortune with a half shrug. "Now that you're no longer a ranger, you're wanting to join our gang?"

Sam let out a slight sigh and said, "That's not at all what I said. I've spent too many years chasing men like you, Turnbaugh."

With his hand poised at his pistol butt, Turnbaugh said, "Yeah, I suppose it's a hard life whichever end of the hunt you're on."

Sam nodded. "Ella's the one who brought it up about riding with you." He paused, then said, "I understand there's other ways a man can make money, but not be on either end of that hunt you mentioned."

Turnbaugh's eyes filled with suspicion. "It

303

might be worth looking into," he said, trying hard not to let that suspicion show.

"What about Max Krey?" Heath asked, the rye causing him to cut right in. "I told him Max is going to kill him."

Turnbaugh gave Heath a cold glance, then, turning back to Sam, said calmly, "What happens between you and Max is your all's business. Are you satisfied with that?"

Sam saw something dark pass across his eyes at the mention of Max Krey's name, but whatever it had been, Sam wouldn't pursue it. It dawned on him that thanks to Ella Lang he had made it to the top men, Freeman Turnbaugh, and soon enough, he'd meet Max Krey. If he wanted to kill them both, he'd soon have the opportunity. Yet he couldn't help but ask himself, since he'd made it this far, how much would it mean to other lawmen if he went ahead and managed to get to that secret mysterious hideout up in the side of Black Mesa?

"I'm satisfied with it," Sam replied.

"Good," said Turnbaugh. "Now where is Ella?" Even as he asked, Sam saw the larger question in his eyes. Freeman Turnbaugh wanted to know how close the two had been, and how close Sam might want them to be again.

Sam kept his eyes riveted on Turnbaugh's, letting him know he had nothing to hide about Ella and him. Nodding at the Monarch Hotel, Sam said, "She's sleeping."

Staring at Sam, Turnbaugh asked, "Is she . . . ?"

"Yeah," Sam said, flatly, "I'm afraid so."

"Did she get it from you?" he asked bluntly.

"Watch your language," Sam replied, the look in his eyes telling Turnbaugh exactly how strongly he disapproved of Ella's appetites.

"Where'd she get it?" he asked, as if assuming Sam would know.

Sam refused to allow his eyes to go to Harvey Fanin. Instead he stared straight into Turnbaugh's eyes and said, "From one of your men, would be my guess."

"I gave it to her," said Harvey Fanin, stepping forward, giving Sam a hard look. "I'm not going to be beholden to this man for not telling. She asked me to pick it up for her from the postal clerk in Hayes City, so I did. Nobody ever told me not to."

Turnbaugh clenched his teeth and said, "I'm telling now, all of yas, don't bring her anymore dope!" He stared back at Sam and said, "I hoped this would be her last spree . . . that she'd get it all out of her

305

system this trip to Dodge."

From the door of the Monarch Hotel, Ella said in a thick voice, "It doesn't work that way, Free."

"Ella," Turnbaugh said, unable to keep himself from smiling at her, in spite of his anger, in spite of the situation. But then he caught himself and said to Sam with a quickly changed expression, "Are we through? Do we understand one another?"

"Yes," said Sam, keeping himself from looking in Ella's direction.

"All right then," said Turnbaugh. He reached over and snatched the bottle from Heath's hand and, stepping wide of the ranger, walked to the front door of the hotel, where he and Ella disappeared inside.

"Well, everybody, there you have it!" Heath said drunkenly, spreading his arms wide. "If Sam Burrack is all right with Free Turnbaugh, he's all right with me!"

Colbert laughed and shook his head. "That's the same Fanin said about Ella!"

"Meaning what?" Fanin asked in a serious tone.

"Meaning nothing, Harvey, damn it," said Colbert. "It just strikes me strange that all of a sudden everybody is warming up to Burrack."

"I'm not," Sugar Townsend said, facing

Sam with his feet spread shoulder width apart, his duster still pulled back behind his holster.

Everybody froze in silence. Sam slipped his thumb over the hammer of his Colt. "Get it said, Sugar Townsend, whatever it is," Sam demanded of him.

"I'm faster than you, Sam Burrack, plain and simple," said Sugar Townsend. "Holster that Colt and I'll prove it."

"Gawddamn it, Sugar," said Fanin, stepping in. "You heard what Free said. Leave this man alone. If you want to see blood, wait until Max gets here." He turned from Townsend to Sam with a cruel grin. "It sounds like Turnbaugh wants to see him and Max go at it."

Sugar Townsend's expression changed slowly as if something had crossed his mind. Again it was something stirred by hearing Max Krey's name mentioned, Sam noted, seeing the gunman's hand relax and drift upward away from his big Walker Colt. "Yeah," said Townsend, "you're right. I want to see that myself."

Chapter 20

Maria and Nat Gilder stood atop a tall rise of grass looking out and down upon the remnants of a trading depot on the valley floor. Having lost the marked horseshoe prints in the tall grass, Maria stared at the empty grasslands and a dry creekbed running alongside the depot, seeing no signs of life.

"I think we are wasting time," she said, just testing the journalist, wanting to know if he really knew his way to the secret outlaw hideout in Black Mesa. "We will ride past Buckton. You will take us straight to Turnbaugh's hideout."

"Oh! Uh, certainly," said Gilder, appearing distressed at the thought of it. "But is that wise, being there's just the two of us?"

Maria gave him a flat stare and said, "You lied to me. You have no idea how to get to the hideout, do you?"

"Of course I do!" said Gilder, sounding

shocked by her blatant accusation. Under Maria's steady gaze, he said, "That is, I know *about* where it's at." He shrugged. "I mean, how hard could it be to —"

"That's it," said Maria, cutting him off. "No more lies. I'm leaving you at Buckton. You are on your own." She turned her horse in the waist-high grass to ride away.

"Wait, please!" said Gilder. "All right, maybe I'm not as familiar with the Black Mesa area as I purported to be. But let's not call it lying. Journalists never lie!" He grinned. "Sometime we just rely on less than accurate information. I've heard so many stories about the place, I'm sure I can take us there."

Maria just stared at him flatly and continued to turn her horse. In doing so, she caught a glimpse of alone rider leading a packhorse and heading toward the fallen depot station. Seeing him caused her to jerk her horse back out of sight behind the edge of the rise. "Get back here, Gilder, quickly!" she whispered, even though there was little chance the rider would have heard her from such a distance.

"What is it?" Gilder asked, hurriedly following her order.

She slipped quickly from her saddle and gazed down at the rider from a position of cover. Recognition came to her and she said under her breath, "Killer Max Krey!"

"Hunh? Really? You mean Freeman Turnbaugh's right-hand man?" Gilder said, ducking with his hand atop his hat as if he risked being seen. "How — how do you know?" His pad and pencil suddenly appeared in his hands.

"The last time I saw him he wore a dead soldier's uniform," Maria said, as if speaking to herself, "but it is him — I know it."

Gilder had spilled down from his saddle and stood crouched, sticking close to her side. "What do you mean, he wore a dead soldier's uniform?" the reporter pried. "Can you explain that more clearly?"

"I will later, if you keep quiet," Maria scolded him. She kept her eyes on Krey, watching him ride up close to the fallen relay shack, pull the packhorse up beside him and step down. Giving a quick look all around, he took down the canvas bags full of money and lugged them over under a corner of the shack's downed tin roof. "I think we may have just found ourselves a piece of luck," Maria said, watching him hurry back to the horse and take down two more bags and hurry back to the shack with them.

"In what way?" Gilder asked, scribbling notes.

"We will follow Krey and see which way his trail leads. It is time for the gang to start getting back together."

The two lay in silence for the next few minutes watching Krey drag brittle brush from the dry creekbed and stuff it under the corner of the fallen roof to hide the bags. Finally, Krey stepped back, looked over the hiding spot, gave one more quick look all around, then stepped over and slapped the extra horse on its rump and sent it bounding away through the tall grass. Krey climbed into his saddle and heeled his horse away.

"He is headed for Buckton," Maria said. "So it looks like we will be going there after all."

"What about the bags he hid down there?" Gilder asked. "Are we going to see what's in them?"

"We will," said Maria, "but I already have a pretty good idea." She thought things over for a moment as she gave Krey a head start. Then she said, "Perhaps Max Krey has gone into business for himself."

When Krey had ridden out of sight in the direction of Buckton, Maria stood up from the ground, dusted bits of grass from herself and walked over to the horses, Gilder right beside her, writing as he stumbled along. "Now will you tell me about the dead soldier's uniform?" he asked.

"Sí," she said, "now I will tell you. Come along, quickly."

They mounted their horses and rode down to the dilapidated trade depot. On the way, Maria told Gilder about the day she and Sam had spotted Turnbaugh's gang riding out across the desert floor. Gilder write furiously as she spoke. When the two of them stepped down from their horses beside the fallen depot, Gilder said, "I can't tell you how distressed I am that lovely Ella Lang had anything to do with such a hideous act."

Maria raised a brow and asked him pointedly. "What exactly do you think she has been doing these years to keep herself in this gang? Is it not you and your kind who named her 'Queen of the Outlaws' and 'the Outlaws' Lady'? What do you think she did to gain such notoriety, make coffee for them?"

Gilder looked embarrassed. "Well, I certainly never suspected that she took part in anything untoward! Certainly nothing as dastardly as murder and robbery!"

"Murder and robbery is what outlaws do,

Mr. Gilder," said Maria. She shook her head, stepped down from her horse and walked over to the corner edge of the fallen tin roof. Stooping down, she struggled with a stiff, dried-out juniper bush until she tossed it aside and pulled out one of the bags of money. After a quick peek at the bag's contents, she closed the bag, set it aside and said to Gilder, "We are moving this to another spot, for safekeeping until everything is settled."

"But why?" said Gilder. "I thought you're in a hurry to follow Krey and find the ranger."

"I see where Krey is headed," said Maria. "If things go wrong, I do not want him riding back, taking this money and riding away with it. This money does not belong to him. It is called stealing, Mr. Gilder," she added, a bit sarcastically. But then she caught herself, and said a little more informatively, "In this business, sometimes just knowing the whereabouts of missing money can save your life."

"Oh, yes, I see," said Gilder, as if he'd never looked at things that way. He snatched up the first clumsy canvas bag and waited for her to hand him another.

"And where do you think we should hide it?" he asked, looking all around.

"In the old creekbed beneath some rocks," said Maria. She hurriedly pulled out bag after bag, then helped Gilder carry them over rocky ground full of thick clumps of wild grass to the dusty, four-foot-deep depression left behind by years of rushing water.

"What if this creek fills?" Gilder asked.

"The money will get wet," Maria said, giving him the shortest possible answer. She smiled thinly to herself, dropped two money bags along the rising side of the creekbed and began gathering rocks to pile over them.

Within moments the bags of money were hidden and the two were back atop their horses, on Krey's trail through the freshly bent grass left in the wake of his horse's hooves. Along the way, Gilder sidled up close to Maria and spoke with one hand planted firmly atop his hat. "Do you realize that if lovely Ella had had anything to do with the deaths of those soldiers, she is subject to hang, the same as Turnbaugh, Max Krey or any other member of the gang?"

"*Sí,* of course I realize that," said Maria, gazing straight ahead.

"Does that not bother you, knowing that this beautiful woman could die on a rough wooden gallows?"

"It bothers me to know that anyone has wasted their life in such a manner as to bring it to the gallows. But then I must consider the terrible things they have done, and the lives of the innocent people that have been destroyed." She glanced sidelong at him. "If Ella Lang hangs, it will be because she has spent her entire life braiding her own noose. She is a reckless *criminal,* Mr. Gilder, not some 'beautiful free spirit,' like the press has called her, 'who lives her life of a wisp of passing prairie wind.' "

Gilder blushed, then said proudly, "That happens to be one of my quotes, in case you didn't already know it."

Maria didn't answer.

"But you *are* right," said Gilder, after having seemed to consider it for a moment. Finally his eyes lit up and he said, "That's one hanging I suppose I owe it to readers to attend . . . in order to tell them the *real* story about Ella Lang. I'm sure she will be repentant in the end, perhaps crying softly as they lead her to the —"

"Plese stop it," Maria said, cutting him off. "You do not have the capabilities of telling a *real* story."

"Well, if that's what you think, you are terribly mistaken," said Gilder, as if offended. "I tell the *real* story. All journalists

315

do. However, you must realize that readers depend on writers like myself to make the story *interesting* as well as truthful."

Maria replied, "Oh? But what if it cannot be both real and interesting . . . which of those two elements must be cut away in order for the other to be read?"

Gilder grew sullen. "I don't want to discuss it with you any further. I am a *journalist.* As such I do not have to *defend my integrity.* The reading public is aware of our high standards of trust, truth and accuracy."

"Of course we are," said Maria, "and it is you journalists who have done a good job telling us about them." She smiled to herself and nudged her horse forward. Gilder grumbled under his breath, but kept up with her.

They stayed back a safe distance from Max Krey and followed his tracks though the grasslands and part of the way across a long stretch of rocky dirt and scrubby brushland surrounding Buckton. Taking shade behind a ten-foot-high upsurge of dirt and rock just off the trail, Maria stepped down from her saddle, grabbed a canteen of tepid water, sipped from it and passed it on to Nat Gilder. Buckton lay no more than a thousand yards ahead.

"Now what do we do?" Gilder asked, after taking a sip of water and swishing it around before swallowing it. "For all we know, the whole gang could already be waiting in there."

"If they are, then I can only hope that Sam is there with them," Maria said. Taking the canteen back, she capped it and hung it back over her saddle horn. She raised her Colt from the holster on her hip, opened the chamber, checked it and closed it.

"Wait a minute," said Gilder in disbelief. "Don't tell me we're riding in there!"

"Not we, perhaps," said Maria. "You are free to choose for yourself." She calmly raised a Winchester repeating rifle from its saddle scabbard, checked it and slipped it back inside.

"In other words, you *are* riding in?" Gilder asked.

"*Sí,*" Maria said quietly, "I am riding in."

"But you can't be serious!" said Gilder. "What about Turnbaugh's men!"

"Buckton is almost a ghost town," said Maria, "but it is still a town. I have as much reason to ride in there as anyone."

"But these men are some awfully tough gunmen. You can't take a chance like this!" Gilder pleaded.

"I take a chance like this every day of my

life, Mr. Gilder," said Maria, leveling her hat on her head. "I may not be the Queen of the Wild West, but I have gone where I please for a long time, in spite of some awfully tough gunmen." She gave him a thin trace of a smile. "If Sam is in there, I must find out, and see what he needs for me to do."

"Oh, dear," Gilder said, rubbing his sweaty forehead with the pencil in his hand. "May I just take a moment here to seek my own counsel? I need to think this thing through a bit." He squinted in contemplation. "You see, I don't want to *die* . . . but *my goodness*, what a *smashing* opportunity for a story this is turning into."

Sam stood at the empty window frame, gazing out across the high rolling scrubland. He wondered just how close Maria was to catching up to him — and he didn't wonder *if* she would ride into Buckton searching for him, he only wondered *when.* He knew she would be on his trail, because he knew that under the same set of circumstances he would have been on hers. Yet something more than simple logic told him she would come riding in. He sensed her coming the same way a man sensed the time of day without being out in the sunlight.

Wrapped in his thoughts, he murmured to himself, "Take your time, Maria." His eyes drifted back in from the wide harsh scrublands and went to the Monarch Hotel, only for a moment. But in that moment, Arlo Heath sidled up to him with two mugs of foaming beer in his thick hand and handed one to the ranger.

"You best forget anything that was ever between you and her, Burrack," Heath said. "She belonged to you once, but she belongs to this gang now. There's nothing you can do that's going to change that."

Sam didn't bother mentioning that his mind had not been on Ella Lang. Instead he took the beer from Heath and said, "That's good advice, Arlo." He sipped the foaming beer and looked the older gunman in the eye. "The talk everywhere is that she's Freeman Turnbaugh's gal. But from what I've seen, it appears she's with whoever is nearest at the time."

"Yeah, well, what could she expect?" Heath said. "There was a time she belonged only to Free Turnbaugh. But she's not a woman that one man can keep happy. I reckon after a while Free reconciled himself to it and settled for what he could get." Heath had drunk enough rye to loosen his tongue. "Ella takes her pick of the gang.

She likes having these tough hombres at her beck and call. I expect it's the thing that makes her feel like she's got any say-so over her life."

Looking out at the hotel again, Sam saw Turnbaugh step out on the porch swinging his gun belt around his waist and buckling it. "I expect everybody needs that," Sam said, sipping his beer. He watched Turnbaugh step off the hotel porch and head toward the saloon.

"Uh-oh," said Heath, seeing Turnbaugh's expression in the failing evening light. "Here comes Free with one of his looks on." Without another word, Heath stepped back, turned away from the window frame and eased over to the bar.

Sam, staying at his spot by the window frame, faced Freeman Turnbaugh when Turnbaugh walked through the door and stopped in the middle of the floor. Staring at the old bartender, he demanded, "You, go chase a hog out in the street or something." The old man batted his eyes blankly, but scuffled out from behind the bar and out the front door.

Once Turnbaugh saw him get out of hearing range, he turned back and said to his men, "Come morning, we're headed out toward Black Mesa, with or without Max

Krey. Does anybody have a problem with that?"

The men only shrugged or shook their heads. But at the corner table Linston McGinty called out, "I thought we were going to hit another army payroll?"

Turnbaugh offered a flat mirthless grin, saying, "I didn't say we would be riding *straight* to Black Mesa, now, did I?"

The men at the bar stirred restlessly in eager anticipation. The McGintys both grinned. "Well, all right then! Cheers!" said Linston, raising a whisky glass as if in a toast.

Turnbaugh faced Sam and said, "If you really want to work with us, this is where you start."

"I made it clear I don't want to ride the outlaw trail," said Sam.

"That you did," said Turnbaugh. "But you've got to do this one job with us." He stared at Sam. "As far as I'm concerned, you're still a lawman until I see you get some blood on your hands working *our* side of the law."

Sam felt the saloon grow tense and silent. He realized every eye was on him. "All right then, one time," he said, "just so you can trust me. After that, I'll draw my pay keeping you informed. Fair enough?"

"More than fair," said Turnbaugh.

The old bartender shuffled back inside the door and stopped. Turnbaugh looked at him and said, "We're not finished talking yet. Go chase another one."

Pointing a finger back along the street, the old bartender said, "I thought you'd want to know, your pard Max Krey is riding in."

Sam noted a dark shadow cross Turnbaugh's face at the sound of Max Krey's name. "Yeah, you're right, I did want to know. Obliged, old man." Looking back at Sam, he said, "All right, Burrack, I think it's time I find out some things for myself. Let's all walk out there and make Killer Max feel welcome."

At the bar, Billy Jones let out a short laugh. The others stared at Sam as if looking at a dead man — all except Arlo Heath. Sam set his mug of beer aside, walked to the middle of the floor and stopped two feet from Freeman Turnbaugh. "After you," he said calmly.

CHAPTER 21

Max Krey saw the men walking toward him as he veered his horse the middle of the street and stepped down from from his saddle at the hitch rail in front of the Monarch Hotel. Free Turnbaugh, at the front of the men, noted that Krey wore a fresh, clean shirt. He also noted that Krey used his left hand to spin his reins and secure his horse to the rail.

Krey offered a trace of a flat grin. "This bunch is a sorry sight for sore eyes," he said, turning, looking all around Buckton. "I see this place has about run its string out."

"Where've you been, Max?" Turnbaugh asked, trying to keep his voice friendly, and not show the rage boiling inside him.

"Oh, just here and there, Free," said Max, taking with his left hand a bottle offered to him by Bill Jones. He pulled the cork with his teeth and spat it into his right hand, not raising his right hand above chest high. "I visited myself a senorita over in the pan-handle I hadn't seen in a while." He managed a smile, but it looked stiff and unreal.

"And what about my nephews, Max?" Turnbaugh asked, keeping his voice level and under control. "Did you get to see them, give them my message like I asked you to?"

As Turnbaugh asked Krey the question, Sugar Townsend, the only other man there who knew what this was all leading up to, took a cautious step to one side, in case Turnbaugh lost his temper or Krey saw through his pretense.

Krey watched Sugar step away, but if he suspected anything he didn't show it. "Yeah, I went by their place," Krey said matter-of-factly. "They weren't there."

"Oh?" said Turnbaugh. "That's odd. They almost always are there . . . unless they're off robbing somewhere." He smiled, able to keep it cordial.

"I thought it was strange," said Krey. As he spoke, he walked back along his horse and reached inside his saddlebags. "I found this bag of trinkets on the mantel above the hearth. Just laying out in the open." He pitched the partially rolled-up bag to Turnbaugh, who caught it with a blank stare.

Turnbaugh unrolled the bag, reached

inside and pulled up a gold heart-shaped locket, a ruby stickpin and a silver bracelet. "Now what do you suppose they meant, leaving this stuff laying around? I'm going to have to talk to them about this. This is sloppy."

"Yeah," said Krey. He glanced all around. "The fact is, I think they hit a train . . . even though you told them to lay low for a while."

"If I find that out, they've got themselves some tall explaining to do," said Turnbaugh. He dropped the jewelry back into the bag, except for the gold locket. He pitched the bag back to Krey.

"I wanted you to have it, Free," said Krey. "I figure you could either keep it, or else give it back to your nephews with a little scolding." He gave a wink, and a sly grin. The grin looked real this time.

But Turnbaugh only stared at him for a second. Then he held the locket up by its chain and said coolly, as he examined it, "I've got something for you too, pard," he said.

"Yeah, what's that?" Krey asked, his senses suddenly alerted by the way Turnbaugh had just called him *pard*.

Turnbaugh gestured a hand back, parting the men, giving Sam room to walk forward into sight. "I've got Sam Burrack here . . . the man who killed your brother, Alvin."

Krey's expression turned to stone as his eyes fell upon the ranger. When he spoke, his voice turned low and guttural in his rage. "Ranger, you son of a bitch!" he growled, his gun hand poising tight, in spite of the fact that his shoulder wound wouldn't allow him full use of his right arm.

"It's me, Krey," Sam said, stepping forward slowly, his big Colt out, cocked and hanging poised in his gun hand, the weight of it seeming to cause his shoulder to droop just a little. "Whatever you and me need to do, let's get it done."

"See?" Turnbaugh said to Krey, eyeing him closely although he'd already seen enough to make him start believing Randall Judd's story. "Here's your chance to settle up."

Sam didn't like the way Turnbaugh had just set this up, and he had no idea what sort of dangerous game these two were playing with each other. But as the rest of the men backed away on either side of him, he held back his sudden impulse to raise the Colt and start firing until the gang lay dead in the street.

Krey swallowed hard, keeping his gun hand poised, having a hard time catching up to the whole situation. He eyed Sam, then shot a glance to Turnbaugh, then to the men, then back to Sam. "What's going here, Free?" he asked. "If this is some sort of joke, I don't like it."

"No joke," said Turnbaugh. "You're my pard. You swore you'd kill this man — here's your chance."

"What's he doing here though? That's what I'm wondering," Krey said, a sheen of sweat forming across his brow.

"Ella brought him to us," said Turnbaugh. "Burrack says he's not a lawman anymore. He wants to work for us, feed us information and whatnot." He studied Krey's face, yet he glanced down every second or so at his gun hand. "I told him he can work for us, but if there's any bad blood to thin out between you and him, he'd have to get it all straightened out first." Turnbaugh gave him a thin, harsh smile. "He says that's all fine by him. How does that sound to you?"

Krey stood stunned for a moment. His intentions had been to get back to the gang, lie up for a while and let his shoulder wound heal without anybody knowing about it. The idea had been risky, but he'd felt he could pull it off. Now all of a sudden, here stood the man who had killed his brother. He had to make a stand. Yet he knew if he tried to throw down with Sam Burrack with a bad shoulder, he'd get himself killed.

"I don't like this, Free," Krey finally said, staring hard at Sam, feeling Sam's eyes just as hard in return.

"Don't like what, Max?" said Turnbaugh, innocently. "It's plain and simple. Either you've got something to settle or you don't. If you've got to kill him, go ahead, do it and we'll ride away. If you're not going to kill him, he's riding with us on an army payroll. Then *he's* going on our *payroll.*"

"What I don't like is that I come riding in here unprepared for this. All of a sudden I'm facing a gunfight! That's part of what I don't like!"

"I've never seen you unprepared for a gunfight, *Killer* Max Krey," Turnbaugh said. "So don't try telling me that."

"Another thing is," said Krey, pointing at the ranger with his left hand, "look at this! He's already drawn and ready!"

"You know what, Burrack?" Turnbaugh said, nodding in agreement. "Hell, he's right. That really doesn't seem fair. How about you holster that big dog, and the two of yas start on even ground?"

Sam stared at Krey, feeling everybody's eyes on him, still asking himself what better opportunity he would have to drop these men in the dirt. "I'm good right here," he replied. "I make it a practice to never holster a cold barrel . . . not when the man I'm facing is still standing upright."

Turnbaugh chuckled; so did some of the men. "We're not going to get this man to do much that he doesn't want to do, Max," he said. "I can see that already." He cocked his head to one side as if seeking another solution, then said to Sam, "How about this? Instead of you holstering, what say we let Max here raise his gun easy-like, and you two start from there?"

Sam said flatly, "His gun comes up, he goes down."

"Damn!" Turnbaugh said with another dark chuckle. "You are one *hard* strip of hide, Burrack!" But then his jovial tone stopped; his voice turned cold. Sam couldn't tell if the change was directed at him or Krey as Turnbaugh said with finality, "I say, let him raise it. I want to *see* him raise it, Burrack — you understand me?"

Sam caught something in Turnbaugh's voice. This wasn't about prodding a gunfight between him and Krey. This was between them. "Raise it then, Krey," said Sam, "nice and easy-like."

"Hold on just one *Gawddamn* minute!" said Krey, his entire face now starting to sweat. "I ain't ready for this! I didn't come here to be shoved into a gunfight by my own men!"

"Raise it, damn you!" shouted Turnbaugh. The rest of the men looked bewildered, except for Sugar Townsend, who stood with his duster pulled back behind his holster.

"I'm not going to, Free!" Krey shouted in reply. "What the hell has gotten into —"

"Raise that Colt or I'll blow your *Gawddamn* head off my *Gawddamn self*!" Turnbaugh bellowed, convinced now that what Randall Judd told him had to be right. As he shouted, his Colt came up fast and unexpected, so unexpected that the move almost drew a bullet from the ranger's Colt. But Sam kept himself together, taking it all in, with no idea what Turnbaugh meant by his move.

"Free, damn it to hell!" Krey raged. "I'm not going to draw this gun!"

"Not going to?" Turnbaugh raged. "You're Gawddamn right you're not! Because you can't!" He took a step forward, his knuckles white around the butt of his pistol. "You can't because you've got a bullet hole in your shoulder! Randall Judd put it there, trying to stop you from killing my nephews, you son of a bitch, you!"

Sugar Townsend's big Walker came up

from his belt and out at arm's length toward Krey. "Say the word, Free. I'll gut-shoot this rotten bastard!" he growled. "I never liked him much anyway." The rest of the men stared in stunned disbelief.

"Free, Jesus!" said Krey. "What are you talking about! I wouldn't do something like that! After all you and me have been to one another! We're like brothers!"

"Yeah," said Turnbaugh, still livid with rage but keeping himself in check, "and that's the only reason your brains aren't already splattered all over the street! Judd lived just long enough to tell me what you did to them! Now you're going to die, you low, double-crossing —"

"Wait, Free! Judd lied! Let me explain it all! You owe me that, don't you?" said Krey, cutting him off, seeing that the more Turnbaugh spoke, the more his rage grew in intensity.

"Explain it all then, *Gawddamn* you!" Turnbaugh raged. "And the minute I catch you trying to lie to me, I'm rubbing you out!"

In the front upstairs hall window of the Monarch Hotel, Ella Lang rubbed her blurry eyes and tried to focus her sight and her mind on the scene playing itself out in the street below. She had been lying stretched out on the bed, naked, recovering slowly from her drugged stupor when the sounds of angry voices penetrated her sleep.

"Oh my God!" she cried out, grabbing on to the windowsill, shaking it, trying to raise it. Looking down at Turnbaugh and Townsend, both holding guns on Max Krey, she cried out louder, "Free! No! Please!"

But through the closed window, Turnbaugh either couldn't hear her or didn't care. He braced himself, ready to kill Krey at any second.

"All right, listen to me, Free!" Krey said, talking quickly, trying to build some sort of story for himself as he went along. "It's true. I shot Randall Judd. But it was because he and your nephews robbed the train after I told them you wanted them to lay low!" His eyes darted back and forth wildly, his left hand almost reached across to his holstered pistol, but he stopped, realizing he wouldn't have a chance.

"And my nephews?" Turnbaugh asked, his voice growing calm, knowing he couldn't believe a single word Max Krey had said. "Tell me that poor Wilbur and Raymond are still alive. Convince me that you didn't kill my sister's only sons."

"I didn't kill them, Free! I swear to God I didn't!" Krey said, his voice taking on a pleading quality.

"You are lying!" Turnbaugh said, his voice growing louder. His hand leveled with purpose; he took aim down the pistol sights.

"Wait! All right, I did kill them! But they were no good, Free! We wouldn't have been able to trust them. They were idiots! Not like us!"

"So long, pard," Turnbaugh said, emptying his gun into Killer Max Krey, Sugar Townsend doing the same thing only a split second behind him. Sam stood watching, his Colt still hanging in his hand. He had some idea of what had just happened, yet for the most part, he was nearly as dumb-founded as the rest of the men standing in the dirt street.

"Oh my God!" Ella screamed, bursting out the front door and flinging herself down onto Max Krey's bloody bullet-riddled body beneath a gray looming drift of burned powder. "What have they done to you? My poor precious Max!"

"Get back away from him, Ella," said Sugar Townsend, stepping forward, reloading his big Walker.

"No, no! You son of a bitch!" she screamed at Sugar, hugging Max's head to her bosom as if shielding him from the gunman. "It's enough, he's dead!"

"Come on, turn him loose, Ella," Turnbaugh coaxed, stooping down, wrenching her free from Krey and lifting her away from him. "He was no good, Ella. He turned on me! I had to do it."

"No! No! No!" Ella swung her head back and forth violently, screaming, fighting, trying to free herself. Her eyes widened as Sugar closed the chamber on his newly loaded Walker, stepped in, lowered the tip of the barrel an inch from Krey's forehead and fired.

Sam stood in silence, as did the rest of the men. The final shot from Sugar Townsend's Walker seemed to drive Krey's death more clearly home to her. She stopped resisting Turnbaugh and collapsed backward against him. Turnbaugh turned her to face him and embraced her protectively.

"He's gone, Ella. Let him go." As he held her against him, he turned his eyes to the ranger, then to the others. "Tomorrow morning," he said in a commanding tone, "everybody be ready to ride."

CHAPTER 22

Maria and Gilder came to a jerking halt at the sound of gunfire coming from Buckton. Maria raised a hand to keep Gilder quiet, although there would have been no need to. The reporter had been riding along, talking and scribbling; but now he sat with his chin dropped and his eyes wide with excitement. The two seemed to be frozen in place in the silence following the cacophony of gunfire, until the single blast from Sugar Townsend's Walker Colt resounded, stirring them back into motion.

"Now that is odd," Gilder commented, his cocked pencil hand going back to the pad, making a quick note. "What do you suppose it all meant?"

Pondering it grimly, Maria replied, "It meant someone has been executed. The last shot was someone making sure that person is dead."

"You can tell all that just from the sound

of the gunshots?" Gilder asked, seeming greatly impressed.

"No, not from the sounds of gunshots," Maria said, giving him a look. "I could tell that from knowing the type of people we are searching for." She nudged the buckskin forward toward town, seeing that the outline of buildings had began to sink into the encroaching evening gloom.

Gilder nudged his horse up alongside her and said, "Say, you don't suppose that could have been . . . ?" He caught himself and said, "No, of course not. Forget I said anything." He tried to brush the matter aside.

Maria gave him another look, and from her expression, Gilder could tell he had touched on a nerve. "I'm sorry," he said meekly. "I didn't mean to worry you."

"I am already worried," Maria said, dismissing the matter with no show of emotion in her voice. Changing the subject, she said, "If we run into Max Krey or Turnbaugh or any of his men in Buckton, you must keep quiet and behave yourself."

"I always behave myself," said Gilder with a thin little smile. "But I can't promise to keep quiet. I feel it my calling to always be on the hunt for a story, and if it becomes necessary for me to probe and question —"

"Please. Just do the best you can," Maria said, cutting him off. "We will try to avoid these men."

Darkness had fallen across Buckton by the time Maria and Nat Gilder rode slowly past the town-limits sign; a dim light glowed in the front window of the Monarch Hotel. At the sight of Sam's white barb standing at the hitch rail, its saddle off and lying on the edge of the boardwalk, Maria felt at least a little relieved.

But when she and Gilder halted their horses at the hitch rail, she saw the bullet holes surrounded with blood on the front of the clapboard-sided building. Stepping down from her saddle, she noted the blood on the boardwalk and the two bloody smears where a body had been dragged away. She gave a searching stare toward the brighter light coming from the open window frame of the saloon and saw men at the poker table and the bar.

"Wait here," she said to Gilder, "while I go inside the hotel and see if Sam is here."

Gilder only nodded and stood between the two horses, looking a bit tense, his pencil and paper in hand.

Inside the hotel, she eased silently up the stairs and looked along the dusty hallway. She found the only room with light seeping from beneath the door and walked to it quietly, staying close to the wall to keep down any creaking from the plank floor.

But in spite of her catlike stealth, as she neared the door, on the other side of it, Sam trimmed the wick down on the lantern in his hand, set it down on a table and drew his Colt. He stepped over beside the door and stood with his back against the wall, waiting, listening, studying the silence until he either read or sensed the barest wisp of motion in the hallway.

Just as Maria started to kneel to see what she could see through the keyhole, the door snapped open a foot and the lantern light found her staring into the barrel of Sam's Colt.

"Freeze," Sam said harshly, yet keeping his voice lowered.

"Sam!" said Maria. "It's me!"

The ranger let his gun slump, his thumb going over the hammer and easing it down. "My goodness, Maria," he said, his voice almost trembling at the sight of her in the darkness of the hallway, "I can't tell you —" But he did not get to finish his words as her arms encircled him, and he returned her embrace, feeling her lips warm on his mouth.

When the kiss ended, they clung to each

other in the open doorway. "Sam, I thought you were . . ."

"Shhh, I know," Sam replied. He closed his eyes for a moment and took in her warmth, her scent, the essence of her; and he repeated softly, "I know . . . I know."

They embraced until across the room Maria saw the sleeping woman lying sprawled on the bed. Feeling her change in his arms and knowing why, Sam said, "That's Ella."

"Oh, I see," said Maria. "And is this her room, or yours?"

"It's hers," Sam said, turning and leading her closer to the bed. He raised the lantern from the table, barely raised the wick and let the light fall upon the sleeping figure. "Lovely Ella Lang," he whispered, gazing down with Maria.

The lantern light, although soft and silken, showed the sleeping woman no kindness. Ella's face looked drawn and sharp-edged, her closed eyes puffy and tortured from too many tears. Sam whispered to Maria, "I came here to try and console her."

Maria saw Sam's impression on the bed, where he'd been lying beside Ella Lang. She envisioned him there, his arms around her. "I understand," Maria said.

"Do you, Maria?" Sam asked in earnest. "It's important to me that you do." He paused, then continued. "Freeman Turn-baugh killed Max Krey a while ago. Ella turned hysterical. I came here to watch her, to make sure she wouldn't do something to hurt herself."

"Hurt herself?" Maria asked.

"It's a long story, Maria." Sam nodded at the needle marks on the inside of Ella's forearm. "We'll go to my room. I'll tell you everything."

Maria took a deep breath, standing at his side. "*Sí,* let's go to your room. I want to know what happened to you. I have been worried."

"I knew you were worried," said Sam, "but there was nothing I could do about it. I couldn't turn loose here." He drew her closer to him. "I knew you'd be coming though." He trimmed the lantern down, then set it beside the bed, and they slipped quietly out the door and down the darkened hallway.

In front of the hotel, Nat Gilder stood between the horses waiting until finally he grew so weary that he sat down on the edge of the boardwalk, folded his arms across his knees, laid his face down and closed his eyes. Moments later he awakened to the sound of Maria's voice as she shook him gently. "Come with me, Mr. Gilder. We're

340

spending the night here."

"We — we *are*?" Gilder sounded rattled and shocked. Maria realized he'd misunderstood her. "*You* will get yourself a room. Sam is here. I will be staying with him."

"Oh, of course," Gilder replied, sounding a little disappointed. He stood up, placed his bowler hat atop his head and shuffled along behind Maria into the hotel.

"That's her! That's the low-down slut that done this to me!" Merlin Wakely said in a harsh whisper. He and Crystal Jack Holder stood back in the dark alley in front of the four bounty hunters they had rounded up between Dodge and Hayes City after Sam shot Blackwell from his saddle.

"Then why didn't you kill her while you just had the chance, mate?" asked an Australian drifter named Taggs Elliot.

"That's the same thing I'm asking myself," said Wakely, giving Holder a scowl in the dark.

"You didn't kill her because it would screw up everything we're here to do — *that's why*," said Holder. He turned a stern gaze to Taggs Elliot. "And you'll keep your comments to yourself, if you want in on this. Nobody is killing anybody until we get Turnbaugh and his men lined up, ready to pluck, gut and broil. Are we all clear on

341

that?" He looked from Taggs to the other three ragged, bristly-bearded men for a response. "Vassey? Shummer? Idaho? Are we?"

The three men nodded in agreement. Idaho Joe Golden said in a gruff tone, "I don't know if you realize this or not, but I'm no Gawddamned idiot. You don't have to repeat everything you say to make sure I heard it." He gave Holder a hard stare.

"Yeah, right," said Holder, dismissing the matter. He stared down along the street at the saloon. "Everybody settle in here for a while and keep still. Soon as they're all drunk enough, we'll move in for the kill." He patted Wakely on his shoulder. "You can wait a little while longer, can't you?"

"Yeah, I expect I can wait all night if I have to," Wakely said, "so long as I *am* the one who gets to cut her black heart out."

"Hey," said Idaho, "I hired on to bring in Freeman Turnbaugh, Max Krey — men with prices on their heads. That woman hasn't done a damn thing to me, and there's not a dime on her head that I ever heard of. We've got no business tangling with her or that ole ranger. They're the kind of sleeping dogs you better let lay if you know what's good for you."

"She cost me my arm," said Wakely. "I'm

sworn to kill her if it means I spend forever in a hot burning hell." He stared across the empty street to the darkened windows on the second floor of the Monarch Hotel.

After introducing the ranger to Nat Gilder, Maria had sent the weary reporter off to his room at the far end of the hall. She then joined Sam in the quiet of his room, where they told each other about everything that had happened to them since he'd left her in Dodge City. When he told about Turnbaugh killing Max Krey earlier in the evening, she shook her head in contemplation.

"Gilder and I happened onto Max Krey and watched him hide four canvas bags full of money — more than likely it is the money from the train robbery."

"That would be my guess," Sam replied. Lying on the bed, the two of them talked quietly in the dim glow of an oil lantern. Sam said, "Before Ella fell asleep, she told me that Turnbaugh wants out. She said he wants this next army payroll robbery to be their last. He wants her to disappear with him . . . catch a ship to Honduras and never be seen or heard from again."

"Does knowing this change anything for you?" Maria asked.

"Yes, it does," said Sam. "As far as I'm

343

concerned, it's too late for either of them to step out. This is no game that Turnbaugh can call off anytime he feels like it. He's left too many bodies along his trail."

"Then you are still going to kill him?" Maria asked.

"No," said Sam, "that's what's changed. I know that's what I was agreeing to when I took off my badge and headed this way." He paused, then said, "But I can't kill a man this way unless he forces me to. If I can get close enough to kill Turnbaugh, I'm close enough to take him in. Now that Krey is dead, Turnbaugh and Ella are all that's going to hold this bunch together. Without them this gang is finished. I'll take Turnbaugh to Fort Smith. Parker will have to figure out what to do next."

Maria offered a small, warm smile. "I am glad to hear you say this," she said softly.

"Tonight is when we have to get it done," Sam said, his voice sounding grim in anticipation. "I had hoped to locate their hideout in Black Mesa. But to do so, I'd have to wait until after the payroll robbery. That would cost more innocent lives."

"I first brought Gilder along with me because he claimed to know the way to the hideout," said Maria. "He has written about it a great deal. But when I pressed him on it

344

right before we came here, he finally admit-
ted that he knows nothing about how to get
there."

"That place must be the world's best-kept
secret," Sam said. "Every lawman and
outlaw knows about it, but it seems nobody
knows how to get there."

"Perhaps when this is over, Ella will agree
to show us the way?" Maria asked.

Looking into her eyes, Sam knew that Maria had other questions about Ella. He knew
this was the time to get them answered.

"I don't want her hurt, Maria, if we can
keep her from it," Sam said

Maria nodded. "What becomes of her af-
terward?"

"Once Turnbaugh is out of the picture, I
want to try to take her somewhere, a place
where they will help her," Sam replied.

"And if she does not want to go?" Maria
asked, both of them knowing the underly-
ing importance of what was being said.

"She's going anyway," said Sam. "I was
willing to step outside the law to take a life.
Surely I can step outside the law to save
one."

Maria didn't respond. But Sam thought
he saw a question in her eyes.

"There's nothing between Ella and me.
That ended a long time ago, Maria," he

said. "I knew that when this all started."

"But still there were things you needed to know?" Maria said softly. She moved closer to him, lifted the edge of a blanket and pulled it over the two of them.

"Yes, I suppose there were," Sam replied. He moved even closer to her.

"Things you cannot even name?" Maria asked, yet Sam knew she was not really asking him a question but rather attempting to put several of *his* questions to rest.

"I suppose there still is." He considered it, slipping an arm around her, feeling her warmth. "Perhaps there always will be. But it doesn't matter. It belongs to the past."

CHAPTER 23

"There goes the ranger," Crystal Jack Holder whispered to the men sitting on the ground behind him in the small alley. "We'll have to make our move now, while they're all together. He's not getting ahead of us this time." Except for Merlin Wakely, whose rage toward Maria had kept him wired tight for the past hour, the bounty hunters had made themselves comfortable against the side of a building and dozed off.

"Get up, Gawddamm it!" Wakely cursed under his breath. He kicked Shummer on his ankle, causing the man's eyes to fly open.

"I'm up, I'm up!" Shummer whispered, rubbing his ankle. He sprang to his feet, Vassey, Taggs Elliot and Idaho Joe Golden right along with him.

Turning to Crystal Jack, Wakely said, "While that ranger is out of the hotel, I couldn't ask for a better time to slip in there and do what I'm sworn to do." As he spoke, he raised a knife from his boot well and held it firmly by its handle.

Crystal Jack stared at him for a minute, then said, "All right, I reckon it's time you get it out of your system. Hurry up and kill her, then come running. "We might need your help at the saloon."

Wakely nodded stiffly, his eyes already having gone to the upper hotel windows and fixed there. He eased out of the alley, then hurried across the dark street in a crouch and along the fronts of the buildings to the hotel, staying in the dark shadows of the boardwalk overhang.

"All right, you men," said Jack Holder, "let's get it done." He drew his Colt and cocked it with stern deliberation. "Remember, once we commence, leave nobody standing." They slipped out of the alley, their respective shotguns, rifles and pistols in hand.

Inside the saloon, Arlo Heath sat passed out at a table by himself, his upper half sprawled forward on the tabletop in a puddle of spilled rye, snoring drunkenly, his mouth open. On a blanket near the wall lay Feathers Hilgi and Michael McGinty, both naked, sleeping entwined in the lantern's flickering glow. In a chair leaned back against a wall, Linston McGinty sat sleep-

348

ing, his head bowed onto his chest.

At the dusty bar stood Freeman Turnbaugh and Sugar Townsend, a half-filled bottle of rye standing on the bar between them. "Well, well," said Townsend, seeing Sam walk through the door with his big Colt drawn, cocked and held down at his side. "Look who has finally decided to join us ole outlaws." His voice sounded thick and whiskey-slurred.

At one end of the bar stood Billy Jones, his head bowed as if asleep, but with a fresh foamy mug of beer standing before him. His gloved right hand rested close to a sawed-off shotgun lying on the bar. At the other end, Tom Colbert stood in almost the same position, an empty shot glass near his left hand, his right hand out of sight beneath the edge of the bar.

"I would offer you a drink, Burrack," Turnbaugh said, staring at Sam, "but that gun in your hand tells me you're not in a drinking mood."

"That's right, Turnbaugh," said Sam. "I'm not in a drinking mood tonight." He looked back and forth from one end of the bar to the other, seeing neither Jones nor Colbert lift their heads or make a move.

"Too bad," said Turnbaugh. He raised a glass of whiskey with his left hand, keeping his right hand near his holstered gun. "I just killed my best pard. I'm running short of folks to drink with."

"Maybe it's time to end the party," said Sam with finality. He spread his feet shoulder-width apart.

Freeman Turnbaugh squinted for closer focus in the dim light and said, "Well, I'll be! Is that a badge on your chest, Burrack?"

"Yes," said Sam. "I pinned it back on. The truth is I felt naked without it."

Turnbaugh gave a dark chuckle. "You law-dogs and your badges," he said, "you're worse than priests with their crosses." He shook his head. "I never could understand why a little ornament like that makes such a difference to yas."

"I don't expect you would," said Sam. He paused, took a breath and gave another glance at either end of the bar. *Here goes,* he said to himself, hoping he'd given Maria enough time to get into position near the empty window frame, in order to back him up. But there was no time to wonder about it now, he thought, clearing his mind, ready-ing himself. "I'm taking you to Fort Smith, Turnbaugh," he said.

Townsend stiffened, his hand poised near his gun butt. Turnbaugh gave another dark chuckle. "Are you now?" he said in a cocky

350

tone, as if it were all a joke. "Care to hear some numbers on how many two-bit lawmen like you has tried that same thing?"

"The numbers don't matter," said Sam, barely shaking his head. "You're going with me. Don't make me kill you."

From their positions at both ends of the bar, Colbert and Jones raised their heads enough for their eyes to cut toward him from beneath their hat brims. Sugar Townsend stood poised, ready, a grim smile on his face. Turnbaugh's hand tensed; Sam saw the move coming.

But before Turnbaugh made his move, a woman's scream resounded along the empty street, coming from the hotel, followed by three pistol shots and breaking glass. "Ella!" Turnbaugh shouted aloud, his eyes going away from Sam and in the direction of the gunshots. The sounds from the hotel brought Linston McGinty up from his chair against the wall. At the same time, Arlo Heath sat upright, rubbing his blurry eyes.

Maria . . . ! Sam said to himself, even as his Colt came up in his hand in answer to Sugar Townsend making a quick grab for the Walker Colt in his belt.

Sam saw his shot nail Sugar Townsend in his chest just as Townsend's big Walker exploded wildly in a loud belch of blue-orange flame. The impact sent Townsend slamming backward into the bar so hard, he flipped up over it, knocking out a row of dirty beer mugs and shot glasses.

Without hesitation, Sam swung first toward the shotgun, realizing full well that something had kept Maria from getting into a backup position. Jones had begun swinging the shotgun toward him, but Sam fired before the double barrels leveled for their shot. Jones staggered backward as Sam's shot struck him low in the chest, the jolt of pain causing Jones to squeeze off both barrels toward the ceiling.

Sam knew he couldn't swing back around toward Tom Colbert in time to keep the man from getting a shot off, but he tried anyway; and to his surprise, Colbert was in no condition to fire. Colbert stood bowed at the waist, staggering backward, both hands clutching a bullet hole in his stomach. From behind him, Sam heard heavy gunfire coming from both the open doorway and the large empty window frame.

Spinning quickly around, his Colt cocked, smoking and ready to fire again, Sam saw Linston McGinty and Arlo Heath fall in a hail of bullets. He heard Feathers Hilgi scream, as she and Michael stood up only to be cut down by gunfire. He saw Turnbaugh on the floor in a widening pool of blood. Past Turnbaugh he saw two men in the window and three in the door, all with their guns blazing.

Ducking away as bullets zipped past his head, one of them nipping at his duster sleeve, Sam saw Turnbaugh trying to crawl away for cover behind the bar. "There he goes!" shouted Holder. "Kill him! Kill them all!"

For reasons he could not have named, Sam's first move was not to get himself out of the gunfire. With his Colt blazing in return fire, he ran in a crouch to where Turnbaugh struggled to get on his feet. Grabbing Turnbaugh by his shoulder, Sam half dragged him along until they both fell behind the bar. Sam caught a glimpse of blood flowing from Turnbaugh's chest, but there was no time to attend to the wound right then. Bullets ripped off chunks of oak and sent splinters flying through the air.

"Stay down!" Sam shouted above the gunfire. He snatched Turnbaugh's pistol from his bloody hand, reached around the lower edge of the bar and fired three rounds, one of them picking up Ed Vassey and pitching him back out through the open window frame. Before ducking back behind cover, he heard the blast of a shotgun and saw Jed

Shummer's buckshot-mangled body come flying in through the open doors.

"Maria!" Sam shouted, somehow knowing that was who had just dropped the hammers on the bounty hunter. No sooner had he called out her name than he heard the gunfire shift toward the street in front of the open door. Unable to take the time to reload, he raced from behind the bar and jumped out through the open window frame.

In the dirt street, he saw Maria facing Idaho Joe, Taggs Elliot and Crystal Jack Holder. As they fired on her, Sam saw her throw her empty shotgun away and draw her Colt from its holster. "Back here, Holder!" Sam shouted, hoping to draw their attention away from her. As he shouted, he fired both guns in his hands at once. Taggs Elliot fell dead on the ground.

Idaho Joe whirled toward Sam, firing, but a shot from Maria caught him high in his side at the same time as a shot from Sam nailed him in the chest. Before Joe hit the ground, Sam turned both guns on Jack Holder, seeing Jack take aim at arm's length on Maria. "This one's for Merlin Wakely!" he bellowed.

Sam pulled the triggers of both guns in his hands, but they were empty. He started to race toward Holder, hoping to knock him down before he could take a shot at Maria. But Sam knew there was no time.

Before he'd gone three steps, the sound of a shotgun blast exploded behind him, and in front of him Jack Holder rose three feet off the ground and flew sidelong in a wide spray of blood. Sam turned quickly and saw Freeman Turnbaugh sag against the saloon's open window frame, a smoking shotgun falling from his hand.

"Maria, are you all right?" Sam called out.

"*Sí,* are you?" Maria asked, hurrying toward him in the middle of the street.

"I'm all right." Sam had already thrown open the chamber on his big Colt and punched out the empty cartridge cases and begun reloading, taking a quick glance along the street for any more bounty hunters. Maria joined him just as his eyes went to Ella Lang lying dead in the dirt, a knife handle sticking up from between her naked breasts. Her pistol lay at her fingertips.

Less than six feet from Ella lay Merlin Wakely, dark blood staining his shirt, his neck twisted at an odd angle. The two lay surrounded by shards of glass from the broken hotel window above them. Standing beside Ella Lang, Nat Gilder looked up from her blank face and toward Sam and Maria, shaking his head slowly, his pencil and pad coming out of his coat, ready to go to work.

Sam and Maria hurried to Freeman Turnbaugh to see if he could be saved. But seeing them approach him, Turnbaugh said in the clearest voice Sam had ever heard come from a dying man, "Take your time, Burrack. I'm not going anywhere." He tried to offer a tired smile. The effort showed his pain. "Is Ella . . . ?"

"Yes," said Sam, knowing from the looks of Turnbaugh that he wouldn't be far behind her. "Take it easy. We'll see what we can do for you."

"No, no, no," Turnbaugh said, shaking his head, staring down at the hard flow of dark blood streaming down his chest. "Don't do anything to slow this down. I'm going. Let me get it over with."

Sam kneeled beside him on the floor inside the window frame.

"*Gracias,* you saved my life," Maria said quietly.

"You're welcome, ma'am," Turnbaugh said. He gazed down as if to check on the flow of blood and gauge how much longer his life would last. Then he looked at Sam and said, "Do me a favor, Burrack?"

356

Sam looked into his eyes, doing some gauging of his own and saying, "If I can. What is it?"

"Take me and Ella off and hide us somewhere. Let the word get around that we just disappeared . . . went off to Honduras maybe?"

"I can't promise anything, Turnbaugh," said Sam. "I'm still a lawman. I have to tell the truth about how all this happened."

"Yeah," said Turnbaugh, "I understand. I just thought that would be a good way to end it, the two of us winning and cashing out." He offered a wistful smile. "Ella would have liked that."

Sam's eyes drifted off to Gilder, who had turned away from Ella's body and came walking toward them. "I'll see what I can do, Turnbaugh," Sam said. "As popular as you and Ella are, I bet there'll be a dozen different stories of what happened to you. Maybe I can see to it that escaping to Honduras is one of them."

Turnbaugh nodded, again checking his wound.

Seeing the man had very little time left, Sam asked flatly, "Now you do me a favor. How do I get to that secret hideout of yours over in Black Mesa?"

"You're in it," Turnbaugh said, giving a

slight chuckle, gesturing a bloody hand all around them.

"Meaning you don't want to tell me?" said Sam.

"Meaning I *am* telling you, Burrack," Turnbaugh replied, his voice starting to take on the strain of losing too much blood. "The secret hideout is here in Buckton, or over in a ghost town named Blue Butte . . . or somewhere in a dozen other places off the main trail — places everybody has left deserted." He gave a sly smile. "There never was a secret hide-out in Black Mesa," he said, "a place all them old bandits disappeared into. That's just something we made up for the Eastern periodicals. We were always highly respected. Hell, we couldn't let folks know the truth, have them thinking that we spent most of our time in shitholes like this." He gazed deeper into Sam's eyes as he felt a terrible weakness creep throughout him. "There's no glamour if the truth . . ."

Sam waited for a second, then reached with his gloved fingertips and closed Turnbaugh's eyes. "Trouble is, even a lot of outlaws believed it," he said, to no one in particular. "They all wanted to be like you . . . and Killer Max Krey." He paused, then said softly, "And like lovely Ella Lang."

"My goodness," said Gilder, standing next to Maria, the two of them looking down at Sam and Turnbaugh, "they certainly had a run of it while it lasted."

Sam turned slowly, looked up at the pencil and paper in Gilder's hand and said, "Do us all a favor and stop writing for now."

"But I have to take notes now, while everything is still fresh in my mind!" said Gilder.

Sam didn't say any more right away. Instead, he looked at Maria and said, "Do you think Mr. Gilder here will make it back to Dodge on his own?"

"Wait!" Gilder cut in. "You're not going to leave me out here alone, are you?"

Sam didn't answer. Instead he said to Maria, "After we get these folks buried, we'll head out, pick up that hidden money you told me about and head back to Dodge."

"*Sí*," said Maria, also ignoring Gilder, "Deputy Mather will be glad to get his horse back from me."

"Hold on, both of you, please!" said Gilder. "Don't leave me out here! I could die!"

"Then put that pencil away and stop writing," said Sam.

"All right then," said Gilder with a sigh, "but you are to blame if I don't get this

359

story accurately reported."

Sam offered a wry smile, saying, "I'm sure you'll manage to get it close enough to tell a *real* good story."

"I'll certainly do the best I can," said Gilder. "Although I have to admit, when it comes to Turnbaugh, Ella and Krey, my reading public is not going to be happy about them meeting this kind of end."

"No kidding?" said Sam, giving Maria a look.

"Oh, absolutely," said Gilder. "These three were *bigger than life*! They needed to have a bigger-than-life finish, not simply die in a dirt street in some abandoned flea-bitten town like this. They should have disappeared into their hideout in Black Mesa and never been heard from again. That would have been so much better, for both them and for my reading public."

Listening to Gilder, Maria gave Sam the same kind of look he'd given her a moment earlier. Sam only nodded slightly at her, then said to Gilder, "Tell me, *Nat,* what do you know about Honduras?"

"Oh, quite a lot actually," said Gilder, beaming at having finally been called by his first name. "I've never been there, but I have heard so much that I feel like I know the place by heart."

"Good," said Sam, as he and Maria turned, Gilder hurrying along with them. "On the way back to Dodge, you can take your pencil out and we'll talk some about Honduras. I think I've got just the bigger-than-life ending you're looking for."

ABOUT THE AUTHOR

Ralph Cotton has been an ironworker, a second mate on a commercial barge, a teamster, a horse trainer, and a lay minister with the Lutheran church. Visit his Web site at www.RalphCotton.com.